SEVENTEEN

Booth Tarkington

Seventeen

Buccaneer Books
Cutchogue, New York

To
S. K. T

Contents

1. William

WILLIAM SYLVANUS BAXTER paused for a moment of thought in front of the drug-store at the corner of Washington Street and Central Avenue. He had an internal question to settle before he entered the store: he wished to allow the young man at the soda-fountain no excuse for saying, "Well, make up your mind what it's goin' to be, can't you?" Rudeness of this kind, especially in the presence of girls and women, was hard to bear, and though William Sylvanus Baxter had borne it upon occasion, he had reached an age when he found it intolerable. Therefore, to avoid offering opportunity for anything of the kind, he decided upon chocolate and strawberry, mixed, before approaching the fountain. Once there, however, and a large glass of these flavors and diluted ice-cream proving merely provocative, he said, languidly—an affectation, for he could have disposed of half a dozen with gusto: "Well, now I'm here, I might as well go one more. Fill 'er up again. Same."

Emerging to the street, penniless, he bent a fascinated and dramatic gaze upon his reflection in the drug-store window, and then, as he turned his back upon the alluring image, his expression altered to one of lofty and uncondescending amusement. That was his glance at the passing public. From the heights, he seemed to bestow upon the world a mysterious derision—for William Sylvanus Baxter was seventeen long years of age, and had learned to present the appearance of one who possesses inside information about life and knows all strangers and most acquaintances to be of inferior caste, costume, and intelligence.

He lingered upon the corner awhile, not pressed for time. Indeed, he found many hours of these summer months heavy upon his hands, for he had no important occupation, unless some intermittent dalliance with a work

1

on geometry (anticipatory of the distant autumn) might be thought important, which is doubtful, since he usually went to sleep on the shady side porch at his home, with the book in his hand. So, having nothing to call him elsewhere, he lounged before the drug-store in the early afternoon sunshine, watching the passing to and fro of the lower orders and bourgeoisie of the middle-sized midland city which claimed him (so to speak) for a native son.

Apparently quite unembarrassed by his presence, they went about their business, and the only people who looked at him with any attention were pedestrians of color. It is true that when the gaze of these fell upon him it was instantly arrested, for no colored person could have passed him without a little pang of pleasure and of longing. Indeed, the tropical violence of William Sylvanus Baxter's tie and the strange brilliancy of his hat might have made it positively unsafe for him to walk at night through the Negro quarter of the town. And though no man could have sworn to the color of that hat, whether it was blue or green, yet its color was a saner thing than its shape, which was blurred, tortured, and raffish; it might have been the miniature model of a volcano that had blown off its cone and misbehaved disastrously on its lower slopes as well. He had the air of wearing it as a matter of course and with careless ease, but that was only an air—it was the apple of his eye.

For the rest, his costume was neutral, subordinate, and even a little neglected in the matter of a detail or two: one pointed flap of his soft collar was held down by a button, but the other showed a frayed thread where the button once had been; his low patent-leather shoes were of a luster not solicitously cherished, and there could be no doubt that he needed to get his hair cut, while something might have been done, too, about the individualized hirsute prophecies which had made independent appearances, here and there, upon his chin. He examined these from time to time by the sense of touch, passing his hand across his face and allowing his finger-tips a slight tapping motion wherever they detected a prophecy. Thus he fell into a pleasant musing and seemed to forget the crowded street.

2. The Unknown

He was roused by the bluff greeting of an acquaintance not dissimilar to himself in age, manner, and apparel.

"H'lo, Silly Bill!" said this person, halting beside William Sylvanus Baxter. "What's the news?"

William showed no enthusiasm; on the contrary, a frown of annoyance appeared upon his brow. The nickname "Silly Bill"—long ago compounded by merry child-comrades from "William" and "Sylvanus"—was not to his taste, especially in public, where he preferred to be addressed simply and manfully as "Baxter." Any direct expression of resentment, however, was difficult, since it was plain that Johnnie Watson intended no offense whatever and but spoke out of custom.

"Don't know any," William replied, coldly.

"Dull times, ain't it?" said Mr. Watson, a little depressed by his friend's manner. "I heard May Parcher was comin' back to town yesterday, though."

"Well, let her!" returned William, still severe.

"They said she was goin' to bring a girl to visit her," Johnnie began in a confidential tone. "They said she was a reg'lar ringdinger and—"

"Well, what if she is?" the discouraging Mr. Baxter interrupted. "Makes little difference to *me,* I guess!"

"Oh no, it don't. *You* don't take any interest in girls! *Oh* no!"

"No, I do not!" was the emphatic and heartless retort. "I never saw one in my life I'd care whether she lived or died!"

"Honest?" asked Johnnie, struck by the conviction with which this speech was uttered. "Honest, is that so?"

"Yes, 'honest'!" William replied, sharply. "They could *all* die, I wouldn't notice!"

Johnnie Watson was profoundly impressed. "Why, *I* didn't know you felt that way about 'em, Silly Bill. I always thought you were kind of—"

"Well, I do feel that way about 'em!" said William Sylvanus Baxter, and, outraged by the repetition of the offen-

3

sive nickname, he began to move away. "You can tell 'em so for me, if you want to!" he added over his shoulder. And he walked haughtily up the street, leaving Mr. Watson to ponder upon this case of misogyny, never until that moment suspected.

It was beyond the power of his mind to grasp the fact that William Sylvanus Baxter's cruel words about "girls" had been uttered because William was annoyed at being called "Silly Bill" in a public place, and had not known how to object otherwise than by showing contempt for any topic of conversation proposed by the offender. This latter, being of a disposition to accept statements as facts, was warmly interested, instead of being hurt, and decided that here was something worth talking about, especially with representatives of the class so sweepingly excluded from the sympathies of Silly Bill.

William, meanwhile, made his way toward the "residence section" of the town, and presently—with the passage of time—found himself eased of his annoyance. He walked in his own manner, using his shoulders to emphasize an effect of carelessness which he wished to produce upon observers. For his consciousness of observers was abnormal, since he had it whether any one was looking at him or not, and it reached a crucial stage whenever he perceived persons of his own age, but of opposite sex, approaching.

A person of this description was encountered upon the sidewalk within a hundred yards of his own home, and William Sylvanus Baxter saw her while yet she was afar off. The quiet and shady thoroughfare was empty of all human life, at the time, save for those two; and she was upon the same side of the street that he was; thus it became inevitable that they should meet, face to face, for the first time in their lives. He had perceived, even in the distance, that she was unknown to him, a stranger, because he knew all the girls in this part of the town who dressed as famously in the mode as that! And then, as the distance between them lessened, he saw that she was ravishingly pretty; far, far prettier, indeed, than any girl he knew. At least it seemed so, for it is, unfortunately, much easier for strangers to be beautiful. Aside from this advantage of mystery, the approaching vision was piquant and graceful enough to have reminded a much older boy of a spotless white kitten, for, in spite of a charmingly managed demureness, there was precisely that kind of playfulness somewhere expressed about her. Just now it was most definite in the look she bent upon the light and fluffy burden which she carried nestled in the inner curve of her right arm: a tiny dog with hair like cotton and a pink ribbon round his neck—an animal sated with indulgence and idiotically unaware of his privilege. He was half asleep!

William did not see the dog, for it is the plain, anatomical truth that when he saw how pretty the girl was, his heart—his physical heart—began to do things the like of which, experienced by an elderly person, would have brought the doctor in haste. In addition, his complexion altered—he broke out in fiery patches. He suffered from breathlessness and from pressure on the diaphragm.

Afterward, he could not have named the color of the little parasol she carried in her left hand, and yet, as it drew nearer and nearer, a rosy haze suffused the neighborhood, and the whole world began to turn an exquisite pink. Beneath this gentle glow, with eyes downcast in thought, she apparently took no note of William, even when she and William had come within a few yards of each other. Yet he knew that she would look up and that their eyes must meet —a thing for which he endeavored to prepare himself by a strange weaving motion of his neck against the friction of his collar—for thus, instinctively, he strove to obtain greater ease and some decent appearance of manly indifference. He felt that his efforts were a failure; that his agitation was ruinous and must be perceptible at a distance of miles, not feet. And then, in the instant of panic that befell, when her dark-lashed eyelids slowly lifted, he had a flash of inspiration.

He opened his mouth somewhat, and as her eyes met his, full and startlingly, he placed three fingers across the orifice, and also offered a slight vocal proof that she had surprised him in the midst of a yawn.

"Oh, hum!" he said.

For the fraction of a second, the deep blue spark in her eyes glowed brighter—gentle arrows of turquoise shot him through and through—and then her glance withdrew from the ineffable collision. Her small, white-shod feet continued to bear her onward, away from him, while his own dimmed shoes peregrinated in the opposite direction—William necessarily, yet with excruciating reluctance, accompanying them. But just at the moment when he and the lovely creature were side by side, and her head turned from him, she spoke—that is, she murmured, but he caught the words.

"You Flopit, wake up!" she said, in the tone of a mother talking baby-talk. *"So* indifferink!"

William's feet and his breath halted spasmodically. For an instant he thought she had spoken to him, and then for the first time he perceived the fluffy head of the dog bobbing languidly over her arm, with the motion of her walking; and he comprehended that Flopit, and not William Sylvanus Baxter, was the gentleman addressed. But—but had she *meant* him?

His breath returning, though not yet operating in its usual manner, he stood gazing after her, while the glamorous parasol passed down the shady street, catching splashes of sunshine through the branches of the maple-trees; and the cottony head of the tiny dog continued to be visible, bobbing rhythmically over a filmy sleeve. Had she meant that William was indifferent? Was it William that she really addressed?

He took two steps to follow her, but a uffocating shyness stopped him abruptly and, in a horror lest she should glance round and detect him in the act, he turned and strode fiercely to the gate of his own home before he dared to look again. And when he did look, affecting great casualness in the action, she was gone, evidently having turned the corner. Yet the street did not seem quite empty; there was still some thing warm and fragrant about it, and a rosy glamor lingered in the air. William rested an elbow upon the gate-post, and with his chin reposing in his hand gazed long in the direction in which the unknown had vanished. And his soul was tremulous, for she had done her work but too well.

" 'Indifferink'!" he murmured, thrilling at his own exceedingly indifferent imitation of her voice. "Indifferink!"

That was just what he would have her think—that he was a cold, indifferent man. It was what he wished all girls to think. And "sarcastic"! He had been envious one day when May Parcher said that Joe Bullitt was "awfully sarcastic." William had spent the ensuing hour in an object-lesson intened to make Miss Parcher see that William Sylvanus Baxter was twice as sarcastic as Joe Bullitt ever thought of being, but this great effort had been unsuccessful, because William failed to understand that Miss Parcher had only been sending a sort of message to Mr. Bullitt. It was a device not unique among her sex; her hope was that William would repeat her remark in such a manner that Joe Bullitt would hear it and call to inquire what she meant.

"'So indifferink'!" murmured William, leaning dreamily upon the gate-post. "Indifferink!" He tried to get the exact cooing quality of the unknown's voice. "Indifferink!" And, repeating the honeyed word, so entrancingly distorted, he fell into a kind of stupor; vague, beautiful pictures rising before him, the one least blurred being of himself, on horseback, sweeping between Flopit and a racing automobile. And then, having restored the little animal to its mistress, William sat carelessly in the saddle (he had the Guardsman's seat) while the perfectly trained steed wheeled about, forelegs in the air, preparing to go. "But shall I not see you again, to thank you more properly?" she cried, pleading. "Some other day—perhaps," he answered.

And left her in a cloud of dust.

3. The Painful Age

"OH, WILL—EE!"

Thus a shrill voice, to his ears hideously different from that other, interrupted and dispersed his visions. Little Jane, his ten-year-old sister, stood upon the front porch, the door open behind her, and in her hand she held a large slab of bread-and-butter covered with apple sauce and powdered sugar. Evidence that she had sampled this compound was upon her cheeks, and to her brother she was a repulsive sight.

"Will—ee!" she shrilled. "Look! *Good!*" And to emphasize the adjective she indelicately patted the region of her
body in which she believed her stomach to be located.
"There's a slice for you on the dining-room table," she informed him, joyously.

Outraged, he entered the house without a word to her,
and, proceeding to the dining-room, laid hands upon the
slice she had mentioned, but declined to eat it in Jane's
company. He was in an exalted mood, and though in no
condition of mind or body would he refuse food of almost
any kind, Jane was an intrusion he could not suffer at this
time.

He carried the refection to his own room and, locking
the door, sat down to eat, while, even as he ate, the spell
that was upon him deepened in intensity.

"Oh, eyes!" he whispered, softly, in that cool privacy and
shelter from the world. "Oh, eyes of blue!"

The mirror of a dressing-table sent him the reflection of
his own eyes, which also were blue; and he gazed upon
them and upon the rest of his image the while he ate his
bread-and-butter and apple sauce and sugar. Thus, watching himself eat, he continued to stare dreamily at the mirror
until the bread-and-butter and apple sauce and sugar had
disappeared, whereupon he rose and approached the dressing-table to study himself at greater advantage.

He assumed as repulsive an expression as he could command, at the same time making the kingly gesture of one
who repels unwelcome attentions; and it is beyond doubt
that he was thus acting a little scene of indifference. Other
symbolic dramas followed, though an invisible observer
might have been puzzled for a key to some of them. One,
however, would have proved easily intelligible: his expression having altered to a look of pity and contrition, he
turned from the mirror, and, walking slowly to a chair
across the room, used his right hand in a peculiar manner,
seeming to stroke the air at a point about ten inches above
the back of the chair. "There, there, little girl," he said in a
low, gentle voice. "I didn't know you cared!"

Then, with a rather abrupt dismissal of this theme, he
returned to the mirror, and, after a questioning scrutiny,
nodded solemnly, forming with his lips the words, "The

real thing—the real thing at last!" He meant that, after many imitations had imposed upon him, Love—the real thing—had come to him in the end. And as he turned away he murmured, "And even her name—unknown!"

This evidently was a thought that continued to occupy him, for he walked up and down the room, frowning; but suddenly his brow cleared and his eye lit with purpose. Seating himself at a small writing-table by the window, he proceeded to express his personality—though with considerable labor—in something which he did not doubt to be a poem.

Three-quarters of an hour having sufficed for its completion, including "rewriting and polish," he solemnly signed it, and then read it several times in a state of hushed astonishment. He had never dreamed that he could do anything like this:

MILADY

I do not know her name
Though it would be the same
Where roses bloom at twilight
And the lark takes his flight
It would be the same anywhere
Where music sounds in air
I was never introduced to the lady
So I could not call her Lass or Sadie
So I will call her Milady
By the sands of the sea
She always will be
Just Milady to me.
    —WILLIAM SYLVANUS BAXTER, Esq., July 14

It is impossible to say how many times he might have read the poem over, always with increasing amazement at his new-found powers, had he not been interrupted by the odious voice of Jane.

"Will—ee!"

To William, in his high and lonely mood, this piercing summons brought an actual shudder, and the very thought of Jane (with tokens of apple sauce and sugar still upon her cheek, probably) seemed a kind of sacrilege. He fiercely swore his favorite oath, acquired from the hero of a work of fiction he admired, "Ye gods!" and concealed his poem in the drawer of the writing-table, for Jane's footsteps were approaching his door.

"Will—ee! Mamma wants you." She tried the handle of the door.

"G'way!" he said.

"Will—ee!" Jane hammered upon the door with her fist. "Will—ee!"

"What you want?" he shouted.

Jane explained, certain pauses indicating that her attention was partially diverted to another slice of bread-and-butter and apple sauce and sugar. "Will—ee, mamma wants you—wants you to go help Genesis bring some washtubs home—and a tin clo'es-boiler—from the second-hand man's store."

"What!"

Jane repeated the outrageous message, adding, "She wants you to hurry—and I got some more bread-and-butter and apple sauce and sugar for comin' to tell you."

William left no doubt in Jane's mind about his attitude in reference to the whole matter. His refusal was direct and infuriated, but, in the midst of a multitude of plain statements which he was making, there was a decisive tapping upon the door at a point higher than Jane could reach, and his mother's voice interrupted:

"Hush, Willie! Open the door, please."

He obeyed furiously, and Mrs. Baxter walked in with a deprecating air, while Jane followed, so profoundly interested that, until almost the close of the interview, she held her bread-and-butter and apple sauce and sugar at a sort of way-station on its journey to her mouth.

"That's a nice thing to ask me to do!" stormed the unfortunate William. "Ye gods! Do you think Joe Bullitt's mother would dare to—"

"Wait, dearie!" Mrs. Baxter begged, pacifically. "I just want to explain—"

" 'Explain'! Ye gods!"

"Now, now, just a minute, Willie!" she said. "What I wanted to explain was why it's necessary for you to go with Genesis for the—"

"Never!" he shouted. "Never! You expect me to walk

through the public streets with that awful-lookin' old nigger—"

"Genesis isn't old," she managed to interpolate. "He—"

But her frantic son disregarded her. "Second-hand wash-tubs!" he vociferated. "And tin clothes-boilers! *That's* what you want your *son* to carry through the public streets in broad daylight! Ye gods!"

"Well, there isn't anybody else," she said. "Please don't rave so, Willie, and say 'Ye gods' so much; it really isn't nice. I'm sure nobody'll notice you—"

" 'Nobody'!" His voice cracked in anguish. "Oh no! Nobody except the whole town! *Why,* when there's anything disgusting has to be done in this family—why do *I* always have to be the one? Why can't Genesis bring the second-hand wash-tubs without *me*? Why can't the second-hand store deliver 'em? Why can't—"

"That's what I want to tell you," she interposed, hurriedly, and as the youth lifted his arms on high in a gesture of ultimate despair, and then threw himself miserably into a chair, she obtained the floor. "The second-hand store doesn't deliver things," she said. "I bought them at an auction, and it's going out of business, and they have to be taken away before half past four this afternoon. Genesis can't bring them in the wheelbarrow, because, he says, the wheel is broken, and he says he can't possibly carry two tubs and a wash-boiler himself; and he can't make two trips because it's a mile and a half, and I don't like to ask him, anyway; and it would take too long, because he has to get back and finish cutting the grass before your papa gets home this evening. Papa said he *had* to! Now, I don't like to ask you, but it really isn't much. You and Genesis can just slip up there and—"

"Slip!" moaned William. " 'Just *slip* up there'! Ye gods!"

"Genesis is waiting on the back porch," she said. "Really it isn't worth your making all this fuss about."

"Oh no!" he returned, with plaintive satire. "It's nothing! Nothing at all!"

"Why, *I* shouldn't mind it," she said, briskly, "if I had the time. In fact, I'll have to, if you won't."

"Ye gods!" He clasped his head in his hands, crushed, for he knew that the curse was upon him and he must go. "Ye gods!"

And then, as he stamped to the door, his tragic eye fell upon Jane, and he emitted a final cry of pain:

"Can't you *ever* wash your face?" he shouted.

4. Genesis and Clematis

GENESIS and his dog were waiting just outside the kitchen door, and of all the world these two creatures were probably the last in whose company William Sylvanus Baxter desired to make a public appearance. Genesis was an out-of-doors man and seldom made much of a toilet; his overalls in particular betraying at important points a lack of the anxiety he should have felt, since only Genesis himself, instead of a supplementary fabric, was directly underneath them. And the aged, grayish, sleeveless and neckless garment which sheltered him from waist to collar-bone could not have been mistaken for a jersey, even though what there was of it was dimly of a jerseyesque character. Upon the feet of Genesis were things which careful study would have revealed to be patent-leather dancing-pumps, long dead and several times buried; and upon his head, pressing down his markedly criminal ears, was a once-derby hat of a brown not far from Genesis's own color, though decidedly without his gloss. A large ring of strange metal, with the stone missing, adorned a finger of his right hand, and from a corner of his mouth projected an unlighted and spreading cigar stub which had the appearance of belonging to its present owner merely by right of salvage.

And Genesis's dog, scratching himself at his master's feet, was the true complement of Genesis, for although he was a youngish dog, and had not long been the property of Genesis, he was a dog that would have been recognized anywhere in the world as a colored person's dog. He was not a special breed of dog—though there was something rather houndlike about him—he was just a dog. His expression was grateful but anxious, and he was unusually bald upon the bosom, but otherwise whitish and brownish, with a gaunt, haunting face and no power to look anybody in the eye.

He rose apprehensively as the fuming William came out

of the kitchen, but he was prepared to follow his master faithfully, and when William and Genesis reached the street the dog was discovered at their heels, whereupon William came to a decisive halt.

"Send that dog back," he said, resolutely. "I'm not going through the streets with a dog like that, anyhow!"

Genesis chuckled. "He ain' goin' back," he said. " 'Ain' nobody kin make 'at dog go back. I ain' had him mo'n two weeks, but I don' b'lieve Pres'dent United States kin make 'at dog go back! I show you." And, wheeling suddenly, he made ferocious gestures, shouting, "G'on back, dog!"

The dog turned, ran back a few paces, halted, and then began to follow again, whereupon Genesis pretended to hurl stones at him; but the animal only repeated his maneuver—and he repeated it once more when William aided Genesis by using actual missiles, which were dodged with almost careless adeptness.

"I'll show him!" said William, hotly. "I'll show him he can't follow *me!*" He charged upon the dog, shouting fiercely, and this seemed to do the work, for the hunted animal, abandoning his partial flights, turned a tucked-under tail, ran all the way back to the alley, and disappeared from sight. "There!" said William. "I guess that'll show him!"

"I ain' bettin' on it!" said Genesis, as they went on. "He nev' did stop foll'in' me yet. I reckon he the foll'indest dog in the worl'! Name Clem."

"Well, he can't follow *me!*" said the surging William, in whose mind's eye lingered the vision of an exquisite doglet, with pink-ribboned throat and a cottony head bobbing gently over a filmy sleeve. "He doesn't come within a mile of *me,* no matter what his name is!"

"Name Clem fer short," said Genesis, amiably. "I trade in a mandoline fer him what had her neck kind o' busted off on one side. I couldn' play her nohow, an' I found her, anyways. Yessuh, I trade in 'at mandoline fer him 'cause always did like to have me a good dog—but I d'in' have me no name fer him; an' this here Blooie Bowers, what I trade in the mandoline to, he say *he* d'in' have no name fer him. Say nev' did know if *was* a name fer him 'tall. So I'z spen' the evenin' at 'at lady's house, Fanny, what used to be cook fer Miz Johnson, nex' do' you' maw's; an'

I ast Fanny what am I go'n' a do about it, an' Fanny say,
'Call him Clematis,' she say. ' 'At's a nice name!' she say.
'Clematis.' So 'at's name I name him, Clematis. Call him
Clem fer short, but Clematis his real name. He'll come,
whichever one you call him, Clem or Clematis. Make no
diff'ence to him, long's he git his vittles. Clem or Clematis,
he ain' carin'!"

William's ear was deaf to this account of the naming of
Clematis; he walked haughtily, but as rapidly as possible,
trying to keep a little in advance of his talkative companion, who had never received the training as a servitor
which should have taught him his proper distance from the
Young Master. William's suffering eyes were fixed upon
remoteness; and his lips moved, now and then, like a
martyr's, pronouncing inaudibly a sacred word. "Milady!
Oh. Milady!"

Thus they had covered some three blocks of their journey—the too-democratic Genesis chatting companionably
and William burning with mortification—when the former
broke into loud laughter.

"What I tell you?" he cried, pointing ahead. "Look
ayonnuh! *No,* suh, Pres'dent United States hisse'f ain' go
tell 'at dog stay home!"

And there, at the corner before them, waited Clematis,
roguishly lying in a mud-puddle in the gutter. He had run
through alleys parallel to their course—and in the face of
such demoniac cunning the wretched William despaired
of evading his society. Indeed, there was nothing to do
but to give up, and so the trio proceeded, with William
unable to decide which contaminated him more, Genesis
or the loyal Clematis. To his way of thinking, he was part
of a dreadful pageant, and he winced pitiably whenever
the eye of a respectable passer-by fell upon him. Everybody seemed to stare—nay, to leer! And he felt that the
whole world would know his shame by nightfall.

Nobody, he reflected, seeing him in such company, could
believe that he belonged to "one of the oldest and best
families in town." Nobody would understand that he was
not walking with Genesis for the pleasure of his companionship—until they got the tubs and the wash-boiler, when
his social condition must be thought even more degraded.
And nobody, he was shudderingly positive, could see that

Clematis was not his dog. Clematis kept himself humbly a
little in the rear, but how was any observer to know that
he belonged to Genesis and not to William?

And how frightful that *this* should befall him on such a
day, the very day that his soul had been split asunder by
the turquoise shafts of Milady's eyes and he had learned
to know the Real Thing at last!

"Milady! Oh, Milady!"

For in the elder teens adolescence may be completed,
but not by experience, and these years know their own
tragedies. It is the time of life when one finds it unendur-
able not to seem perfect in all outward matters: in worldly
position, in the equipments of wealth, in family, and in
the grace, elegance, and dignity of all appearances in
public. And yet the youth is continually betrayed by the
child still intermittently insistent within him, and by the
child which undiplomatic people too often assume him
to be. Thus with William's attire: he could ill have borne
any suggestion that it was not of the mode, but taking
care of it was a different matter. Also, when it came to
his appetite, he could and would eat anything at any time,
but something younger than his years led him—often in
semi-secrecy—to candy-stores and soda-water fountains
and ice-cream parlors; he still relished green apples and
knew cravings for other dangerous inedibles. But these
survivals were far from painful to him; what injured his
sensibilities was the disposition on the part of people
—especially his parents, and frequently his aunts and
uncles—to regard him as a little boy. Briefly, the deference
his soul demanded in its own right, not from strangers
only, but from his family, was about that which is supposed to be shown a Grand Duke visiting his Estates.
Therefore William suffered often.

But the full ignominy of the task his own mother had
set him this afternoon was not realized until he and Genesis
set forth upon the return journey from the second-hand
shop, bearing the two wash-tubs, a clothes-wringer (which
Mrs. Baxter had forgotten to mention), and the tin boiler
—and followed by the lowly Clematis.

5. Sorrows within a Boiler

THERE WAS something really pageant-like about the little excursion now, and the glittering clothes-boiler, borne on high, sent flashing lights far down the street. The wash-tubs were old-fashioned, of wood; they refused to fit one within the other; so William, with his right hand, and Genesis, with his left, carried one of the tubs between them; Genesis carried the heavy wringer with his right hand, and he had fastened the other tub upon his back by means of a bit of rope which passed over his shoulder; thus the tin boiler, being a lighter burden, fell to William.

The cover would not stay in place, but continually fell off when he essayed to carry the boiler by one of its handles, and he made shift to manage the accursed thing in various ways—the only one proving physically endurable being, unfortunately, the most grotesque. He was forced to carry the cover in his left hand and to place his head partially within the boiler itself, and to support it —tilted obliquely to rest upon his shoulders—as a kind of monstrous tin cowl or helmet. This had the advantage of somewhat concealing his face, though when he leaned his head back, in order to obtain clearer vision of what was before him, the boiler slid off and fell to the pavement with a noise that nearly caused a runaway, and brought the hot-cheeked William much derisory attention from a passing street-car. However, he presently caught the knack of keeping it in position, and it fell no more.

Seen from the rear, William was unrecognizable—but interesting. He appeared to be a walking clothes-boiler, armed with a shield and connected, by means of a wash-tub, with a Negro of informal ideas concerning dress. In fact, the group was whimsical, and three young people who turned in behind it, out of a cross-street, indulged immediately in fits of inadequately suppressed laughter, though neither Miss May Parcher nor Mr. Johnnie Watson even remotely suspected that the legs beneath the clothes-boiler belonged to an acquaintance. And as for the third

16

of this little party, Miss Parcher's visitor, those peregrinating legs suggested nothing familiar to her.

"Oh, see the fun-ee laundrymans!" she cried, addressing a cottony doglet's head that bobbed gently up and down over her supporting arm. "Sweetest Flopit must see, too! Flopit, look at the fun-ee laundrymans!"

"'Sh!" murmured Miss Parcher, choking. "He might hear you."

He might, indeed, since they were not five yards behind him and the dulcet voice was clear and free. Within the shadowy interior of the clothes-boiler were features stricken with sudden, utter horror. *"Flopit!"*

The attention of Genesis was attracted by a convulsive tugging of the tub which he supported in common with William; it seemed passionately to urge greater speed. A hissing issued from the boiler, and Genesis caught the words, huskily whispered:

"Walk faster! You got to walk faster."

The tub between them tugged forward with a pathos of appeal wasted upon the easy-going Genesis.

"I got plenty time cut 'at grass befo' you' pa gits home," he said, reassuringly. "Thishere rope what I got my extry tub slung to is 'mos' wo' plum thew my hide."

Having uttered this protest, he continued to ambulate at the same pace, though somewhat assisted by the forward pull of the connecting tub, an easance of burden which he found pleasant; and no supplementary message came from the clothes-boiler, for the reason that it was incapable of further speech. And so the two groups maintained for a time their relative positions, about fifteen feet apart.

The amusement of the second group having abated through satiety, the minds of its components turned to other topics. "Now Flopit must have his darlin' 'ickle run," said Flopit's mistress, setting the doglet upon the ground. "That's why sweetest Flopit and I and all of us came for a walk, instead of sitting on the nice, cool porchkins. *See* the sweetie toddle! Isn't he adorable, May? *Isn't* he adorable, Mr. Watson?"   ....

Mr. Watson put a useless sin upon his soul, since all he needed to say was a mere "Yes." He fluently avowed himself to have become insane over the beauty of Flopit.

Flopit, placed upon the ground, looked like something that had dropped from a Christmas tree, and he automatically made use of fuzzy legs, somewhat longer than a caterpillar's, to patter after his mistress. He was neither enterprising nor inquisitive; he kept close to the rim of her skirt, which was as high as he could see, and he wished to be taken up and carried again. He was in a half-stupor; it was his desire to remain in that condition, and his propulsion was almost wholly subconscious, though surprisingly rapid, considering his dimensions.

"My goo'ness!" exclaimed Genesis, glancing back over his shoulder. " 'At li'l' think ack like he think he go'n a *git* somewheres!" And then, in answer to a frantic pull upon the tub, "Look like you mighty strong t'day," he said. "I cain' go no fastuh!" He glanced back again, chuckling. " 'At li'l bird do well not mix up nothin' 'ith ole man Clematis!"

Clematis, it happened, was just coming into view, having been detained round the corner by his curiosity concerning a set of Louis XVI furniture which some housemovers were unpacking upon the sidewalk. A curl of excelsior, in fact, had attached itself to his nether lip, and he was pausing to remove it—when his roving eye fell upon Flopit. Clematis immediately decided to let the excelsior remain where it was, lest he miss something really important.

He approached with glowing eagerness at a gallop.

Then, having almost reached his goal, he checked himself with surprising abruptness and walked obliquely beside Flopit, but upon a parallel course, his manner agitated and his brow furrowed with perplexity. Flopit was about the size of Clematis's head, and although Clematis was certain that Flopit was something alive, he could not decide what.

Flopit paid not the slightest attention to Clematis. The self-importance of dogs, like that of the minds of men, is in directly inverse ratio to their size; and if the self-importance of Flopit could have been taken out of him and given to an elephant, that elephant would have been insufferable.

Flopit continued to pay no attention to Clematis.

All at once, a rougish and irresponsible mood seized upon Clematis; he laid his nose upon the ground, deliberating a bit of gaiety, and then, with a little rush, set a large, rude paw upon the sensitive face of Flopit and capsized him. Flopit uttered a bitter complaint in an asthmatic voice.

"Oh, nassy dray bid Horror!" cried his mistress, turning quickly at this sound and waving a pink parasol at Clematis. "Shoo! *Dirty* dog! Go 'way!" And she was able somehow to connect him with the wash-tub and boiler, for she added, "Nassy laundrymans to have bad doggies!"

Mr. Watson rushed upon Clematis with angry bellowings and imaginary missiles. "You disgusting brute!" he roared. "How *dare* you?"

Apparently much alarmed, Clematis lowered his ears, tucked his tail underneath him, and fled to the rear, not halting once or looking back until he disappeared round the corner whence he had come. "There!" said Mr. Watson. "I guess *he* won't bother us again very soon!"

It must be admitted that Milady was one of those people who do not mind being overheard, no matter what they say. "Lucky for us," she said, "we had a nice dray bid *mans* to protect us, wasn't it, Flopit?" And she thought it necessary to repeat something she had already made sufficiently emphatic.

"Nassy laundrymans!"

"I expect I gave that big mongrel the fright of his life," said Mr. Watson, with complacency. "He'll probably run a mile!"

The shoulders of Genesis shook as he was towed along by the convulsive tub. He knew from previous evidence that Clematis possessed both a high quality and a large quantity of persistence, and it was his hilarious opinion that the dog had not gone far. As a matter of fact, the head of Clematis was at this moment cautiously extended from behind the fence-post at the corner whither he had fled. Viewing with growing assurance the scene before him, he permitted himself to emerge wholly, and sat down, with his head tilted to one side in thought. Almost at the next corner the clothes-boiler with legs, and the wash-tubs, and Genesis were marching on; and just behind them went three figures not so familiar to Clematis, and connected in his mind with a vague, mild apprehension. But all backs were safely toward him, and behind them pattered that small live thing which had so profoundly interested him.

He rose and came on apace, silently.

When he reachced the side of Flopit, some eight or nine seconds later, Clematis found himself even more fascinated and perplexed than during their former interview, though again Flopit seemed utterly to disregard him. Clematis was not at all sure that Flopit *was* a dog, but he felt that it was his business to find out. Heaven knows, so far, Clematis had not a particle of animosity in his heart, but he considered it his duty to himself—in case Flopit turned out not to be a dog—to learn just what he was. The thing might be edible.

Therefore, again pacing obliquely beside Flopit (while the human beings ahead went on, unconscious of the approaching climax behind them) Clematis sought to detect, by senses keener than sight, some evidence of Flopit's standing in the zoological kingdom; and, sniffing at the top of Flopit's head—though Clematis was uncertain about its indeed being a head—he found himself baffled and mentally much disturbed.

Flopit did not smell like a dog; he smelled of violets.

6. Truculence

CLEMATIS frowned and sneezed as the infinitesimal particles of sachet powder settled in the lining of his nose. He became serious, and was conscious of a growing feeling of dislike; he began to be upset over the whole matter. But his conscience compelled him to persist in his attempt to solve the mystery; and also he remembered that one should be courteous, no matter what some other thing chooses to be. Hence he sought to place his nose in contact with Flopit's, for he had perceived on the front of the mysterious stranger a buttony something which might possibly be a nose.

Flopit evaded the contact. He felt that he had endured about enough from this Apache, and that it was nearly time to destroy him. Having no experience of battle, save with bedroom slippers and lace handkerchiefs, Flopit had little doubt of his powers as a warrior. Betrayed by his majestic self-importance, he had not the remotest idea that he was small. Usually he saw the world from a window, or from the seat of an automobile, or over his mistress's arm. He looked down on all dogs, thought them ruffianly, despised them; and it is the miraculous truth that not only was he unaware that he was small, but he did not even know that he was a dog, himself. He did not think about himself in that way.

From these various ignorances of his sprang his astonishing, his incredible, valor. Clematis, with head lowered close to Flopit's, perceived something peering at him from beneath the tangled curtain of cottony, violet-scented stuff which seemed to be the upper part of Flopit's face. It was Flopit's eye, a red-rimmed eye and sore—and so demoniacally maligant that Clematis, indescribably startled, would have withdrawn his own countenance at once—but it was too late. With a fearful oath Flopit sprang upward and annexed himself to the under lip of the horrified Clematis.

Horror gave place to indignation instantly; and as Miss Parcher and her guest turned, screaming, Clematis's self-command went all to pieces.

Miss Parcher became faint and leaned against the hedge along which they had been passing, but her visitor continued to scream, while Mr. Watson endeavored to kick Clematis without ruining Flopit—a difficult matter.

Flopit was baresark from the first, and the mystery is where he learned the dog-cursing that he did. In spite of the David-and-Goliath difference in size it would be less than justice to deny that a very fair dog-fight took place. It was so animated, in truth, that the one expert in such matters who was present found himself warmly interested. Genesis relieved himself of the burden of the wash-tub upon his back, dropped the handle of that other in which he had a half-interest, and watched the combat; his mouth, like his eyes, wide open in simple pleasure.

He was not destined to enjoy the spectacle to the uttermost; a furious young person struck him a frantic, though harmless, blow with a pink parasol.

"You stop them!" she screamed. "You make that horrible dog stop, or I'll have you arrested!"

Genesis rushed forward.

"You *Clem!*" he shouted.

And instantly Clematis was but a whitish and brownish streak along the hedge. He ran like a dog in a moving picture when they speed the film, and he shot from sight, once more, round the corner, while Flopit, still cursing, was seized and squeezed in his mistress's embrace.

But she was not satisfied. "Where's that laundryman with the tin thing on his head?" she demanded. "He ought to be arrested for having such a dog. It's *his* dog, isn't it? Where is he?"

Genesis turned and looked round about the horizon, mystified. William Sylvanus Baxter and the clothes-boiler had disappeared from sight.

"If he owns that dog," asserted the still furious owner of Flopit, "I *will* have him arrested. Where he is? Where is that laundryman?"

"Why, he," Genesis began slowly, "*he* ain' no laundrym—" He came to an uncertain pause. If she chose to assume, with quick feminine intuition, that the dog was William's and that William was a laundryman, it was not Genesis's place to enlighten her. " 'Tic-larly," he reflected, "since she talk so free about gittin' people 'rested!" He became aware that William had squirmed through the hedge and now lay prostrate on the other side of it, but this, likewise, was something within neither his duty nor his inclination to reveal.

"Thishere laundryman," said Genesis, resuming—"thishere laundryman what own the dog, I reckon he mus' hopped on 'at street-car what went by."

"Well, he *ought* to be arrested!" she said, and, pressing her cheek to Flopit's, she changed her tone. "Izzum's ickle heart a-beatin' so floppity! Um's own mumsy make ums all right, um's p'eshus Flopit!"

Then with the consoling Miss Parcher's arm about her, and Mr. Watson even more dazzled with love than when he had first met her, some three hours past, she made her way between the tubs, and passed on down the street. Not till the three (and Flopit) were out of sight did William come forth from the hedge.

"Hi yah!" exclaimed Genesis. " 'At lady go'n a 'rest ev'y man what own a dog, 'f she had her way!"

But William spoke no word.

In silence, then, they resumed their burdens and their journey. Clematis was waiting for them at the corner ahead.

7. Mr. Baxter's Evening Clothes

THAT EVENING, at about half-past seven o'clock, dinner being over and Mr. and Mrs. Baxter (parents of William) seated in the library, Mrs. Baxter said:

"I think it's about time for you to go and dress for your Emerson Club meeting, papa, if you intend to go."

"Do I have to dress?" Mr. Baxter asked, plaintively.

"I think nearly all the men do, don't they?" she insisted.

"But I'm getting old enough not to have to, don't you think, mamma?" he urged, appealingly. "When a man's my age—"

"Nonsense!" she said. "Your figure is exactly like William's. It's the figure that really shows age first, and yours hasn't begun to." And she added, briskly, "Go along like a good boy and get it over!"

Mr. Baxter rose submissively and went upstairs to do as he was told. But, after fifteen or twenty minutes, during which his footsteps had been audible in various parts of the house, he called down over the banisters:

"I can't find 'em."

"Can't find what?"

"My evening clothes. They aren't anywhere in the house."

"Where did you put them the last time you wore them?" she called.

"I don't know. I haven't had 'em on since last spring."

"All right; I'll come," she said, putting her sewing upon the table and rising. "Men never can find anything," she observed, additionally, as she ascended the stairs. "Especially their own things!"

On this occasion, however, as she was obliged to admit a little later, women were not more efficacious than the duller sex. Search high, search low, no trace of Mr. Baxter's evening clothes was to be found. "Perhaps William could find them," said Mrs. Baxter, a final confession of helplessness.

But William was no more to be found than the missing apparel. William, in fact, after spending some time in the lower back hall, listening to the quest above, had just gone out through the kitchen door. And after some ensuing futile efforts, Mr. Baxter was forced to proceed to his club in the accouterments of business.

He walked slowly, enjoying the full moon, which sailed up a river in the sky—the open space between the trees that lined the street—and as he passed the house of Mr. Parcher he noted the fine white shape of a masculine evening bosom gleaming in the moonlight on the porch. A dainty figure in white sat beside it, and there was another white figure present, though this one was so small that Mr. Baxter did not see it at all. It was the figure of a tiny doglet, and it reposed upon the black masculine knees that belonged to the evening bosom.

Mr. Baxter heard a dulcet voice.

"He *is* indifferink, isn't he, sweetest Flopit? Seriously, though, Mr. Watson was telling me about you to-day. He says you're the most indifferent man he knows. He says you don't care two minutes whether a girl lives or dies. Isn't he a mean ole wicked sing, p'eshus Flopit!"

The reply was inaudible, and Mr. Baxter passed on, having recognized nothing of his own.

"These *young* fellows don't have any trouble finding their dress-suits, I guess," he murmured. "Not on a night like this!"

... Thus William, after a hard day, came to the gates of his romance, entering those portals of the moon in triumph. At one stroke his dashing raiment gave him high superiority over Johnnie Watson and other rivals who might loom. But if he had known to what undoing this great coup exposed him, it is probable that Mr. Baxter would have appeared at the Emerson Club, that night, in evening clothes.

8. Jane

WILLIAM'S period of peculiar sensitiveness dated from that evening, and Jane, in particular, caused him a great deal of anxiety. In fact, he began to feel that Jane was a mortification which his parents might have spared him, with no loss to themselves or to the world. Not having shown that consideration for anybody, they might at least have been less spinelessly indulgent of her. William's bitter conviction was that he had never seen a child so starved of discipline or so lost to etiquette as Jane.

For one thing, her passion for bread-and-butter, covered with apple sauce and powdered sugar, was getting to be a serious matter. Secretly, William was not yet so changed by love as to be wholly indifferent to this refection himself, but his consumption of it was private, whereas Jane had formed the habit of eating it in exposed places—such as the front yard or the sidewalk. At no hour of the day was it advisable for a relative to approach the neighborhood in fastidious company, unless prepared to acknowledge kinship with a spindly young person either eating bread-and-butter and apple sauce and powdered sugar, or all too visibly just having eaten bread-and-butter and apple sauce and powdered sugar. Moreover, there were times when Jane had worse things than apple sauce to answer for, as William made clear to his mother in an oration as hot as the July noon sun which looked down upon it.

Mrs. Baxter was pleasantly engaged with a sprinkling-can and some small flower-beds in the shady back yard, and Jane, having returned from various sidewalk excursions, stood close by as a spectator, her hands replenished with the favorite food and her chin rising and falling in gentle motions, little prophecies of slight distensions which passed down her slender throat with slow, rhythmic regularity. Upon this calm scene came William, plunging round a corner of the house, furious yet plaintive.

"You've got to do something about that child!" he began. "I *cannot* stand it!"

Jane looked at him dumbly, not ceasing, however, to

eat; while Mrs. Baxter thoughtfully continued her sprinkling.

"You've been gone all morning, Willie," she said. "I thought your father mentioned at breakfast that he expected you to put in at least four hours a day on your mathematics and—"

"That's neither here nor there," William returned, vehemently. "I just want to say this: if you don't do something about Jane, I will! Just look at her! *Look* at her, I ask you! That's just the way she looked half an hour ago, out on the public sidewalk in front of the house, when I came by here with Miss *Pratt!* That was pleasant, wasn't it? To be walking with a lady on the public street and meet a member of my family looking like that! Oh, *lovely!*"

In the anguish of this recollection his voice cracked, and though his eyes were dry his gestures wept for him. Plainly, he was about to reach the most lamentable portion of his narrative. "And then she *hollered* at me! She hollered, 'Oh, *Will—ee!*'" Here he gave an imitation of Jane's voice, so damnatory that Jane ceased to eat for several moments and drew herself up with a kind of dignity. "She hollered, 'Oh, *Will—ee*' at me" he stormed. "Anybody would think I was about six years old! She hollered, 'Oh, Will—ee' and she rubbed her stomach and slushed apple sauce all over her face, and she kept hollering, "Will—ee!' with her mouth full. "Will—ee, look! Good! Bread-and-butter and apple sauce and sugar! I bet you wish *you* had some. Will—ee!'"

"You did eat some, the other day," said Jane. "You ate a whole lot. You eat it every chance you get!"

"You hush up!" he shouted, and returned to his description of the outrage. "She kept *following* us! She followed us, hollering, '*Will—ee!*' till it's a wonder we didn't go deaf! And just look at her! I don't see how you can stand it to have her going around like that and people knowing it's your child! Why, she hasn't got enough *on!*"

Mrs. Baxter laughed. "Oh, for this very hot weather, I really don't think people notice or care much about—"

" 'Notice'!" he wailed. "I guess Miss *Pratt* noticed! Hot weather's no excuse for—for outright obesity!" (As Jane was thin, it is probable that William had mistaken the meaning of this word.) "Why, half o' what she *has* got on has come unfastened—especially that frightful thing hanging around her leg—and look at her back, I just beg you! I ask you to look at her back. You can see her spinal cord!"

"Column," Mrs. Baxter corrected. "Spinal column, Willie."

"What do *I* care which it is?" he fumed. "People aren't supposed to go around with it *exposed,* whichever it is! And with apple sauce on their ears!"

"There is not!" Jane protested, and at the moment when she spoke she was right. Naturally, however, she lifted her hands to the accused ears, and the unfortunate result was to justify William's statement.

"*Look!*" he cried, "I just ask you to look! Think of it: that's the sight I have to meet when I'm out walking with Miss *Pratt!* She asked me who it was, and I wish you'd seen her face. She wanted to know who 'that curious child' was, and I'm glad you didn't hear the way she said it. 'Who *is* that curious child?' she said, and I had to tell her it was my sister. I had to tell Miss *Pratt* it was my only *sister!*"

"Willie, who is Miss Pratt?" asked Mrs. Baxter, mildly. "I don't think I've ever heard of—"

Jane had returned to an admirable imperturbability, but she chose this moment to interrupt her mother, and her own eating, with remarks delivered in a tone void of emphasis or expression.

"Willie's mashed on her," she said, casually. "And she wears false side-curls. One almost came off."

At this unspeakable desecration William's face was that of a high priest stricken at the altar.

"She's visitin' Miss May Parcher," added the deadly Jane. "But the Parchers are awful tired of her. They wish she'd go home, but they don't like to tell her so."

One after another these insults from the canaille fell upon the ears of William. That slanders so atrocious could soil the universal air seemed unthinkable.

He became icily calm.

"*Now* if you don't punish her," he said, deliberately, "it's because you have lost your sense of duty!"

Having uttered these terrible words, he turned upon his heel and marched toward the house. His mother called after him:

"Wait, Willie. Jane doesn't mean to hurt your feelings—"

"My feelings!" he cried, the iciness of his demeanor giving way under the strain of emotion. "You stand there and allow her to speak as she did of one of the—one of the—" For a moment William appeared to be at a loss, and the fact is that it always has been a difficult matter to describe *the* bright, ineffable divinity of the world to one's mother, especially in the presence of an inimical third party of tender years. "One of the—" he said; "one of the—the noblest —one of the noblest—"

Again he paused.

"Oh, Jane didn't mean anything," said Mrs. Baxter. "And if you think Miss Pratt is so nice, I'll ask May Parcher to bring her to tea with us some day. If it's too hot, we'll have iced tea, and you can ask Johnnie Watson, if you like. Don't get so upset about things, Willie!"

"'Upset'!" he echoed, appealing to heaven against this word. "'Upset'!" And he entered the house in a manner most dramatic.

"What made you say that?" Mrs. Baxter asked, turning curiously to Jane when William had disappeared. "Where did you hear any such things?"

"I was there," Jane replied, gently eating on and on. William could come and William could go, but Jane's alimentary canal went on forever.

"You were where, Jane?"

"At the Parchers'."

"Oh, I see."

"Yesterday afternoon," said Jane, "when Miss Parcher had the Sunday-school class for lemonade and cookies."

"Did you hear Miss Parcher say—"

"No'm," said Jane. "I ate too many cookies, I guess, maybe. Anyways, Miss Parcher said I better lay down—"

"*Lie* down, Jane."

"Yes'm. On the sofa in the libberry, an' Mrs. Parcher an' Mr. Parcher came in there an' sat down, after while, an' it was kind of dark, an' they didn't hardly notice me, or I guess they thought I was asleep, maybe. Anyways, they didn't talk loud, but Mr. Parcher would sort of grunt an' ack cross. He said he just wished he knew when he was goin' to have a home again. Then Mrs. Parcher said May *had* to ask her Sunday-school class, but he said he never meant the Sunday-school class. He said since Miss Pratt came to visit, there wasn't anywhere he could go, because Willie Baxter an' Johnnie Watson an' Joe Bullitt an' all the other ones like that were there all the time, an' it made him just sick at the stummick, an' he did wish there was some way to find out when she was goin' home, because he couldn't stand much more talk about love. He said Willie an' Johnnie Watson an' Joe Bullitt an' Miss Pratt were always arguin' somep'm about love, an' he said Willie was the worst. Mamma, he said he didn't like the rest of it, but he said he guessed he could stand it if it wasn't for Willie. An' he said the reason they were all so in love of Miss Pratt was because she talks baby-talk, an' he said he couldn't stand much more baby-talk. Mamma, she has the loveliest little white dog, an' Mr. Parcher doesn't like it. He said he couldn't go anywhere around the place without steppin' on the dog or Willie Baxter. An' he said he couldn't sit on his own porch any more; he said he couldn't sit even in the liberry but he had to hear baby-talk goin' on *some*wheres an' then either Willie Baxter or Joe Bullitt or somebody or another arguin' about love. Mamma, he said"—Jane became impressive—"he said, mamma, he said he didn't mind the Sunday-school class, but he couldn't stand those dam boys!"

"Jane!" Mrs. Baxter cried, "you *mustn't* say such things!"

"I didn't, mamma. Mr. Parcher said it. He said he couldn't stand those da—"

"*Jane!* No matter what he said, you mustn't repeat—"

"But I'm not. I only said Mr. *Parcher* said he couldn't stand those d—"

Mrs. Baxter cut the argument short by imprisoning Jane's mouth with a firm hand. Jane continued to swallow quietly until released. Then she said:

"But, mamma, how can I tell you what he said unless I say—"

"Hush!" Mrs. Baxter commanded. "You must never, never again use such a terrible and wicked word."

"I won't, mamma," Jane said, meekly. Then she brightened. "Oh, *I* know! I'll say 'word' instead. Won't that be all right?"

"I—I suppose so."

"Well, Mr. Parcher said he couldn't stand those word boys. That sounds all right, doesn't it, mamma?"

Mrs. Baxter hesitated, but she was inclined to hear as complete as possible a report of Mr. and Mrs. Parcher's conversation, since it seemed to concern William so nearly; and she well knew that Jane had her own way of telling things—or else they remained untold.

"I—I suppose so," Mrs. Baxter said again.

"Well, they kind of talked along," Jane continued, much pleased; "an' Mr. Parcher said when he was young he wasn't any such a—such a word fool as these young word fools were. He said in all his born days Willie Baxter was the wordest fool he ever saw!"

Willie Baxter's mother flushed a little. "That was very unjust and very wrong of Mr. Parcher," she said, primly.

"Oh no, mamma!" Jane protested. "Mrs. Parcher thought so, too."

"Did she, indeed!"

"Only she didn't say word or wordest or anything like that," Jane explained. "She said it was because Miss Pratt had coaxed him to be so in love of her; an' Mr. Parcher said he didn't care whose fault it was, Willie was a—a word calf an' so were all the rest of 'em, Mr. Parcher said. An' he said he couldn't stand it any more. Mr. Parcher said that a whole lot of times, mamma. He said he guess' pretty soon he'd haf to be in the lunatic asylum if Miss Pratt stayed a few more days with her word little dog an' her word Willie Baxter an' all the other word calfs. Mrs. Parcher said he oughtn't to say 'word,' mamma. She said, 'Hush, hush!' to him, mamma. He talked liked this, mamma: he said, 'I'll be word if I stand it!' An' he kept gettin' crosser, and he said, 'Word! Word! *Word!* Wor—'"

"There!" Mrs. Baxter interrupted, sharply. "That will do, Jane! We'll talk about something else now, I think."

Jane looked hurt; she was taking great pleasure in this confidential interview, and gladly would have continued to quote the harried Mr. Parcher at great length. Still, she was not entirely uncontent: she must have had some perception that her performance—merely as a notable bit of reportorial art—did not wholly lack style, even if her attire did. Yet, brilliant as Jane's work was, Mrs. Baxter felt no astonishment; several times ere this Jane had demonstrated a remarkable faculty for the retention of details concerning William. And running hand in hand with a really superb curiosity, this powerful memory was making Jane an even greater factor in William's life than he suspected.

During the glamors of early love, if there be a creature more deadly than the little brother of a budding woman, that creature is the little sister of a budding man. The little brother at least tells in the open all he knows, often at full power of his lungs, and even that may be avoided, since he is wax in the hands of bribery; but the little sister is more apt to save her knowledge for use upon a terrible occasion; and, no matter what bribes she may accept, she is certain to tell her mother everything. All in all, a young lover should arrange, if possible, to be the only child of elderly parents; otherwise his mother and sister are sure to know a great deal more about him than he knows that they know.

This was what made Jane's eyes so disturbing to William during lunch that day. She ate quietly and competently, but all the while he was conscious of her solemn and inscrutable gaze fixed upon him; and she spoke not once. She could not have rendered herself more annoying, especially as William was trying to treat her with silent scorn, for nothing is more irksome to the muscles of the face than silent scorn, when there is no means of showing it except by the expression. On the other hand, Jane's inscrutability gave her no discomfort whatever. In fact, inscrutability is about the most comfortable expression that a person can wear, though the truth is that just now Jane was not really inscrutable at all.

She was merely looking at William and thinking of Mr. Parcher.

9. Little Sisters Have Big Ears

THE CONFIDENTIAL talk between mother and daughter at
noon was not the last to take place that day. At nightfall
—eight o'clock in this pleasant season—Jane was saying
her prayers beside her bed, while her mother stood close
by, waiting to put out the light.

"An' bless mamma and papa an'—" Jane murmured,
coming to a pause. "An'—an' bless Willie," she added,
with a little reluctance.

"Go on, dear," said her mother. "You haven't finished."

"I know it, mamma," Jane looked up to say. "I was just
thinkin' a minute. I want to tell you about somep'm."

"Finish your prayers first, Jane."

Jane obeyed with a swiftness in which there was no
intentional irreverence. Then she jumped into bed and
began a fresh revelation.

"It's about papa's clo'es, mamma."

"What clothes of papa's? What do you mean, Jane?"
asked Mrs. Baxter, puzzled.

"The ones you couldn't find. The ones you been lookin'
for 'most every day."

"You mean papa's evening clothes?"

"Yes'm," said Jane. "Willie's got 'em on."

"What!"

"Yes, he has!" Jane assured her with emphasis. "I bet
you he's had 'em on every single evening since Miss Pratt
came to visit the Parchers! Anyway, he's got 'em on now,
cause I saw 'em."

Mrs. Baxter bit her lip and frowned. "Are you sure,
Jane?"

"Yes'm. I saw him in 'em."

"How?"

"Well, I was in my bare feet after I got undressed
—before you came up-stairs—mamma, an' I was kind of
walkin' around in the hall—"

"You shouldn't do that, Jane."

"No'm. An' I heard Willie say somep'm kind of to himself, or like deckamation. He was inside his room, but the

32

door wasn't quite shut. He started out once, but he went
back for somep'm an' forgot to, I guess. Anyway, I thought
I better look an' see what was goin' on, mamma. So I just
kind of peeked in—"

"But you shouldn't do that, dear," Mrs. Baxter said,
musingly. "It isn't really quite honorable."

"No'm. Well, what you think he was doin'?" (Here
Jane's voice betrayed excitement and so did her eyes.)
"He was standin' up there in papa's clo'es before the
lookin'-glass, an' first he'd lean his head over on one side,
an' then he'd lean it over on the other side, an' then he'd
bark, mamma."

"He'd what?"

"Yes'm!" said Jane. "He'd give a little teeny *bark*,
mamma—kind of like a puppy, mamma."

"What?" cried Mrs. Baxter.

"Yes'm, he did!" Jane asserted. "He did it four or five
times. First he'd lean his head way over on his shoulder
like this—look, mamma!—an' then he'd lean it way over
the other shoulder, an' every time he'd do it he'd bark.
'Berp-werp!' he'd say, mamma, just like that, only not loud
at all. He said, 'Berp-werp! *Berp-werp-werp!*' You could
tell he meant it for barkin', but it wasn't very good,
mamma. What you think he meant, mamma?"

"Heaven knows!" murmured the astonished mother.

"An' then," Jane continued, "he quit barkin' all of a
sudden, an' didn't lean his head over any more, an' com-
menced actin' kind of solemn, an' kind of whispered to
himself. I think he was kind of pretendin' he was talkin'
to Miss Pratt, or at a party, maybe. Anyways, he spoke
out loud after while—not just exactly *loud,* I mean, but
anyway so's 't I could hear what he said. Mamma—he said,
'Oh, my baby-talk lady!' Just like that, mamma. Listen,
mamma, here's the way he said it: 'Oh, my baby-talk
lady!' "

Jane's voice, in this impersonation, became sufficiently
soft and tremulous to give Mrs. Baxter a fair idea of
the tender yearning of the original. " '*Oh, my baby-talk
lady!*' " cooed the terrible Jane.

"Mercy!" Mrs. Baxter exclaimed. "Perhaps it's no wonder Mr. Parcher—" She broke off abruptly, then inquired,
"What did he do next, Jane?"

"Next," said Jane, "he put the light out, an' I had to—well, I just waited kind of squeeged up against the wall, an' he never saw me. He went on out to the back stairs, an' went down the stairs tiptoe, mamma. You know what I think, mamma? I think he goes out that way an' through the kitchen on account of papa's clo'es."

Mrs. Baxter paused, with her hand upon the key of the shaded electric lamp. "I suppose so," she said. "I think perhaps—" For a moment or two she wrapped herself in thought. "Perhaps"—she repeated, musingly—"perhaps we'll keep this just a secret between you and me for a little while, Jane, and not say anything to papa about the clothes. I don't think it will hurt them, and I suppose Willie feels they give him a great advantage over the other boys—and papa uses them so very little, especially since he's grown a wee bit stouter. Yes, it will be our secret, Jane. We'll think it over till to-morrow."

"Yes'm."

Mrs. Baxter turned out the light, then came and kissed Jane in the dark. "Good night, dear."

"G' night, mamma." But as Mrs. Baxter reached the door Jane's voice was heard again.

"Mamma?"

"Yes?" Mrs. Baxter paused.

"Mamma," Jane said, slowly, "I think—I think Mr. Parcher is a very nice man. Mamma?"

"Yes, dear?"

"Mamma, what do you s'pose Willie barked at the lookin'-glass for?"

"That," said Mrs. Baxter, "is beyond me. Young people and children do the strangest things, Jane! And then, when they get to be middle-aged, they forget all those strange things they did, and they can't understand what the new young people—like you and Willie—mean by the strange things *they* do."

"Yes'm. I bet *I* know what he was barkin' for, mamma."

"Well?"

"You know what I think? I think he was kind of practisin'. I think he was practisin' how to bark at Mr. Parcher."

"No, no!" Mrs. Baxter laughed. "Who ever could think

of such a thing but you, Jane! You go to sleep and forget your nonsense!"

Nevertheless, Jane might almost have been gifted with clairvoyance, her preposterous idea came so close to the actual fact, for at that very moment William was barking. He was not barking directly at Mr. Parcher, it is true, but within a short distance of him and all too well within his hearing.

10. Mr. Parcher and Love

MR. PARCHER, that unhappy gentleman, having been driven indoors from his own porch, had attempted to read *Plutarch's Lives* in the library, but, owing to the adjacency of the porch and the summer necessity for open windows, his escape spared only his eyes and not his suffering ears. The house was small, being but half of a double one, with small rooms, and the "parlor," library, and dining-room all about equally exposed to the porch which ran along the side of the house. Mr. Parcher had no refuge except bed or the kitchen, and as he was troubled with chronic insomnia, and the cook had callers in the kitchen, his case was desperate. Most unfortunately, too, his reading-lamp, the only one in the house, was a fixture near a window, and just beyond that window sat Miss Pratt and William in sweet unconsciousness, while Miss Parcher entertained the overflow (consisting of Mr. Johnnie Watson) at the other end of the porch. Listening perforce to the conversation of the former couple—though "conversation" is far from the expression later used by Mr. Parcher to describe what he heard— he found it impossible to sit still in his chair. He jerked and twitched with continually increasing restlessness; sometimes he gasped, and other times he moaned a little, and there were times when he muttered huskily.

"Oh, cute-ums!" came the silvery voice of Miss Pratt from the likewise silvery porch outside, underneath the summer moon. "Darlin' Flopit, look! Ickle boy Baxter goin' make imitations of darlin' Flopit again. See! Ickle boy Baxter puts head one side, then other side, just like darlin' Flopit. Then barks just like darlin' Flopit! Ladies and 'entlemen, imitations of darlin' Flopit by ickle boy Baxter."

"Berp-werp! Berp-werp!" came the voice of William Sylvanus Baxter.

And in the library *Plutarch's Lives* moved convulsively, while with writhing lips Mr. Parcher muttered to himself.

"More, more!" cried Miss Pratt, clapping her hands. "Do it again, ickle boy Baxter!"

"Berp-werp! Berp-werp-werp!"

"*Word!*" muttered Mr. Parcher.

Miss Pratt's voice became surcharged with honeyed wonder. "How did he learn such marv'lous, *marv'lous* imitations of darlin' Flopit? He ought to go on the big, big stage and be a really actor, oughtn't he, darlin' Flopit? He could make milyums and milyums of dollardies, couldn't he, darlin' Flopit?"

William's modest laugh disclaimed any great ambition for himself in this line. "Oh, I always could think up imitations of animals; things like that—but I hardly would care to—to adop' the stage for a career. Would—you?" (There was a thrill in his voice when he pronounced the ineffably significant word "you.")

Miss Pratt became intensely serious.

"It's my *dream!*" she said.

William, seated upon a stool at her feet, gazed up at the amber head, divinely splashed by the rain of moonlight. The fire with which she spoke stirred him as few things had ever stirred him. He knew she had just revealed a side of herself which she reserved for only the chosen few who were capable of understanding her, and he fell into a hushed rapture. It seemed to him that there was a sacredness about this moment, and he sought vaguely for something to say that would live up to it and not be out of keeping. Then, like an inspiration, there came into his head some words he had read that day and thought beautiful. He had found them beneath an illustration in a magazine, and he spoke them almost instinctively.

"It was wonderful of you to say that to me," he said. "I shall never forget it!"

"It's my *dream!*" Miss Pratt exclaimed, again, with the same enthusiasm. "It's my *dream.*"

"You would make a glorious actress!" he said.

At that her mood changed. She laughed a laugh like a sweet little girl's laugh (not Jane's) and, setting her rocking-chair in motion, cuddled the fuzzy white doglet in her arms. "Ickle boy Baxter t'yin' flatterbox us, tunnin' Flopit! No'ty, no'ty flatterbox!"

"No, no!" William insisted, earnestly. "I mean it. But—but—"

"But whatcums?"

"What do you think about actors and actresses making love to each other on the stage? Do you think they have to really feel it, or do they just pretend?"

"Well," said Miss Pratt, weightily, "sometimes one way, sometimes the other."

William's gravity became more and more profound. "Yes, but how can they pretend like that? Don't you think love is a sacred thing, Cousin Lola?"

Fictitious sisterships, brotherships, and cousinships are devices to push things along, well known to seventeen and even more advanced ages. On the wonderful evening of their first meeting William and Miss Pratt had cozily arranged to be called, respectively, "Ickle boy Baxter" and "Cousin Lola." (Thus they had broken down the tedious formalities of their first twenty minutes together.)

"Don't you think love is sacred?" he repeated in the deepest tone of which his vocal cords were capable.

"Ess," said Miss Pratt.

"*I* do!" William was emphatic. "I think love is the most sacred thing there is. I don't mean *some* kinds of love. I mean *real* love. You take some people, I don't believe they ever know what real love means. They *talk* about it, maybe, but they don't understand it. Love is something nobody can understand unless they feel it and—and if they don't understand it they don't feel it. Don't *you* think so?"

"Ess."

"Love," William continued, his voice lifting and thrilling to the great theme—"love is something nobody can ever have but one time in their lives, and if they don't have it then, why prob'ly they never will. Now, if a man *really* loves a girl, why he'd do anything in the world she wanted him to. Don't *you* think so?"

"Ess, 'deedums!" said the silvery voice.

"But if he didn't, then he wouldn't," said William vehemently. "But when a man really loves a girl he will. Now, you take a man like that and he can generally do just about anything the girl he loves wants him to. Say, f'rinstance, she wants him to love her even more than he does already—or almost anything like that—and supposin' she asks him to. Well, he would go ahead and do it. If they really loved each other he would!"

He paused a moment, then in a lowered tone he said, "I think *real* love is sacred, don't you?"

"Ess."

"Don't you think love is the most sacred thing there is —that is, if it's *real* love?"

"Ess."

"*I* do," said William, warmly. "I—I'm glad you feel like that, because I think real love is the kind nobody could have but just once in their lives, but if it isn't *real* love, why—why most people never have it at all, because—" He paused, seeming to seek for the exact phrase which would express his meaning. "—Because the *real* love a man feels for a girl and a girl for a man, if they *really* love each other, and, you look at a case like that, of course they would *both* love each other, or it wouldn't be real love —well, what *I* say is, if it's *real* love, well, it's—it's sacred because I think that kind of love is always sacred. Don't you think love is sacred if it's the real thing?"

"Ess," said Miss Pratt. "Do Flopit again. Be Flopit!"

"Berp-werp! Berp-werp-werp."

And within the library an agonized man writhed and muttered:

"*Word! Word!* WORD—"

This hoarse repetition had become almost continuous.

. . . But out on the porch, that little, jasmine-scented bower in Arcady where youth cried to youth and golden heads were haloed in the moonshine, there fell a silence. Not utter silence, for out there an ethereal music sounded constantly, unheard and forgotten by older ears. Time was when the sly playwrights used "incidental music" in their dramas; they knew that an audience would be moved so long as the music played; credulous while that crafty enchantment lasted. And when the galled Mr. Parcher wondered how those young people out on the porch could listen to each other and not die, it was because he did not hear and had forgotten the music that throbs in the veins of youth. Nevertheless, it may not be denied that despite his poor memory this man of fifty was deserving of a little sympathy.

It was William who broke the silence. "How—" he began, and his voice trembled a little. "How—how do you—how do you think of me when I'm not with you?"

"Think nice-cums," Miss Pratt responded. "Flopit an' me think nice-cums."

"No," said William; "I meant what name do you have for me when you're—when you're thinking about me?"

Miss Pratt seemed to be puzzled, perhaps justifiably, and she made a cooing sound of interrogation.

"I mean like this," William explained. "F'rinstance, when you first came, I always thought of you as 'Milady'—when I wrote that poem, you know."

"Ess. Boo'fums."

"But now I don't," he said. "Now I think of you by another name when I'm alone. It—it just sort of came to me. I was kind of just sitting around this afternoon, and I didn't know I was thinking about anything at all very much, and then all of a sudden I said it to myself out loud. It was about as strange a thing as I ever knew of. Don't *you* think so?"

"Ess. It uz dest *weird!*" she answered. "What *are* dat pitty names?"

"I called you," said William, huskily and reverently, "I called you 'My Baby-Talk Lady.' "

Bang!

They were startled by a crash from within the library; a heavy weight seemed to have fallen (or to have been hurled) a considerable distance. Stepping to the window, William beheld a large volume lying in a distorted attitude at the foot of the wall opposite to that in which the reading-lamp was a fixture. But of all human life the room was empty; for Mr. Parcher had given up, and was now hastening to his bed in the last faint hope of saving his reason.

His symptoms, however, all pointed to its having fled; and his wife, looking up from some computations in laundry charges, had but a vision of windmill gestures as he passed the door of her room. Then, not only for her, but for the inoffensive people who lived in the other half of the house, the closing of his own door took place in a really memorable manner.

William, gazing upon the fallen Plutarch, had just offered the explanation, "Somebody must 'a' thrown it at a bug or something, I guess," when the second explosion sent its reverberations through the house.

"My goodness!" Miss Pratt exclaimed, jumping up.

William laughed reassuringly, remaining calm. "It's only a door blew shut up-stairs," he said. "Let's sit down again—just the way we were?"

Unfortunately for him, Mr. Joe Bullitt now made his appearance at the other end of the porch. Mr. Bullitt, though almost a year younger than either William or Johnnie Watson, was of a turbulent and masterful disposition. Moreover, in regard to Miss Pratt his affections were in as ardent a state as those of his rivals, and he lacked Johnnie's meekness. He firmly declined to be shunted by Miss Parcher, who was trying to favor William's cause, according to a promise he had won of her by strong pleading. Regardless of her efforts, Mr. Bullitt descended upon William and his Baby-Talk Lady, and received from the latter a honeyed greeting, somewhat to the former's astonishment and not at all to his pleasure.

"Oh, goody-cute!" cried Miss Pratt. "Here's big Bruvva Josie-Joe!" And she lifted her little dog close to Mr. Bullitt's face, guiding one of Flopit's paws with her fingers. "Stroke big Bruvva Josie-Joe's pint teeks, darlin' Flopit." (Josie-Joe's pink cheeks were indicated by the expression "pint teeks," evidently, for her accompanying action was to pass Flopit's paw lightly over those glowing surfaces.) "'At's nice!" she remarked. "Stroke him gently, p'eshus Flopit, an' nen we'll coax him to make pitty singin' for us, like us did yestiday."

She turned to William.

"*Coax* him to make pitty singin'? I *love* his voice—I'm dest *crazy* over it. Isn't oo?"

William's passion for Mr. Bullitt's voice appeared to be under control. He laughed coldly, almost harshly. "Him sing?" he said. "Has he been tryin' to sing around *here?* I wonder the family didn't call for the police!"

It was to be seen that Mr. Bullitt did not relish the sally.

"Well, they will," he retorted, "if you ever spring one o' your solos on 'em!" And turning to Miss Pratt, he laughed loudly and bitterly. "You ought to hear Silly Bill sing— some time when you don't mind goin' to bed sick for a couple o' days!"

Symptoms of truculence at once became alarmingly pronounced on both sides. William was naturally incensed, and as for Mr. Bullitt, he had endured a great deal from William every evening since Miss Pratt's arrival. William's evening clothes were hard enough for both Mr. Watson and Mr. Bullitt to bear, without any additional insolence on the part of the wearer. Big Bruvva Josie-Joe took a step toward his enemy and breathed audibly.

"Let's *all* sing," the tactful Miss Pratt proposed, hastily. "Come on, May and Cousin Johnnie-Jump-Up," she called to Miss Parcher and Mr. Watson. "Singin'-school, dirls an' boys! Singin'-school! Ding, ding! Singin'-school bell's a-wingin'!"

The diversion was successful. Miss Parcher and Mr. Watson joined the other group with alacrity, and the five young people were presently seated close together upon the steps of the porch, sending their voices out upon the air and up to Mr. Parcher's window in the song they found loveliest that summer.

Miss Pratt carried the air. William also carried it part of the time and hunted for it the rest of the time, though never in silence. Miss Parcher "sang alto," Mr. Bullitt "sang bass," and Mr. Watson "sang tenor"—that is, he sang as high as possible, often making the top sound of a chord and always repeating the last phrase of each line before the others finished it. The melody was a little too sweet, possibly; while the singers thought so highly of the words that Mr. Parcher missed not one, especially as the vocal rivalry between Josie-Joe and Ickle Boy Baxter incited each of them to prevent Miss Pratt from hearing the other.

William sang loudest of all; Mr. Parcher had at no time any difficulty in recognizing his voice.

Oh, I love my love in the morning,
  And I love my love at night,
I love my love in the dawning,

And when the stars are bright.
Some may love the sunshine,
Others may love the dew.
Some may love the raindrops,
But I love only you-*oo*-oo!
By the stars up above
It is you I luh-*huv!*
Yes, *I* love own-*lay* you!

They sang it four times; then Mr. Bullitt sang his solo, "Tell her, O Golden Moon, how I Adore her," William following with "The violate loves the cowslip, but *I* love *yew*," and after that they all sang "Oh, I love my love in the morning" again.

All this while that they sang of love, Mr. Parcher was moving to and fro upon his bed, not more than eighteen feet in an oblique upward-slanting line from the heads of the serenaders. Long, long he tossed, listening to the young voices singing of love; long, long he thought of love, and many, many times he spoke of it aloud, though he was alone in the room. And in thus speaking of it, he would give utterance to phrases and Words probably never before used in connection with love since the world began.

His thoughts, and, at intervals, his mutterings, continued to be active far into the night, long after the callers had gone, and though his household and the neighborhood were at rest, with never a katydid outside to rail at the waning moon. And by a coincidence not more singular than most coincidences, it happened that at just about the time he finally fell asleep, a young lady at no great distance from him awoke to find herself thinking of him.

II. Beginning a True Friendship

THIS WAS Miss Jane Baxter. She opened her eyes upon the new-born day, and her first thoughts were of Mr. Parcher. That is, he was already in her mind when she awoke, a circumstance to be accounted for on the ground that his conversation, during her quiet convalescence in his library, had so fascinated her that in all likelihood she had been dreaming of him. Then, too, Jane and Mr. Parcher had a bond in common, though Mr. Parcher did not know it. Not without result had William repeated Miss Pratt's inquiry in Jane's hearing: "Who *is* that curious child?" Jane had preserved her *sang-froid,* but the words remained with her, for she was one of those who ponder and retain in silence.

She thought almost exclusively of Mr. Parcher until breakfast-time, and resumed her thinking of him at intervals during the morning. Then, in the afternoon, a series of quiet events not unconnected with William's passion caused her to think of Mr. Parcher more poignantly than ever; nor was her mind diverted to a different channel by another confidential conversation with her mother. Who can say, then, that it was not by design that she came face to face with Mr. Parcher on the public highway at about five o'clock that afternoon? Everything urges the belief that she deliberately set herself in his path.

Mr. Parcher was walking home from his office, and he walked slowly, gulping from time to time, as he thought of the inevitable evening before him. His was not a rugged constitution, and for the last fortnight or so he had feared that it was giving way altogether. Each evening he felt that he was growing weaker, and sometimes he thought piteously that he might go away for a while. He did not much care where, though what appealed to him most, curiously enough, was not the thought of the country, with the flowers and little birds; no, what allured him was the idea that perhaps he could find lodgment for a time in an Old People's Home, where the minimum age for inmates was about eighty.

Walking more and more slowly, as he approached the dwelling he had once thought of as home, he became aware of a little girl in a checkered dress approaching him at a gait varied by the indifferent behavior of a barrel-hoop which she was disciplining with a stick held in her right hand. When the hoop behaved well, she came ahead rapidly; when it affected to be intoxicated, which was most often its whim, she zigzagged with it, and gained little ground. But all the while, and without reference to what went on concerning the hoop, she slowly and continuously fed herself (with her left hand) small, solemnly relished bites of a slice of bread-and-butter covered with apple sauce and powdered sugar.

Mr. Parcher looked upon her, and he shivered slightly; for he knew her to be Willie Baxter's sister.

Unaware of the emotion she produced in him, Jane checked her hoop and halted.

"G'd afternoon, Mister Parcher," she said gravely.

"Good afternoon," he returned, without much spirit.

Jane looked up at him trustfully and with a strange, unconscious fondness. "You goin' home now, Mr. Parcher?" she asked, turning to walk at his side. She had suspended the hoop over her left arm and transferred the bread-and-butter and apple sauce and sugar to her right, so that she could eat even more conveniently than before.

"I suppose so," he murmured.

"My brother Willie's been at your house all afternoon," she remarked.

He repeated, "I suppose so," but in a tone which combined the vocal tokens of misery and of hopeless animosity.

"He just went home," said Jane. "I was 'cross the street from your house, but I guess he didn't see me. He kept lookin' back at your house. Miss Pratt was on the porch."

"I suppose so." This time it was a moan.

Jane proceeded to give him some information. "My brother Willie isn't coming back to your house to-night, but he doesn't know it yet."

"What!" exclaimed Mr. Parcher.

"Willie isn't goin' to spend any more evenings at your house at all," said Jane, thoughtfully. "He isn't, but he doesn't know it yet."

Mr. Parcher gazed fixedly at the wonderful child, and something like a ray of sunshine flickered over his seamed and harried face. "Are you *sure* he isn't?" he said. "What makes you think so?"

"I know he isn't," said demure Jane. "It's on account of somep'm I told mamma."

And upon this a gentle glow began to radiate throughout Mr. Parcher. A new feeling budded within his bosom; he was warmly attracted to Jane. She was evidently a child to be cherished, and particularly to be encouraged in the line of conduct she seemed to have adopted. He wished the Bullitt and Watson families each had a little girl like this. Still, if what she said of William proved true, much had been gained and life might be tolerable, after all.

"He'll come in the afternoons, I guess," said Jane. "But you aren't home then, Mr. Parcher, except late—like you were that day of the Sunday-school class. It was on account of what you said that day. I told mamma."

"Told mamma what?"

"What you said. "

Mr. Parcher's perplexity continued. "What about?"

"About Willie. *You* know!" Jane smiled fraternally.

"No, I don't."

"It was when I was layin' in the liberry, that day of the Sunday-school class," Jane told him. "You an' Mrs. Parcher was talkin' in there about Miss Pratt an' Willie an' everything."

"Good heavens!" Mr. Parcher, summoning his memory, had placed the occasion and Jane together. "Did you *hear* all that?"

"Yes." Jane nodded. "I told mamma all what you said."

"Murder!"

"Well," said Jane, "I guess it's good I did, because look—that's the very reason mamma did somep'm so's he can't come any more except in daytime. I guess she thought Willie oughtn't to behave so's 't you said so many things about him like that; so to-day she did somep'm, an' now he can't come any more to behave that loving way of Miss Pratt that you said you would be in the lunatic asylum if he didn't quit. But he hasn't found it out yet."

"Found what out, please?" asked Mr. Parcher, feeling more affection for Jane every moment.

"He hasn't found out he can't come back to your house to-night; an' he can't come back to-morrow night, nor day-after-to-morrow night, nor—"

"Is it because your mamma is going to tell him he can't?"

"No, Mr. Parcher. Mamma says he's too old—an' she said she didn't like to, anyway. She just *did* somep'm."

"What? What did she do?"

"It's a secret," said Jane. "I could tell you the first part of it—up to where the secret begins, I expect."

"Do!" Mr. Parcher urged.

"Well, it's about somep'm Willie's been *wearin'*," Jane began, moving closer to him as they slowly walked onward. "I can't tell you what they were, because that's the secret—but he had 'em on him every evening when he

came to see Miss Pratt, but they belong to papa, an' papa
doesn't know a word about it. Well, one evening papa
wanted to put 'em on, because he had a right to, Mr.
Parcher, an' Willie didn't have any right to at all, but
mamma couldn't find 'em; an' she rummidged an' rummidged 'most all next day an' pretty near every day since
then an' never did find 'em, until don't you believe I saw
Willie inside of 'em only last night! He was startin' over to
your house to see Miss Pratt in 'em! So I told mamma, an'
she said it'd haf to be a secret, so that's why I can't tell you
what they were. Well, an' then this afternoon, early, I was
with her, an' she said, long as I had told her the secret in
the first place, I could come in Willie's room with her, an'
we both were already in there anyway, 'cause I was kind of
thinkin' maybe she'd go in there to look for 'em, Mr.
Parcher—"

"I see," he said, admiringly. "I see."

"Well, they were under Willie's window-seat, all folded
up; an' mamma said she wondered what she better do, an'
she was worried because she didn't like to have Willie behave so's you an' Mrs. Parcher thought that way about
him. So she said the—the secret—what Willie wears, you
know, but they're really papa's an' aren't Willie's any
more'n they're *mine*—well, she said the secret was gettin' a
little teeny bit too tight for papa, but she guessed they—I
mean the secret—she said she guessed it was already pretty
loose for Willie; so she wrapped it up, an' I went with her,
an' we took 'em to a tailor, an' she told him to make 'em
bigger, for a surprise for papa, 'cause then they'll fit him
again, Mr. Parcher. She said he must make 'em a whole lot
bigger. She said he must let 'em way, *way* out! So I guess
Willie would look too funny in 'em after they're fixed; an'
anyway, Mr. Parcher, the secret won't be home from the
tailor's for two weeks, an' maybe by that time Miss Pratt'll
be gone."

They had reached Mr. Parcher's gate; he halted and
looked down fondly upon this child who seemed to have
read his soul. "Do you honestly think so?" he asked.

"Well, anyway, Mr. Parcher," said Jane, "mamma said
—well, she said she's sure Willie wouldn't come here in the
evening any more—when *you're* at home, Mr. Parcher—
'cause after he'd been wearin' the secret every night this

way he wouldn't like to come and not have the secret on.
Mamma said the reason he would feel like that was because
he was seventeen years old. An' she isn't goin' to tell him
anything about it, Mr. Parcher. She said that's the best
way."

Her new friend nodded and seemed to agree. "I suppose
that's what you meant when you said he wasn't coming
back but didn't know it yet?"

"Yes, Mr. Parcher."

He rested an elbow upon the gate-post, gazing down
with ever-increasing esteem. "Of course I know your last
name," he said, "but I'm afraid I've forgotten your other
one."

"It's Jane."

"Jane," said Mr. Parcher, "I should like to do something for you."

Jane looked down, and with eyes modestly lowered she
swallowed the last fragment of the bread-and-butter and
apple sauce and sugar which had been the constantly eva-
nescent companion of their little walk together. She was
not mercenary; she had sought no reward.

"Well, I guess I must run home," she said. And with
one lift of her eyes to his and a shy laugh—laughter being a
rare thing for Jane—she scampered quickly to the corner
and was gone.

But though she cared for no reward, the extraordinary
restlessness of William, that evening, after dinner, must at
least have been of great interest to her. He ascended to his
own room directly from the table, but about twenty minutes
later came down to the library, where Jane was sitting
(her privilege until half after seven) with her father and
mother. William looked from one to the other of his
parents and seemed about to speak, but did not do so.
Instead, he departed for the upper floor again and presently could be heard moving about energetically in various
parts of the house, a remote thump finally indicating that
he was doing something with a trunk in the attic.

After that he came down to the library again and once
more seemed about to speak, but did not. Then he went
upstairs again, and came down again, and he was still
repeating this process when Jane's time-limit was reached
and she repaired conscientiously to her little bed. Her

mother came to hear her prayers and to turn out the light; and when Mrs. Baxter had passed out into the hall, after that, Jane heard her speaking to William, who was now conducting what seemed to be excavations on a serious scale in his own room.

"Oh, Willie, perhaps I didn't tell you, but—you remember I'd been missing papa's evening clothes and looking everywhere—for days and days?"

"Ye-es," huskily from William.

"Well, I found them! And where do you suppose I'd put them? I found them under your window-seat. Can you think of anything more absurd than putting them there and then forgetting it? I took them to the tailor's to have them let out. They were getting too tight for papa, but they'll be all right for him when the tailor sends them back."

What the stricken William gathered from this it is impossible to state with accuracy; probably he mixed some perplexity with his emotions. Certainly he was perplexed the following evening at dinner.

Jane did not appear at the table. "Poor child! she's sick in bed," Mrs. Baxter explained to her husband. "I was out, this afternoon, and she ate nearly *all* of a five-pound box of candy."

Both the sad-eyed William and his father were dumb-founded. "Where on earth did she get a five-pound box of candy?" Mr. Baxter demanded.

"I'm afraid Jane has begun her first affair," said Mrs. Baxter. "A gentleman sent it to her."

"What gentleman?" gasped William.

And in his mother's eyes, as they slowly came to rest on his in reply, he was aware of an inscrutability strongly remindful of that inscrutable look of Jane's.

"Mr. Parcher," she said, gently.

12. Progress of the Symptoms

MRS. BAXTER'S little stroke of diplomacy had gone straight to the mark; she was a woman of insight. For every reason she was well content to have her son spend his evenings at home, though it cannot be claimed that his presence enlivened the household, his condition being one of strange, trancelike irrascibility. Evening after evening passed, while he sat dreaming painfully of Mr. Parcher's porch; but in the daytime, though William did not literally make hay while the sun shone, he at least gathered a harvest somewhat resembling hay in general character.

Thus:

One afternoon, having locked his door to secure himself against intrusion on the part of his mother or Jane, William seated himself at his writing-table, and from a drawer therein took a small cardboard box, which he uncovered, placing the contents in view before him upon the table. (How meager, how chilling a word is "contents"!) In the box were:

A faded rose.

Several other faded roses, disintegrated into leaves.

Three withered "four-leaf clovers."

A white ribbon still faintly smelling of violets.

A small silver shoe-buckle.

A large pearl button.

A small pearl button.

A tortoise-shell hair-pin.

A cross-section from the heel of a small slipper.

A stringy remnant, probably once an improvised wreath of daisies.

Four or five withered dandelions.

Other dried vegetation, of a nature now indistinguishable.

William gazed reverently upon this junk of precious souvenirs; then from the inner pocket of his coat he brought forth, warm and crumpled, a lumpish cluster of red geranium blossoms, still aromatic and not quite dead, though naturally, after three hours of such intimate confinement, they wore an unmistakable look of suffering. With a tenderness which his family had never observed in him since that piteous day in his fifth year when he tried to mend his broken doll, William laid the geranium blossoms in the cardboard box among the botanical and other relics.

His gentle eyes showed what the treasures meant to him, and yet it was strange that they should have meant so much, because the source of supply was not more than a quarter of a mile distant, and practically inexhaustible. Miss Pratt had now been a visitor at the Parchers' for something less than five weeks, but she had made no mention of prospective departure, and there was every reason to suppose that she meant to remain all summer. And as any foliage or anything whatever that she touched, or that touched her, was thenceforth suitable for William's museum, there appeared to be some probability that autumn might see it so enlarged as to lack that rarity in the component items which is the underlying value of most collections.

William's writing-table was beside an open window, through which came an insistent whirring, unagreeable to his mood; and, looking down upon the sunny lawn, he beheld three lowly creatures. One was Genesis; he was cutting the grass. Another was Clematis; he had assumed a transient attitude, curiously triangular, in order to scratch his ear, the while his anxious eyes never wavered from the third creature.

This was Jane. In one hand she held a little stack of sugar-sprinkled wafers, which she slowly but steadily depleted, unconscious of the increasingly earnest protest, at last nearing agony, in the eyes of Clematis. Wearing unaccustomed garments of fashion and festivity, Jane stood, in speckless, starchy white and a blue sash, watching the lawnmower spout showers of grass as the powerful Genesis easily propelled it along overlapping lanes, back and forth, across the yard.

From a height of illimitable loftiness the owner of the cardboard treasury looked down upon the squat commonplaceness of those three lives. The condition of Jane and Genesis and Clematis seemed almost laughably pitiable to him, the more so because they were unaware of it. They breathed not the starry air that William breathed, but what did it matter to them? The wretched things did not know that they meant nothing to Miss Pratt!

Clematis found his ear too pliable for any great solace from his foot, but he was not disappointed; he had expected little, and his thoughts were elsewhere. Rising, he permitted his nose to follow his troubled eyes, with the result that it touched the rim of the last wafer in Jane's external possession.

This incident annoyed William. "Look there!" he called

from the window. "You mean to eat that cake after the dog's had his face on it?"

Jane remained placid. "It wasn't his face."

"Well, if it wasn't his face, I'd like to know what—"

"It wasn't his face," Jane repeated. "It was his nose. It wasn't all of his nose touched it, either. It was only a little outside piece of his nose."

"Well, are you going to eat that cake, I ask you?"

Jane broke off a small bit of the wafer. She gave the bit to Clematis and slowly ate what remained, continuing to watch Genesis and apparently unconscious of the scorching gaze from the window.

"I never saw anything as disgusting as long as I've lived!" William announced. "I wouldn't 'a' believed it if anybody'd told me a sister of mine would eat after—"

"I didn't," said Jane. "I like Clematis, anyway."

"Ye gods!" her brother cried. "Do you think that makes it any better? And, *by* the *way,*" he continued, in a tone of even greater severity, "I'd like to know where you got those cakes. Where'd you get 'em, I'd just like to inquire?"

"In the pantry." Jane turned and moved toward the house. "I'm goin' in for some more, now."

William uttered a cry; these little cakes were sacred. His mother, growing curious to meet a visiting lady of whom (so to speak) she had heard much and thought more, had asked May Parcher to bring her guest for iced tea, that afternoon. A few others of congenial age had been invited: there was to be a small matinée, in fact, for the honor and pleasure of the son of the house, and the cakes of Jane's onslaught were part of Mrs. Baxter's preparations. There was no telling where Jane would stop; it was conceivable that Miss Pratt herself might go waferless.

William returned the cardboard box to its drawer with reverent haste; then, increasing the haste, but dropping the reverence, he hied himself to the pantry with such advantage of longer legs that within the minute he and the wafers appeared in conjunction before his mother, who was arranging fruit and flowers upon a table in the "living-room."

William entered in the stained-glass attitude of one bearing gifts. Overhead, both hands supported a tin pan, well laden with small cakes and wafers, for which Jane was silently but repeatedly and systematically jumping. Even under the stress of these efforts her expression was cool and collected; she maintained the self-possession that was characteristic of her.

Not so with William; his cheeks were flushed, his eyes indignant. "You see what this child is doing?" he demanded. "Are you going to let her ruin everything?"

"Ruin?" Mrs. Baxter repeated, absently, refreshing with fair water a bowl of flowers upon the table. "Ruin?"

"Yes, ruin!" William was hotly emphatic. "If you don't do something with her it'll all be ruined before Miss Pr— before they even get here!"

Mrs. Baxter laughed. "Set the pan down, Willie."

"Set it *down?*" he echoed, incredulously. "With that child in the room and grabbing like—"

"There!" Mrs. Baxter took the pan from him, placed it upon a chair, and with the utmost coolness selected five wafers and gave them to Jane. "I'd already promised her she could have five more. You know the doctor said Jane's digestion was the finest he'd ever misunderstood. They won't hurt her at all, Willie."

This deliberate misinterpretation of his motives made it difficult for William to speak. "Do *you* think," he began, hoarsely, "do you *think*—"

"They're so small, too," Mrs. Baxter went on. *"She* probably wouldn't be sick if she ate them all."

"My heavens!" he burst forth. "Do you think I was worrying about—" He broke off, unable to express himself save by a few gestures of despair. Again finding his voice, and a great deal of it, he demanded: "Do you realize that Miss *Pratt* will be here within less than half an hour? What do you suppose she'd think of the people of this town if she was invited out, expecting decent treatment, and found two-thirds of the cakes eaten up before she got there, and what was left of 'em all mauled and pawed over and crummy and chewed-up lookin' from some wretched *child?*" Here William became oratorical, but not with marked effect, since Jane regarded him with unmoved eyes, while Mrs. Baxter continued to be mildly preoccupied in arranging the table. In fact, throughout this episode in controversy the ladies' party had not only the numerical but the emotional advantage. Obviously, the approach of Miss

Pratt was not to them what it was to William. "I tell you," he declaimed—"yes, I tell you that it wouldn't take much of this kind of thing to make Miss Pratt think the people of this town were—well, it wouldn't take much to make her think the people of this town hadn't learned much of how to behave in society and were pretty uncilivized!" He corrected himself. "Uncivilized! And to think Miss Pratt has to find that out in *my* house! To think—"

"Now, Willie," said Mrs. Baxter, gently, "you'd better go up and brush your hair again before your friends come. You mustn't let yourself get so excited."

" 'Excited!' " he cried, incredulously. "Do you think I'm *excited?* Ye gods!" He smote his hands together, and in his despair of her intelligence, would have flung himself down upon a chair, but was arrested half-way by simultaneous loud cries from his mother and Jane.

"Don't sit on the CAKES!" they both screamed.

Saving himself and the pan of wafers by a supreme contortion at the last instant, William decided to remain upon his feet. "What do I care for the cakes?" he demanded, contemptuously, beginning to pace the floor. "It's the question of principle I'm talking about! Do you think it's right to give the people of this town a poor name when strangers like Miss *Pratt* come to vis—"

"Willie!" His mother looked at him hopelessly. "Do go and brush your hair. If you could see how you've tousled it you would."

He gave her a dazed glance and strode from the room.

Jane looked after him placidly. "Didn't he talk funny!" she murmured.

"Yes, dear," said Mrs. Baxter. She shook her head and uttered the enigmatic words, "They do."

"I mean Willie, mamma," said Jane. "If it's anything about Miss Pratt, he always talks awful funny. Don't you think Willie talks awful funny if it's anything about Miss Pratt, mamma?"

"Yes, but—"

"What, mamma?" Jane asked as her mother paused.

"Well—it happens. People do get like that at his age, Jane."

"Does everybody?"

"No, I suppose not everybody. Just some."

Jane's interest was roused. "Well, do those that do, mamma," she inquired, "do they all act like Willie?"

"No," said Mrs. Baxter. "That's the trouble; you can't tell what's coming."

Jane nodded. "I think I know," she said. "You mean Willie—"

William himself interrupted her. He returned violently to the doorway, his hair still tousled, and, standing upon the threshold, said, sternly:

"What is that child wearing her best dress for?"

"Willie!" Mrs. Baxter cried. "Go brush your hair!"

"I wish to know what that child is all dressed up for?" he insisted.

"To please you! Don't you want her to look her best at your tea?"

"I thought that was it!" he cried, and upon this confirmation of his worst fears he did increased violence to his rumpled hair. "I suspected it, but I wouldn't 'a' believed it! You mean to let this child—you mean to let—" Here his agitation affected his throat and his utterance became clouded. A few detached phrases fell from him: "—Invite *my* friends—children's party—ye gods!—think Miss Pratt plays dolls—"

"Jane will be very good," his mother said. "I shouldn't think of not having her, Willie, and you needn't bother about your friends; they'll be very glad to see her. They all know her, except Miss Pratt, perhaps, and—" Mrs. Baxter paused; then she asked, absently: "By the way, haven't I heard somewhere that she likes pretending to be a little girl, herself?"

"*What!*"

"Yes," said Mrs. Baxter, remaining calm; "I'm sure I've heard somewhere that she likes to talk 'baby-talk.' "

Upon this a tremor passed over William, after which he became rigid. "You ask a lady to your house," he began, "and even before she gets here, before you've ever seen her, you pass judgment upon one of the—one of the noblest—"

"Good gracious! *I* haven't 'passed judgment.' If she does talk 'baby-talk,' I imagine she does it very prettily, and I'm sure I've no objection. And if she does do it, why should you be insulted by my mentioning it?"

"It was the way you said it," he informed her, icily.

"Good gracious! I just said it!" Mrs. Baxter laughed, and then, probably a little out of patience with him, she gave way to that innate mischieviousness in such affairs which is not unknown to her sex. "You see, Willie, if she pretends to be a cunning little girl, it will be helpful to Jane to listen and learn how."

William uttered a cry; he knew that he was struck, but he was not sure how or where. He was left with a blank mind and no repartee. Again he dashed from the room.

In the hall, near the open front door, he came to a sudden halt, and Mrs. Baxter and Jane heard him calling loudly to the industrious Genesis:

"Here! You go cut the grass in the back yard, and for Heaven's sake, take that dog with you!"

"Grass aweady cut roun' back," responded the amiable voice of Genesis, while the lawn-mower ceased not to whir. "Cut all 'at back yod 's mawnin'."

"Well, you can't cut the front yard now. Go around in the back yard and take that dog with you."

"Nemmine 'bout 'at back yod! Ole Clem ain' trouble nobody."

"You hear what I tell you?" William shouted. "You do what I say and you do it quick!"

Genesis laughed gaily. "I got my grass to cut!"

"You decline to do what I command you?" William roared.

"Yes, indeedy! Who pay me my wages? 'At's *my* boss. You ma say, 'Genesis, you git all 'at lawn mowed b'fo' sundown.' No, suh! Nee'n' was'e you' bref on me, 'cause I'm got all *my* time good an' took up!"

Once more William presented himself fatefully to his mother and Jane. "May I just kindly ask you to look out in the front yard?"

"I'm familiar with it, Willie," Mrs. Baxter returned, a little wearily.

"I mean I want you to look at Genesis."

"I'm familiar with his appearance, too," she said. "Why in the world do you mind his cutting the grass?"

William groaned. "Do you honestly want guests coming to this house to see that awful old darky out there and know that *he's* the kind of servants we employ? Ye gods!"

"Why, Genesis is just a neighborhood outdoors darky, Willie; he works for half a dozen families besides us. Everybody in this part of town knows him."

"Yes," he cried, "but a lady that didn't live here wouldn't. Ye gods! What do you suppose she *would* think? You know what he's got on!"

"It's a sort of sleeveless jersey he wears, Willie, I think."

"No, you *don't* think that!" he cried, with great bitterness. "You know it's not a jersey! You know perfectly well what it is, and yet you expect to keep him out there when —when one of the—one of the nobl—when my friends arrive! And they'll think that's our *dog* out there, won't they? When intelligent people come to a house and see a dog sitting out in front, they think it's the family in the house's dog, don't they?" William's condition becoming more and more disordered, he paced the room, while his agony rose to a climax. "Ye gods! What do you think Miss Pratt will think of the people of this town, when she's invited to meet a few of my friends and the first thing she sees is a nigger in his undershirt? What'll she think when she finds that child's eaten up half the food, and the people have to explain that the dog in the front yard belongs to the darky—" He interrupted himself with a groan: "And prob'ly she wouldn't believe it. Anybody'd *say* they didn't own a dog like that! And that's what you want her to see, before she even gets inside the house! Instead of a regular gardener in livery like we ought to have, and a bulldog or a good Airedale or a fox-hound, or something, the first things you want intelligent people from out of town to see are that awful old darky and his mongrel scratchin' fleas and like as not lettin' 'em get on other people! *That'd* be nice, wouldn't it? Go out to tea expecting decent treatment and get fl—"

"*Willie!*"

Mrs. Baxter managed to obtain his attention. "If you'll go and brush your hair I'll send Genesis and Clematis away for the rest of the afternoon. And then if you'll sit down quietly and try to keep cool until your friends get here, I'll—"

" 'Quietly'!" he echoed, shaking his head over this mystery. "I'm the only one that *is* quiet around here. Things'd be in a fine condition to receive guests if I didn't keep pretty cool, I guess!"

"There, there," she said, soothingly. "Go and brush your hair. And change your collar, Willie; it's all wilted. I'll send Genesis away."

His wandering eye failed to meet hers with any intelligence. "Collar," he muttered, as if in soliloquy. "Collar."

"Change it!" said Mrs. Baxter, raising her voice. "It's *wilted.*"

He departed in a dazed manner.

Passing through the hall, he paused abruptly, his eye having fallen with sudden disapproval upon a large, heavily framed, glass-covered engraving, "The Battle of Gettysburg," which hung upon the wall, near the front door. Undeniably, it was a picture feeble in decorative quality; no doubt, too, William was right in thinking it as unworthy of Miss Pratt, as were Jane and Genesis and Clematis. He felt that she must never see it, especially as the frame had been chipped and had a corner broken, but it was more pleasantly effective where he found it than where (in his nervousness) he left it. A few hasty jerks snapped the elderly green cords by which it was suspended; then he laid the picture upon the floor and with his handkerchief made a curious labryinth of avenues in the large oblong area of fine dust which this removal disclosed upon the wall. Pausing to wipe his hot brow with the same implement, he remembered that some one had made allusions to his collar and hair, whereupon he sprang to the stairs, mounted two at a time, rushed into his own room, and confronted his streaked image in the mirror.

13. At Home to His Friends

AFTER ABLUTIONS, he found his wet hair plastic, and easily obtained the long, even sweep backward from the brow, lacking which no male person, unless bald, fulfilled his definition of a man of the world. But there ensued a period of vehemence and activity caused by a bent collar-button, which went on strike with a desperation that was downright savage. The day was warm and William was warmer; moisture bedewed him afresh. Belated victory no sooner arrived than he perceived a fatal dimpling of the new collar, and was forced to begin the operation of exchanging it for a successor. Another exchange, however, he unfortunately forgot to make: the handkerchief with which he had wiped the wall remained in his pocket.

Voices from below, making polite laughter, warned him that already some of the bidden party had arrived, and, as he completed the fastening of his third consecutive collar, an ecstasy of sound reached him through the open window —and then, oh then! his breath behaved in an abnormal manner and he began to tremble. It was the voice of Miss Pratt, no less!

He stopped for one heart-struck look from his casement. All in fluffy white and heliotrope she was—a blonde rapture floating over the sidewalk toward William's front gate. Her little white cottony dog, with a heliotrope ribbon round his neck, bobbed his head over her cuddling arm; a heliotrope parasol shielded her infinitesimally from the amorous sun. Poor William!

Two youths entirely in William's condition of heart accompanied the glamorous girl and hung upon her rose-leaf lips, while Miss Parcher appeared dimly upon the outskirts of the group, the well-known penalty for hostesses who entertain such radiance. Probably it serves them right.

To William's reddening ear Miss Pratt's voice came clearly as the chiming of tiny bells, for she spoke whimsically to her little dog in that tinkling childlike fashion which was part of the spell she cast.

"Darlin' Flopit," she said, "wake up! Oo tummin' to tea-potty wiz all de drowed-ups. P'eshus Flopit, wake up!"

Dizzy with enchantment, half suffocated, his heart melting within him, William turned from the angelic sounds and fairy vision of the window. He ran out of the room, and plunged down the front stairs. And the next moment the crash of breaking glass and the loud thump-bump of a heavily falling human body resounded through the house.

Mrs. Baxter, alarmed, quickly excused herself from the tea-table, round which were gathered four or five young people, and hastened to the front hall, followed by Jane.

Through the open door were seen Miss Pratt, Miss Parcher, Mr. Johnnie Watson and Mr. Joe Bullitt coming leisurely up the sunny front walk, laughing and unaware of the catastrophe which had just occurred within the shadows of the portal. And at a little distance from the foot of the stairs William was seated upon the prostrate "Battle of Gettysburg."

"It slid," he said, hoarsely. "I carried it upstairs with me"—he believed this—"and somebody brought it down and left it lying flat on the floor by the bottom step on purpose to trip me! I stepped on it and it slid." He was in a state of shock: it seemed important to impress upon his mother the fact that the picture had not remained firmly in place when he stepped upon it. "It *slid*, I tell you!"

"Get up, Willie!" she urged, under her breath, and as he summoned enough presence of mind to obey, she beheld ruins other than the wrecked engraving. She stifled a cry. *"Willie!* Did the glass cut you?"

He felt himself. "No'm."

"It did your trousers! You'll have to change them. Hurry!"

Some of William's normal faculties were restored to him by one hasty glance at the back of his left leg, which had a dismantled appearance. A long blue strip of cloth hung there, with white showing underneath.

"Hurry!" said Mrs. Baxter. And hastily gathering some fragments of glass, she dropped them upon the engraving, pushed it out of the way, and went forward to greet Miss Pratt and her attendants.

As for William, he did not even pause to close his mouth, but fled with it open. Upward he sped, unseen, and came to a breathless halt upon the landing at the top of the stairs.

As it were in a dream he heard his mother's hospitable greetings at the door, and then the little party lingered in the hall, detained by Miss Pratt's discovery of Jane.

"Oh, tweetums tootums ickle dirl!" he heard the ravishing voice exclaim. "Oh, tootums ickle blue sash!"

"It cost a dollar and eighty-nine cents," said Jane. "Willie sat on the cakes."

"Oh no, he didn't," Mrs. Baxter laughed. "He didn't *quite!"*

"He had to go up-stairs," said Jane. And as the stricken listener above smote his forehead, she added placidly, "He tore a hole in his clo'es."

She seemed about to furnish details, her mood being communicative, but Mrs. Baxter led the way into the "living-room"; the hall was vacated, and only the murmur of voices and laughter reached William. What descriptive information Jane may have added was spared his hearing, which was a mercy.

And yet it may be that he could not have felt worse than he did; for there *is* nothing worse than to be seventeen and to hear one of the Noblest girls in the world told by a little child that you sat on the cakes and tore a hole in your clo'es.

William leaned upon the banister railing and thought thoughts about Jane. For several long, seething moments he thought of her exclusively. Then, spurred by the loud laughter of rivals and the agony of knowing that even in his own house they were monopolizing the attention of one of the Noblest, he hastened into his own room and took account of his reverses.

Standing with his back to the mirror, he obtained over his shoulder a view of his trousers which caused him to break out in a fresh perspiration. Again he wiped his forehead with the handkerchief, and the result was instantly visible in the mirror.

The air thickened with sounds of frenzy, followed by a torrential roar and great sputterings in a bath-room, which tumult subsiding, William returned at a tragic gallop to his room and, having removed his trousers, began a feverish examination of the garments hanging in a clothes-closet. There were two pairs of flannel trousers which would probably again be white and possible, when cleaned and pressed, but a glance showed that until then they were not to be considered as even the last resort of desperation. Beside them hung his "last year's summer suit" of light gray.

Feverishly he brought it forth, threw off his coat, and then—deflected by another glance at the mirror—began to change his collar again. This was obviously necessary, and to quicken the process he decided to straighten the bent collar button. Using a shoe-horn as a lever, he succeeded in bringing the little cap or head of the button into its proper plane, but, unfortunately, his final effort dislodged the cap from the rod between it and the base, and it flew off malignantly into space. Here was a calamity; few things are more useless than a decapitated collar-button, and William had no other. He had made sure that it was his last before he put it on that day; also he had ascertained that there was none in, on, or about his father's dressing-table. Finally, in the possession of neither William nor his father was there a shirt with an indigenous collar.

For decades, collar-buttons have been on the hand-me-down shelves of humor; it is a mistake in the catalogue. They belong to pathos. They have done harm in the world, and there have been collar-buttons that failed when the destinies of families hung upon them. There have been collar-buttons that thwarted proper matings. There have been collar-buttons that bore last hopes, and, falling to the floor, *never* were found! William's broken collar-button was really the only collar-button in the house, except such as were engaged in serving his male guests below.

At first he did not realize the extent of his misfortune. How could he? Fate is always expected to deal its great blows in the grand manner. But our expectations are fustian spangled with pinchbeck; we look for tragedy to be theatrical. Meanwhile, every day before our eyes, fate works on, employing for its instruments the infinitesimal, the ignoble and the petty—in a word, collar-buttons.

Of course William searched his dressing-table and his father's, although he had been thoroughly over both once before that day. Next he went through most of his mother's and Jane's accessories to the toilette; through trinket-boxes, glove-boxes, hairpin-boxes, handkerchief-cases—even through sewing-baskets. Utterly he convinced himself that ladies not only use no collar-buttons, but also never pick them up and put them away among their own belongings. How much time he consumed in this search is difficult to reckon—it is almost impossible to believe that there is absolutely no collar-button in a house.

And what William's state of mind had become is matter for exorbitant conjecture. Jane, arriving at his locked door upon an errand, was bidden by a thick, unnatural voice to depart.

"Mamma says, 'What in mercy's name is the matter?'"
Jane called. "She whispered to me, 'Go an' see what in
mercy's name is the matter with Willie; an' if the glass cut
him, after all; an' why don't he come down'; an' why don't
you, Willie? We're all havin' the nicest time!"

"You g'way!" said the strange voice within the room.
"G'way!"

"Well, did the glass cut you?"

"No! Keep quiet! G'way!"

"Well, are you *ever* comin' down to your party?"

"Yes, I am! G'way!"

Jane obeyed, and William somehow completed the task
upon which he was engaged. Genius had burst forth from
his despair; necessity had become a mother again, and
William's collar was in place. It was tied there. Under his
necktie was a piece of string.

He had lost count of time, but he was frantically aware
of its passage; agony was in the thought of so many rich
moments frittered away up-stairs, while Joe Bullitt and
Johnnie Watson made hay below. And there was another
spur to haste in his fear that the behavior of Mrs. Baxter
might not be all that the guest of honor would naturally
expect of William's mother. As for Jane, his mind filled
with dread; shivers passed over him at intervals.

It was a dismal thing to appear at a "party" (and that
his own) in "last summer's suit," but when he had hastily
put it on and faced the mirror, he felt a little better—for
three or four seconds. Then he turned to see how the back
of it looked.

And collapsed in a chair, moaning.

14. Time Does Fly

HE REMEMBERED now what he had been too hurried to
remember earlier. He had worn these clothes on the previous Saturday, and, returning from a glorified walk with
Miss Pratt, he had demonstrated a fact to which his near
demolition of the wafers, this afternoon, was additional tes-
timony. This fact, roughly stated, is that a person of seventeen, in love, is liable to sit down anywhere. William had

dreamily seated himself upon a tabouret in the library, without noticing that Jane had left her open paint-box there. Jane had just been painting sunsets: naturally all the little blocks of color were wet, and the effect upon William's pale-gray trousers was marvelous—far beyond the capacity of his coat to conceal. Collar-buttons and children's paint-boxes—those are the trolls that lie in wait!

The gray clothes and the flannel trousers had been destined for the professional cleaner, and William, rousing himself from a brief stupor, made a piteous effort to substitute himself for that expert so far as the gray trousers were concerned. He divested himself of them and brought water, towels, bath-soap, and a rubber bath-sponge to the bright light of his window; and there, with touching courage and persistence, he tried to scrub the paint out of the cloth. He obtained cloud studies and marines which would have interested a Post-Impressionist, but upon trousers they seemed out of place.

There came one seeking and calling him again; raps sounded upon the door, which he had not forgotten to lock.

"Willie," said a serious voice, "mamma wants to know what in mercy's name is the matter! She wants to know if you know for mercy's name what time it is! She wants to know what in mercy's name you think they're all goin' to think! She says—"

"G'way!"

"Well, she said I had to find out what in mercy's name you're doin', Willie."

"You tell her," he shouted, hoarsely—"tell her I'm playin' dominoes! What's she *think* I'm doin'?"

"I guess"—Jane paused, evidently to complete the swallowing of something—"I guess she thinks you're goin' crazy. I don't like Miss Pratt, but she lets me play with that little dog. Its name's Flopit!"

"You go 'way from that door and stop bothering me," said William. "I got enough on my mind!"

"Mamma looks at Miss Pratt," Jane remarked. "Miss Pratt puts cakes in that Mr. Bullitt's mouth and Johnnie Watson's mouth, too. She's awful."

William made it plain that these bulletins from the party found no favor with him. He bellowed, "If you don't get away from that *door*—"

Jane was interested in the conversation, but felt that it would be better to return to the refreshment-table. There she made use of her own conception of a whisper to place before her mother a report which was considered interesting and even curious by every one present; though, such was the courtesy of the little assembly, there was a general pretense of not hearing.

"I told him," thus whispered Jane, "an' he said, 'You g'way from that door or I'll do somep'm'—he didn't say what, mamma. He said, 'What do you think I'm doin'? I'm playin' dominoes.' He didn't mean he was playin' dominoes, mamma. He just said he was. I think maybe he was just lookin' in the lookin'-glass some more."

Mrs. Baxter was becoming embarrassed. She resolved to go to William's room herself at the first opportunity; but for some time her conscientiousness as a hostess continued to occupy her at the table, and then, when she would have gone, Miss Pratt detained her by a roguish appeal to make Mr. Bullitt and Mr. Watson behave. Both refused all nourishment except such as was placed in their mouths by the delicate hand of one of the Noblest, and the latter said that really she wanted to eat a little tweetie now and then herself, and not to spend her whole time feeding the Men. For Miss Pratt had the same playfulness with older people that she had with those of her own age; and she elaborated her pretended quarrel with the two young gentlemen, taking others of the dazzled company into her confidence about it, and insisting upon "Mamma Batster's" acting formally as judge to settle the difficulty. However, having thus arranged matters, Miss Pratt did not resign the center of interest, but herself proposed a compromise: she would continue to feed Mr. Bullitt and Mr. Watson "every other tweetie"—that is, each must agree to eat a cake "all by him own self," after every cake fed to him. So the comedietta went on, to the running accompaniment of laughter, with Mr. Bullitt and Mr. Watson swept by such gusts of adoration they were like to perish where they sat. But Mrs. Baxter's smiling approval was beginning to be painful to the muscles of her face, for it was hypocritical. And if William had known her thoughts about one of the Noblest, he could only have attributed them to that demon of groundless prejudice which besets all females, but most particularly and outrageously the mothers and sisters of Men.

A colored serving-maid entered with a laden tray, and, having disposed of its freight of bon-bons among the guests, spoke to Mrs. Baxter in a low voice.

"Could you manage step in the back hall a minute, please, ma'am?"

Mrs. Baxter managed and, having closed the door upon the laughing voices, asked, quickly: "What is it, Adelia? Have you seen Mr. William? Do you know why he doesn't come down?"

"Yes'm," said Adelia. "He gone mighty near out his head, Miz Baxter."

"What!"

"Yes'm. He come floppin' down the back stairs in his baf-robe li'l' while ago. He jes' gone up again. He ain't got no britches, Miz Baxter."

"No *what?*"

"No'm," said Adelia. "He 'ain't got no britches at all."

A statement of this kind is startling under almost any circumstances, and it is unusually so when made in reference to a person for whom a party is being given. Therefore it was not unreasonable of Mrs. Baxter to lose her breath.

"But—it can't *be!*" she gasped. "He has! He has plenty!"

"No'm, he 'ain't," Adelia assured her. "An' he's carryin' on so I don't scarcely think he knows much what he's doin', Miz Baxter. He brung down some gray britches to the kitchen to see if I couldn' press an' clean 'em right quick: they was the ones Miss Jane, when she's paintin' all them sunsets, lef' her paint-box open, an' one them sunsets got on these here gray britches, Miz Bazter; an' hones'ly, Miz Baxter, he's fixed 'em in a condishum, tryin' to git that paint out, I don't believe it 'll be no use sendin' 'em to the cleaner. 'Clean 'em an' press 'em *quick?*' I says. 'I couldn' clean 'em by Resurreckshum, let alone pressin' em!' No'm! Well, he had his blue britches, too, but they's so ripped an' tore an' kind o' shredded away in one place, the cook she jes' hollered when he spread 'em out, an' he didn' even ast me could I mend 'em. An' he had two pairs o' them white flannen britches, but hones'ly, Miz Baxter, I don't scarcely

think Genesis would wear 'em, the way they is now! 'Well,'
I says, 'ain't but one thing lef' to do *I* can see,' I says. 'Why
don't you go put on that nice black suit you had last
winter?' "

"Of course!" Mrs. Baxter cried. "I'll go and—"

"No'm," said Adelia. "You don' need to. He's up in the
the attic now, r'arin' roun' 'mongs' them trunks, but seem
to me like I remember you put that suit away under the
heavy blankets in that big cedar ches' with the padlock. If
you jes' tell me where is the key, I take it up to him."

"Under the bureau in the spare room," said Mrs. Baxter. *"Hurry!"*

Adelia hurried; and, fifteen minutes later, William, for
the last time that afternoon, surveyed himself in his mirror.
His face showed the strain that had been upon him and
under which he still labored; the black suit was a map of
creases, and William was perspiring more freely than ever
under the heavy garments. But at least he was clothed.

He emptied his pockets, disgorging upon the floor a
multitude of small white spheres, like marbles. Then, as
he stepped out into the hall, he discovered that their odor
still remained about him; so he stopped and carefully
turned his pockets inside out, one after the other, but finding that he still smelled vehemently of the "moth-balls,"
though not one remained upon him, he went to his
mother's room and sprinkled violet toilet-water upon his
chest and shoulders. He disliked such odors, but that left
by the moth-balls was intolerable, and, laying hands upon
a canister labeled "Hyacinth," he contrived to pour a quantity of scented powder inside his collar, thence to be dis-
tributed by the force of gravity so far as his dampness
permitted.

Lo, William was now ready to go to his party! Moist,
wilted, smelling indeed strangely, he was ready.

But when he reached the foot of the stairs he discovered
that there was one thing more to be done. Indignation
seized him, and also a creeping fear chilled his spine, as
he beheld a lurking shape upon the porch, stealthily moving toward the open door. It was the lowly Clematis, dog
unto Genesis.

William instantly divined the purpose of Clematis. It was
debatable whether Clematis had remained upon the prem-

ises after the departure of Genesis, or had lately returned thither upon some errand of his own, but one thing was certain, and the manner of Clematis—his attitude, his every look, his every gesture—made it as clear as day. Clematis had discovered, by one means or another, the presence of Flopit in the house, and had determined to see him personally.

Clematis wore his most misleading expression; a stranger would have thought him shy and easily turned from his purpose—but William was not deceived. He knew that if Clematis meant to see Flopit, a strong will, a ready brain, and stern action were needed to thwart him; but at all costs that meeting must be prevented. Things had been awful enough, without that!

He was well aware that Clematis could not be driven away, except temporarily, for nothing was further fixed upon Clematis than his habit of retiring under pressure, only to return and return again. True, the door could have been shut in the intruder's face, but he would have sought other entrance with possible success, or, failing that, would have awaited in the front yard the dispersal of the guests and Flopit's consequent emerging. This was a contretemps not to be endured.

The door of the living-room was closed, muffling festal noises and permitting safe passage through the hall. William cast a hunted look over his shoulder; then he approached Clematis.

"Good ole doggie," he said, huskily. "Hyuh, Clem! Hyuh, Clem!"

Clematis moved sidelong, retreating with his head low and his tail denoting anxious thoughts.

"Hyuh, Clem!" said William, trying, with only fair success, to keep his voice from sounding venomous. "Hyuh, Clem!"

Clematis continued his deprecatory retreat.

Thereupon William essayed a ruse—he pretended to nibble at something, and then extended his hand as if it held forth a gift of food. "Look, Clem," he said. "Yum-yum! Meat, Clem! Good meat!"

For once Clematis was half credulous. He did not advance, but he elongated himself to investigate the extended hand, and the next instant found himself seized viciously by the scruff of the neck. He submitted to capture in absolute silence. Only the slightest change of countenance betrayed his mortification at having been found so easy a gull; this passed, and a look of resolute stoicism took its place.

He refused to walk, but offered merely nominal resistance, as a formal protest which he wished to be of record, though perfectly understanding that it availed nothing at present. William dragged him through the long hall and down a short passageway to the cellar door. This he opened, thrust Clematis upon the other side of it, closed and bolted it.

Immediately a stentorian howl raised blood-curdling echoes and resounded horribly through the house. It was obvious that Clematis intended to make a scene, whether he was present at it or not. He lifted his voice in sonorous dolor, stating that he did not like the cellar and would continue thus to protest as long as he was left in it alone. He added that he was anxious to see Flopit and considered it an unexampled outrage that he was withheld from the opportunity.

Smitten with horror, William reopened the door and charged down the cellar stair after Clematis, who closed his caitiff mouth and gave way precipitately. He fled from one end of the cellar to the other and back, while William pursued; choking, and calling in low, ferocious tones: "Good doggie! Good ole doggie! Hyuh, Clem! Meat, Clem, meat—"

There was dodging through coal-bins; there was squirming between barrels; there was high jumping and broad jumping, and there was a final aspiring but baffled dash for the top of the cellar stairs, where the door, forgotten by William, stood open. But it was here that Clematis, after a long and admirable exhibition of ingenuity, no less than agility, submitted to capture. That is to say, finding himself hopelessly pinioned, he resumed the stoic.

Grimly the panting and dripping William dragged him through the kitchen, where the cook cried out unintelligibly, seeming to summon Adelia, who was not present. Through the back yard went captor and prisoner, the latter now maintaining a seated posture—his pathetic conception of dignity under duress. Finally, into a small shed or toolhouse, behind Mrs. Baxter's flower-beds, went Clematis in a hurried and spasmodic manner. The instant the door slammed he lifted his voice—and was bidden to use it now as much as he liked.

Adelia, with a tray of used plates, encountered the son of the house as he passed through the kitchen on his return, and her eyes were those of one who looks upon miracles.

William halted fiercely.

"What's the matter?" he demanded. "Is my face dirty?"

"You mean, are it too dirty to go in yonduh to the party?" Adelia asked slowly. "No suh; you look all right to go in there. You lookin' jes' fine to go in there now, Mist' Willie!"

Something in her tone struck him as peculiar, even as ominous, but his blood was up—he would not turn back now. He strode into the hall and opened the door of the "living-room."

Jane was sitting on the floor, busily painting sunsets in a large blank-book which she had obtained for that exclusive purpose.

She looked up brightly as William appeared in the doorway, and in answer to his wild gaze she said:

"I got a little bit sick, so mamma told me to keep quiet a while. She's lookin' for you all over the house. She told papa she don't know what in mercy's name people are goin' to think about you, Willie."

The distraught youth strode to her. "The party—" he choked. "*Where—*"

"They all stayed pretty long," said Jane, "but the last ones said they had to go home to their dinners when papa came, a little while ago. Johnnie Watson was carryin' Flopit for that Miss Pratt."

William dropped into the chair beside which Jane had established herself upon the floor. Then he uttered a terrible cry and rose.

Again Jane had painted a sunset she had not intended.

15. Romance of Statistics

ON A WARM morning, ten days later, William stood pensively among his mother's flower-beds behind the house, his attitude denoting a low state of vitality. Not far away, an aged Negro sat upon a wheelbarrow in the hot sun, tremulously yet skilfully whittling a piece of wood into the shape of a boat, labor more to his taste, evidently, than that which he had abandoned at the request of Jane. Allusion to his preference for a lighter task was made by Genesis, who was erecting a trellis on the border of the little garden.

"Pappy whittle all day," he chuckled. "Whittle all night, too! Pappy, I thought you 'uz goin' to git 'at long bed all spade' up fer me by noon. Ain't 'at what you tole me?"

"You let him alone, Genesis," said Jane, who sat by the old man's side, deeply fascinated. "There's goin' to be a great deal of rain in the next few days, maybe, an' I haf to have this boat ready."

The aged darky lifted his streaky and diminished eyes to the burnished sky, and laughed. "Rain come some day, anyways," he said. "We git de boat ready 'fo' she fall, dat sho." His glance wandered to William and rested upon him with feeble curiosity. "Dat ain' yo' pappy, is it?" he asked Jane.

"I should say it isn't!" she exclaimed. "It's Willie. He was only seventeen about two or three months ago, Mr. Genesis." This was not the old man's name, but Jane had evolved it, inspired by respect for one so aged and so kind about whittling. He was the father of Genesis, and the latter, neither to her knowledge nor to her imagination, possessed a surname.

"I got cat'rack in my lef' eye," said Mr. Genesis, "an' de right one, she kine o' tricksy, too. Tell black man f'um white man, little f'um big."

"I'd hate it if he was papa," said Jane, confidentially. "He's always cross about somep'm, because he's in love." She approached her mouth to her whittling friend's ear and continued in a whisper: "He's in love of Miss Pratt.

70

She's out walkin' with Joe Bullitt. I was in the front yard
with Willie, an' we saw 'em go by. He's mad."

William did not hear her. Moodily, he had discovered
that there was something amiss with the buckle of his belt,
and, having ungirded himself, he was biting the metal
tongue of the buckle in order to straighten it. This fell
under the observation of Genesis, who remonstrated.

"You break you' teef on 'at buckle," he said.

"No, I won't, either," William returned, crossly.

"Ain' my teef," said Genesis. "Break 'em, you want to!"

The attention of Mr. Genesis did not seem to be attracted to the speakers; he continued his whittling in a
craftsmanlike manner, which brought praise from Jane.

"You can see to whittle, Mr. Genesis," she said. "You
whittle better than anybody in the world."

"I speck so, mebbe," Mr. Genesis returned, with a little
complacency. "How ole yo' pappy?"

"Oh, he's *old!*" Jane explained.

William deigned to correct her. "He's not old; he's
middle-aged."

"Well, suh," said Mr. Genesis, "I had three chillum 'fo'
I 'uz twenty. I had two when I 'uz eighteem."

William showed sudden interest. "You did!" he exclaimed. "How old were you when you had the first one?"

"I 'uz jes' yo' age," said the old man. "I 'uz seventeem."

"By George!" cried William.

Jane seemed much less impressed than William, seventeen being a long way from ten, though, of course, to
seventeen itself hardly any information could be imagined
as more interesting than that conveyed by the words of the
aged Mr. Genesis. The impression made upon William was
obviously profound and favorable.

"By George!" he cried again.

"Genesis he de youngis' one," said the old man. "Genesis he 'uz bawn when I 'uz sixty-one."

William moved closer. "What became of the one that
was born when you were seventeen?" he asked.

"Well, suh," said Mr. Genesis, "I nev' did know."

At this, Jane's interest equaled William's. Her eyes
consented to leave the busy hands of the aged darky, and,
much enlarged, rose to his face. After a little pause of awe
and sympathy she inquired:

"Was it a boy or a girl?"

The old man deliberated within himself. "Seem like it mus' been a boy."

"Did it die?" Jane asked, softly.

"I reckon it mus' be dead by now," he returned, musingly. "Good many of 'em dead: what I *knows* is dead. Yes'm, I reckon so."

"How old were you when you were married?" William asked, with a manner of peculiar earnestness—it was the manner of one who addresses a colleague.

"Me? Well, suh, dat 'pen's." He seemed to search his memory. "I rickalect I 'uz ma'ied once in Looavle," he said.

Jane's interest still followed the first child. "Was that where it was born, Mr. Genesis?" she asked.

He looked puzzled, and paused in his whittling to rub his deeply corrugated forehead. "Well, suh, mus' been some bawn in Looavle. Genesis," he called to his industrious son, "whaih 'uz *you* bawn?"

"Right'n 'is town," laughed Genesis. "You fergit a good deal, pappy, but I notice you don' fergit come to meals!"

The old man grunted, resuming his whittling busily. "Hain' much use," he complained. "Cain' eat nuff'm 'lessen it all gruely. Man cain' eat nuff'm 'lessen he got teef. Genesis, di'n' I hyuh you tellin' dis white gemmum take caih his teef—not bite on no i'on?"

William smiled in pity. "I don't need to bother about that, I guess," he said. "I can crack nuts with my teeth."

"Yes, suh," said the old man. "You kin now. Ev'y nut you crack now goin' cos' you a yell when you git 'long 'bout fawty an' fifty. You crack nuts now an' you'll holler den!"

"Well, I guess I won't worry myself much now about what won't happen till I'm forty or fifty," said William. "My teeth'll last *my* time, I guess."

That brought a chuckle from Mr. Genesis. "Jes' listen!" he exclaimed. "Young man think he ain' nev' goin' be ole man. Else he think, 'Dat ole man what I'm goin' to be, dat ain' goin' be me 'tall—dat goin' be somebody else! What I caih 'bout dat ole man? I ain't a-goin' take caih o' no teef fer *him!*' Yes, suh, an' den when he *git* to be ole man, he say, 'What become o' dat young man I yoosta be? Where is dat young man agone to? He 'uz a fool, dat's what—an' *I* ain' no fool, so he mus' been somebody else, not me; but I do jes' wish I had him hyuh 'bout two minutes—long enough to lam him fer not takin' caih o' my teef fer me!' Yes, suh!'"

William laughed; his good humor was restored and he found the conversation of Mr. Genesis attractive. He seated himself upon an upturned bucket near the wheelbarrow, and reverted to a former theme. "Well, I *have* heard of people getting married even younger'n you were," he said. "You take India, for instance. Why, they get married in India when they're twelve, and even seven and eight years old."

"They do not!" said Jane, promptly. "Their mothers and fathers wouldn't let 'em, an' they wouldn't want to, anyway."

"I suppose you been to India and know all about it!" William retorted. "For the matter o' that, there was a young couple got married in Pennsylvania the other day; the girl was only fifteen, and the man was sixteen. It was in the papers, and their parents consented, and said it was a good thing. Then there was a case in Fall River, Massachusetts, where a young man eighteen years old married a woman forty-one years old; it was in the papers, too. And I heard of another case somewhere in Iowa—a boy began shaving when he was thirteen, and shaved every day for four years, and now he's got a full beard, and he's goin' to get married this year—before he's eighteen years old. Joe Bullitt's got a cousin in Iowa that knows about this case—he knows the girl this fellow with the beard is goin' to marry, and he says he expects it'll turn out the best thing could have happened. They're goin' to live on a farm. There's hunderds of cases like that, only you don't hear of more'n just a few of 'em. People used to get married at sixteen, seventeen, eighteen—anywhere in there—and never think anything of it at all. Right up to about a hunderd years ago there were more people married at those ages than there were along about twenty-four and twenty-five, the way they are now. For instance, you take Shakespeare—"

William paused.

Mr. Genesis was scraping the hull of the miniature boat

with a piece of broken glass, in lieu of sandpaper, but he seemed to be following his young friend's remarks with attention. William had mentioned Shakespeare impulsively, in the ardor of demonstrating his point; however, upon second thought he decided to withdraw the name.

"I mean, you take the olden times," he went on; "hardly anybody got married after they were nineteen or twenty years old, unless they were widowers, because they were all married by that time. And right here in our own county, there were eleven couples married in the last six months under twenty-one years of age. I've got a friend named Johnnie Watson; his uncle works down at the court-house and told him about it, so it can't be denied. Then there was a case I heard of over in—"

Mr. Genesis uttered a loud chuckle. "My goo'ness!" he exclaimed. "How you c'leck all dem fac's? Lan' name! What puzzlin' *me* is how you 'member 'em after you done c'leck 'em. Ef it 'uz me I couldn't c'leck 'em in de firs' place, an' ef I could, dey wouldn' be no use to me 'cause I couldn't rickalect 'em!"

"Well, it isn't so hard," said William, "if you kind of get the hang of it." Obviously pleased, he plucked a spear of grass and placed it between his teeth, adding, "I always did have a pretty good memory."

"Mamma says you're the most forgetful boy she ever heard of," said Jane, calmly. "She says you can't remember anything two minutes."

William's brow darkened. "Now look here—" he began, with severity.

But the old darky intervened. "Some folks got good rickaleckshum an' some folks got bad," he said, pacifically. "Young white gemmum rickalect mo' in two minute dan what I kin in two years!"

Jane appeared to accept this as settlement of the point at issue, while William bestowed upon Mr. Genesis a glance of increased favor. William's expression was pleasant to see; in fact, it was the pleasantest expression Jane had seen him wearing for several days. Almost always, lately, he was profoundly preoccupied, and so easily annoyed that there was no need to be careful of his feelings, because—as his mother observed—he was "certain to break out about every so often, no matter what happened!"

"I remember pretty much everything," he said, as if in modest explanation of the performance which had excited the aged man's admiration. "I can remember things that happened when I was four years old."

"So can I," said Jane. "I can remember when I was two. I had a kitten fell down the cistern and papa said it hurt the water."

"My goo'ness!" Mr. Genesis exclaimed. "An' you 'uz on'y two year ole, honey! Bes' *I* kin do is rickalect when I 'uz 'bout fifty."

"Oh no!" Jane protested. "You said you remembered havin' a baby when you were seventeen, Mr. Genesis."

"Yes'm," he admitted. "I mean rickalect good like you do 'bout yo' li'l' cat an' all how yo' pappy tuck on 'bout it. I kin rickalect *some,* but I cain' rickalect *good.*"

William coughed with a certain importance. "Do you remember," he asked, "when you were married, how did you feel about it? Were you kind of nervous, or anything like that, beforehand?"

Mr. Genesis again passed a wavering hand across his troubled brow.

"I mean," said William, observing his perplexity, "were you sort of shaky—f'rinstance, as if you were taking an important step in life?"

"Lemme see." The old man pondered for a moment. "I felt mighty shaky once. I rickalect; dat time yalla m'latta man shootin' at me f'um behime a snake-fence."

"Shootin' at you!" Jane cried, stirred from her accustomed placidity. "Mr. Genesis! What *did* he do that for?"

"Nuff'm!" replied Mr. Genesis, with feeling. "Nuff'm in de wide worl'! He boun' to shoot *some*body, an' pick on me 'cause I 'uz de handies'."

He closed his knife, gave the little boat a final scrape with the broken glass, and then a soothing rub with the palm of his hand. "Dah, honey," he said—and simultaneously factory whistles began to blow. "Dah yo' li'l' steamboat good as I kin git her widout no b'iler ner no smokestack. I reckon yo' pappy'll buy 'em for you."

Jane was grateful. "It's a beautiful boat, Mr. Genesis. I do thank you!"

Genesis, the son, laid aside his tools and approached. "Pappy finish whittlin' spang on 'em noon whistles," he chuckled. "Come 'long, pappy. I bet you walk fas' 'nuff goin' todes dinnuh. I hear fry-cakes ploppin' in skillet!"

Mr. Genesis laughed loudly, his son's words evidently painting a merry and alluring picture; and the two, followed by Clematis, moved away in the direction of the alley gate. William and Jane watched the brisk departure of the antique with sincere esteem and liking.

"He must have been sixteen," said William musingly.

"When?" Jane asked.

William, in deep thought, was still looking after Mr. Genesis; he was almost unconscious that he had spoken aloud and he replied, automatically:

"When he was married."

Then, with a start, he realized into how great a condescension he had been betrayed, and hastily added, with pronounced hauteur, "Things you don't understand. You run in the house."

Jane went into the house, but she did not carry her obedience to the point of running. She walked slowly, and in that state of profound reverie which was characteristic of her when she was immersed in the serious study of William's affairs.

16. The Shower

SHE CONTINUED to be thoughtful until after lunch, when, upon the sun's disappearance behind a fat cloud, Jane and the heavens exchanged dispositions for the time—the heavens darkened and Jane brightened. She was in the front hall, when the sunshine departed rather abruptly, and she jumped for joy, pointing to the open door. "Look! Looky there!" she called to her brother. Richly ornamented, he was descending the front stairs, his embellishments including freshly pressed white trousers, a new straw hat, unusual shoes, and a blasphemous tie. "I'm goin' to get to sail my boat," Jane shouted. "It's goin' to rain."

"It is not," said William, irritated. "It's not going to anything like rain. I s'pose you think it ought to rain just to let you sail that chunk of wood!"

"It's goin' to rain—it's goin' to rain!" (Jane made a

little singsong chant of it.) "It's goin' to rain—it gives
Willie a pain—it's goin' to rain—it gives Willie a pain—
it's goin' to—"

He interrupted her sternly. "Look here! You're old
enough to know better. I s'pose you think there isn't anything as important in the world as your gettin' the chance
to sail that little boat! I s'pose you think business and
everything else has got to stop and get ruined, maybe, just
to please you!" As he spoke he walked to an umbrella-
stand in the hall and deliberately took therefrom a bamboo
walking-stick of his father's. Indeed, his denunciation of
Jane's selfishness about the weather was made partly to
reassure himself and settle his nerves, strained by the unusual procedure he contemplated, and partly to divert
Jane's attention. In the latter effort he was unsuccessful;
her eyes became strange and unbearable.

She uttered a shriek:

"Willie's goin' to carry a *cane!*"

"You hush up!" he said, fiercely, and hurried out
through the front door. She followed him to the edge of
the porch; she stood there while he made his way to the
gate, and she continued to stand there as he went down
the street, trying to swing the cane in an accustomed and
unembarrassed manner.

Jane made this difficult.

"Willie's got a *cane!*" she screamed. "He's got papa's
cane!" Then, resuming her little chant, she began to sing:
"It's goin' to rain—Willie's got papa's cane—it's goin' to
rain—Willie's got papa's cane!" She put all of her voice
into a final effort. *"Miss Pratt'll get wet if you don't take
an umbereller-r-r!"*

The attention of several chance pedestrians had been
attracted, and the burning William, breaking into an
agonized half-trot, disappeared round the corner. Then
Jane retired within the house, feeling that she had done
her duty. It would be his own fault if he got wet.

Rain was coming. Rain was in the feel of the air—and
in Jane's hope.

She was not disappointed. Mr. Genesis, so secure of fair
weather in the morning, was proved by the afternoon to be
a bad prophet. The fat cloud was succeeded by others,
fatter; a corpulent army assailed the vault of heaven,

heavy outriders before a giant of evil complexion and devastating temper.

An hour after William had left the house, the dust in the streets and all loose paper and rubbish outdoors rose suddenly to a considerable height and started for somewhere else. The trees had colic; everything became as dark as winter twilight; streaks of wildfire ran miles in a second, and somebody seemed to be ripping up sheets of copper and tin the size of farms. The rain came with a swish, then with a rattle, and then with a roar, while people listened at their garret doorways and marveled. Windowpanes turned to running water—it poured.

Then it relented, dribbled, shook down a few last drops; and passed on to the countryside. Windows went up; eaves and full gutters plashed and gurgled; clearer light fell; then, in a moment, sunshine rushed upon shining green trees and green grass; doors opened—and out came the children!

Shouting, they ran to the flooded gutters. Here were rivers, lakes, and oceans for navigation; easy pilotage, for the steersman had but to wade beside his craft and guide it with a twig. Jane's timely boat was one of the first to reach the water.

Her mother had been kind, and Jane, with shoes and stockings left behind her on the porch, was a happy sailor as she waded knee-deep along the brimming curbstones. At the corner below the house of the Baxters, the street was flooded clear across, and Jane's boat, following the current, proceeded gallantly onward here, sailed down the next block, and was thoughtlessly entering a sewer when she snatched it out of the water. Looking about her, she perceived a gutter which seemed even lovelier than the one she had followed. It was deeper and broader and perhaps a little browner, wherefore she launched her ship upon its dimpled bosom and explored it as a far as the next sewer-hole or portage. Thus the voyage continued for several blocks with only one accident—which might have happened to anybody. It was an accident in the nature of a fall, caused by the sliding of Jane's left foot on some slippery mud. This treacherous substance, covered with water, could not have been anticipated; consequently Jane's emotions were those of indignation rather than of culpability.

Upon rising, she debated whether or not she should return to her dwelling, inclining to the opinion that the authorities there would have taken the affirmative; but as she was wet not much above the waist, and the guilt lay all upon the mud, she decided that such an interruption of her journey would be a gross injustice to herself. Navigation was reopened.

Presently the boat wandered into a miniature whirlpool, grooved in a spiral and pleasant to see. Slowly the water went round and round, and so did the boat without any assistance from Jane. Watching this movement thoughtfully, she brought forth from her drenched pocket some sodden whitish disks, recognizable as having been crackers, and began to eat them. Thus absorbed, she failed at first to notice the approach of two young people along the sidewalk.

They were the entranced William and Miss Pratt; and their appearance offered a suggestive contrast in relative humidity. In charming and tender-colored fabrics, fluffy and cool and summery, she was specklessly dry; not a drop had touched even the little pink parasol over her shoulder, not one had fallen upon the tiny white doglet drowsing upon her arm. But William was wet—he was still more than merely damp, though they had evidently walked some distance since the rain had ceased to fall. His new hat was a mucilaginous ruin; his dank coat sagged; his shapeless trousers flopped heavily, and his shoes gave forth marshy sounds as he walked.

No brilliant analyst was needed to diagnose this case. Surely any observer must have said: "Here is a dry young lady, and at her side walks a wet young gentleman who carries an umbrella in one hand and a walking-stick in the other. Obviously the young lady and gentleman were out for a stroll for which the stick was sufficient, and they were caught by the rain. Before any fell, however, he found her a place of shelter—such as a corner drug-store—and then himself gallantly went forth into the storm for an umbrella. He went to the young lady's house, or to the house where she may be visiting, for if he had gone to his own he would have left his stick. It may be, too, that at his own, his mother would have detained him, since he is still at the age when it is just possible sometimes for mothers to get their sons into the house when it rains. He returned with the umbrella to the corner drug-store at probably about the time when the rain ceased to fall, because his extreme moistness makes necessary the deduction that he was out in all the rain that rained. But he does not seem to care."

The fact was that William did not even know that he was wet. With his head sidewise and his entranced eyes continuously upon the pretty face so near, his state was almost somnambulistic. Not conscious of his soggy garments or of the deluged streets, he floated upon a rosy cloud, incense about him, far-away music enchanting his ears.

If Jane had not recognized the modeling of his features she might not have known them to be William's, for they had altered their grouping to produce an expression with which she was totally unfamiliar. To be explicit, she was unfamiliar with this expression in that place—that is to say, upon William, though she had seen something like it upon other people, once or twice, in church.

William's thoughts might have seemed to her as queer as his expression, could she have known them. They were not very definite, however, taking the form of sweet, vague pictures of the future. These pictures were of married life; that is, married life as William conceived it for himself and Miss Pratt—something strikingly different from that he had observed as led by his mother and father, or their friends and relatives. In his rapt mind he beheld Miss Pratt walking beside him "through life," with her little parasol and her little dog—her exquisite face always lifted playfully toward his own (with admiration underneath the playfulness), and he heard her voice of silver always rippling "baby-talk" throughout all the years to come. He saw her applauding his triumphs—though these remained indefinite in his mind, and he was unable to foreshadow the business or profession which was to provide the amazing mansion (mainly conservatory) which he pictured as their home. Surrounded by flowers, and maintaining a private orchestra, he saw Miss Pratt and himself growing old together, attaining to such ages as thirty and even thirty-five, still in perfect harmony, and always either dancing in the evenings or strolling hand in hand in the moonlight.

Sometimes they would visit the nursery, where curly-headed, rosy cherubs played upon a white-bear rug in the firelight. These were all boys and ready-made, the youngest being three years old and without a past.

They would be beautiful children, happy with their luxurious toys on the bear rug, and they would *never* be seen in any part of the house except the nursery. Their deportment would be flawless, and—

"*Will-ee!*"

The aviator struck a hole in the air; his heart misgave him. Then he came to earth—a sickening drop, and instantaneous.

"*Will-ee!*"

There was Jane, a figurine in a plastic state and altogether disgraceful—she came up out of the waters and stood before them with feet of clay, indeed; pedestaled upon the curbstone.

"Who *is* that *curious* child?" said Miss Pratt, stopping. William shuddered.

"Was she calling *you?*" Miss Pratt asked, incredulously.

"Willie, I told you you better take an umbereller," said Jane, "instead of papa's cane." And she added triumphantly, "Now you see!"

Moving forward, she seemed to have in mind a dreadful purpose; there was something about her that made William think she intended casually to accompany him and Miss Pratt.

"You go home!" he commanded, hoarsely.

Miss Pratt uttered a little scream of surprise and recognition. "It's your little sister!" she exclaimed, and then, reverting to her favorite playfulness of enunciation, " 'Oor ickle sissa!" she added, gaily, as a translation. Jane misunderstood it; she thought Miss Pratt meant "*our* little sister."

"Go home!" said William.

"No'ty, no'ty!" said Miss Pratt, shaking her head. "Me 'fraid oo's a no'ty, no'ty ickle dirl! All datie!"

Jane advanced. "I wish you'd let me carry Flopit for you," she said.

Giving forth another gentle scream, Miss Pratt hopped prettily backward from Jane's extended hands. "Oo-oo!" she cried, chidingly. "Mustn't touch! P'eshus Flopit all soap-water-wash clean. Ickle dirly all muddy-nassy! Ickle

dirly must doe home, det all soap-water-wash clean like
nice ickle sissa. Evabody will love 'oor ickle sissa *den,*"
she concluded, turning to William. "Tell 'oor ickle sissa
mus' doe home det soap-water-wash!"

Jane stared at Miss Pratt with fixed solemnity during
the delivery of these admonitions, and it was to be seen
that they made an impression upon her. Her mouth slowly
opened, but she spake not. An extraordinary idea had just
begun to make itself at home in her mind. It was an idea
which had been hovering in the neighborhood of that
domain ever since William's comments upon the conversation of Mr. Genesis, in the morning.

"Go home!" repeated William, and then, as Jane stood
motionless and inarticulate, transfixed by her idea, he said,
almost brokenly, to his dainty companion, "I *don't* know
what you'll think of my mother! To let this child—"

Miss Pratt laughed comfortingly as they started on
again. "Isn't mamma's fault, foolish boy Baxter. Ickle
dirlies will det datie!"

The profoundly mortified William glanced back over
his shoulder, bestowing upon Jane a look in which bitterness was mingled with apprehension. But she remained
where she was, and did not follow. That was a little to be
thankful for, and he found some additional consolation in
believing that Miss Pratt had not caught the frightful
words, "papa's cane," at the beginning of the interview.
He was encouraged to this belief by her presently taking
from his hand the decoration in question and examining
it with tokens of pleasure. " 'Oor pitty walk'-'tick," she
called it, with a tact he failed to suspect. And so he began
to float upward again; glamors enveloped him and the
earth fell away.

He was alone in space with Miss Pratt once more.

17. Jane's Theory

THE PALE end of sunset was framed in the dining-room
windows, and Mr. and Mrs. Baxter and the rehabilitated
Jane were at the table, when William made his belated
return from the afternoon's excursion. Seating himself, he

waived his mother's references to the rain, his clothes, and probable colds, and after one laden glance at Jane—denoting a grievance so elaborate that he despaired of setting it forth in a formal complaint to the Powers—he fell into a state of trance. He took nourishment automatically, and roused himself but once during the meal, a pathetic encounter with his father resulting from this awakening.

"Everybody in town seemed to be on the streets, this evening, as I walked home," Mr. Baxter remarked, addressing his wife. "I suppose there's something in the clean air after a rain that brings 'em out. I noticed one thing, though; maybe it's the way they dress nowadays, but you certainly don't see as many pretty girls on the streets as there used to be."

William looked up absently. "I used to think that, too," he said, with dreamy condescension, "when I was younger."

Mr. Baxter stared.

"Well, I'll be darned!" he said.

"Papa, papa!" his wife called, reprovingly.

"When you were younger!" Mr. Baxter repeated, with considerable irritation. "How old d' you think you are?"

"I'm going on eighteen," said William, firmly. "I know plenty of cases—cases where—" He paused, relapsing into lethargy.

"What's the matter with him?" Mr. Baxter inquired, heatedly, of his wife.

William again came to life. "I was saying that a person's age is different according to circumstances," he explained with dignity, if not lucidity. "You take Genesis's father. Well, he was married when he was sixteen. Then there was a case over in Iowa that lots of people know about and nobody thinks anything of. A young man over there in Iowa that's seventeen years old began shaving when he was thirteen and shaved every day for four years, and now—"

He was interrupted by his father, who was no longer able to contain himself. "And now I suppose he's got *whiskers!*" he burst forth. "There's an ambition for you! My soul!"

It was Jane who took up the tale. She had been listening with growing excitement, her eyes fixed piercingly upon William. "He's got a beard!" she cried, alluding not to her brother, but to the fabled Iowan. "I heard Willie tell ole Mr. Genesis about it."

"It seems to lie heavily on your mind," Mr. Baxter said to William. "I suppose you feel that in the face of such an example, your life between the ages of thirteen and seventeen has been virtually thrown away?"

William had again relapsed, but he roused himself feebly. "Sir?" he said.

"What *is* the matter with him?" Mr. Baxter demanded. "Half the time lately he seems to be hibernating, and only responds by a slight twitching when poked with a stick. The other half of the time he either behaves like I-don't-know-what or talks about children growing whiskers in Iowa! Hasn't that girl left town yet?"

William was not so deep in trance that this failed to stir him. He left the table.

Mrs. Baxter looked distressed, though, as the meal was about concluded, and William had partaken of his share in spite of his dreaminess, she had no anxieties connected with his sustenance. As for Mr. Baxter, he felt a little remorse, undoubtedly, but he was also puzzled. So plain a man was he that he had no perception of the callous brutality of the words *"that girl"* when applied to some girls. He referred to his mystification a little later, as he sat with his evening paper in the library.

"I don't know what I said to that tetchy boy to hurt him," he began in an apologetic tone. "I don't see that there was anything to rough for him to stand in a little sarcasm. He needn't be so sensitive on the subject of whiskers, it seems to me."

Mrs. Baxter smiled faintly and shook her head.

It was Jane who responded. She was seated upon the floor, disporting herself mildly with her paint-box. "Papa, I know what's the matter with Willie," she said.

"Do you?" Mr. Baxter returned. "Well, if you make it pretty short, you've got just about long enough to tell us before your bedtime."

"I think he's married," said Jane.

"What!" And her parents united their hilarity.

"I do think he's married," Jane insisted, unmoved. "I think he's married with that Miss Pratt."

"Well," said her father, "he does seem upset, and it may be that her visit and the idea of whiskers, coming so close together, is more than mere coincidence, but I hardly think Willie is married, Jane!"

"Well, then," she returned, thoughtfully, "he's *almost* married. I know that much, anyway."

"What makes you think so?"

"Well, because! I *kind* of thought he must be married, or anyways somep'm, when he talked to Mr. Genesis this mornin'. He said he knew how some people got married in Pennsylvania an' India, an' he said they were only seven or eight years old. He said so, an' I heard him; an' he said there were eleven people married that were only seventeen, an' this boy in Iowa got a full beard an' got married, too. An' he said Mr. Genesis was only sixteen when *he* was married. He talked all about gettin' married when you're seventeen years old, an' he said how people thought it was the best thing could happen. So I just *know* he's almost married!"

Mr. Baxter chuckled, and Mrs. Baxter smiled, but a shade of thoughtfulness, a remote anxiety, fell upon the face of the latter.

"You haven't any other reason, have you, Jane?" she asked.

"Yes'm," said Jane, promptly. "An' it's a more reason than any! Miss Pratt calls you 'mamma' as if you were *her* mamma. She does it when she talks to Willie."

"Jane!"

"Yes'm, I *heard* her. An' Willie said, 'I don't know what you'll think about mother.' He said, 'I don't know what you'll think about mother,' to Miss Pratt."

Mrs. Baxter looked a little startled, and her husband frowned. Jane mistook their expression for incredulity. "They *did,* mamma," she protested. "That's just the way they talked to each other. I heard 'em this afternoon, when Willie had papa's cane."

"Maybe they were doing it to tease you, if you were with them," Mr. Baxter suggested.

"I wasn't with 'em. I was sailin' my boat, an' they came along, an' first they never saw me, an' Willie looked —oh, papa, I wish you'd seen him!" Jane rose to her feet in her excitement. "His face was so funny, you never saw anything like it! He was walkin' along with it turned sideways, an' all the time he kept walkin' frontways, he kept his face sideways—like this, papa. Look, papa!" And she gave what she considered a faithful imitation of William walking with Miss Pratt. "Look, papa! This is the way Willie went. He had it sideways so's he could see Miss Pratt, papa. An' his face was just like this. Look, papa!" She contorted her features in a terrifying manner. "Look, papa!"

"Don't, Jane!" her mother exclaimed.

"Well, I haf to show papa how Willie looked, don't I?" said Jane, relaxing. "That's just the way he looked. Well an' then they stopped an' talked to me, an' Miss Pratt said, 'It's our little sister.' "

"Did she really?" Mrs. Baxter asked, gravely.

"Yes'm, she did. Soon as she saw who I was, she said, 'Why, it's our little sister!' Only she said it that way she talks—sort of foolish. 'It's our 'ittle sissy'—somep'm like that, mamma. She said it twice an' told me to go home an' get washed up. An' Miss Pratt told Willie—Miss Pratt said, 'It isn't mamma's fault Jane's so dirty,' just like that. She—"

"Are you sure she said 'our little sister'?" said Mrs. Baxter.

"Why, you can ask Willie! She said it that funny way. 'Our 'ittle sissy'; that's what she said. An' Miss Pratt said, 'Ev'rybody would love our little sister if mamma washed her in soap an' water!' You can ask Willie; that's exackly what Miss Pratt said, an' if you don't believe it you can ask *her*. If you don't want to believe it, why, you can ask—"

"Hush, dear," said Mrs. Baxter. "All this doesn't mean anything at all, especially such nonsense as Willie's thinking of being married. It's your bedtime."

"Well, but, *mamma*—"

"Was that all they said?" Mr. Baxter inquired.

Jane turned to him eagerly. "They said all lots of things like that, papa. They—"

"Nonsense!" Mrs. Baxter interrupted. "Come, it's bedtime. I'll go up with you. You mustn't think such nonsense."

"But, mamma—"

"Come along, Jane!"

Jane was obedient in the flesh, but her spirit was free; her opinions were her own. Disappointed in the sensation she had expected to produce, she followed her mother out of the room wearing the expression of a person who says, "You'll *see*—some day when everything's ruined!"

Mr. Baxter, left alone, laughed quietly, lifted his neglected newspaper to obtain the light at the right angle, and then allowed it to languish upon his lap again. Frowning, he began to tap the floor with his shoe.

He was trying to remember what things were in his head when he was seventeen, and it was difficult. It seemed to him that he had been a steady, sensible young fellow— really quite a man—at that age. Looking backward at the blur of youthful years, the period from sixteen to twenty-five appeared to him as "pretty much all of a piece." He could not recall just when he stopped being a boy; it must have been at about fifteen, he thought.

All at once he sat up stiffly in his chair, and the paper slid from his knee. He remembered an autumn, long ago, when he had decided to abandon the educational plans of his parents and become an actor. He had located this project exactly, for it dated from the night of his seventeenth birthday, when he saw John McCullough play "Virginius."

Even now Mr. Baxter grew a little red as he remembered the remarkable letter he had written, a few weeks later, to the manager of a passing theatrical company. He had confidently expected an answer, and had made his plans to leave town quietly with the company and afterward reassure his parents by telegraph. In fact, he might have been on the stage at this moment, if that manager had taken him. Mr. Baxter began to look nervous.

Still, there is a difference between going on the stage and getting married. "I don't know, though!" Mr. Baxter thought. "And Willie's certainly not so well balanced in a *general* way as I was." He wished his wife would come down and reassure him, though of course it was all nonsense.

But when Mrs. Baxter came down-stairs she did not

reassure him. "Of course Jane's too absurd!" she said.
"I don't mean that she 'made it up'; she never does that,
and no doubt this little Miss Pratt did say about what
Jane thought she said. But it all amounts to nothing."

"Of course!"

"Willie's just going through what several of the other
boys about his age are going through—like Johnnie Watson and Joe Bullitt and Wallace Banks. They all seem to
be frantic over her."

"I caught a glimpse of her the day you had her to tea.
She's rather pretty."

"Adorably! And perhaps Willie has been just a *little*
bit more frantic than the others."

"He certainly seems in a queer state!"

At this his wife's tone became serious. "Do you think
he *would* do as crazy a thing as that?"

Mr. Baxter laughed. "Well, I don't know what he'd
do it *on!* I don't suppose he has more than a dollar in
his possession."

"Yes, he has," she returned, quickly. "Day before yesterday there was a second-hand furniture man here, and
I was too busy to see him, but I wanted the storeroom in
the cellar cleared out, and I told Willie he could have
whatever the man would pay him for the junk in there,
if he'd watch to see that they didn't *take* anything. They
found some old pieces that I'd forgotten, underneath things,
and altogether the man paid Willie nine dollars and eighty-
five cents."

"But, mercy-me!" exclaimed Mr. Baxter, "the girl may
be an idiot, but she wouldn't run away and marry a boy
just barely seventeen on nine dollars and eighty-five cents!"

"Oh no!" said Mrs. Baxter. "At least, I don't *think* so.
Of course girls do as crazy things as boys sometimes—in
their way. I was thinking—" She paused. "Of *course* there
couldn't be anything in it, but it did seem a little strange."

"What did?"

"Why, just before I came down-stairs, Adelia came for
the laundry; and I asked her if she'd seen Willie; and she
said he'd put on his dark suit after dinner, and he went
out through the kitchen, carrying his suit-case."

"He did?"

"Of course," Mrs. Baxter went on, slowly, "I *couldn't* believe he'd do such a thing, but he really is in a preposterous way over this little Miss Pratt, and he *did* have that money—"

"By George!" Mr. Baxter got upon his feet. "The way he talked at dinner, I could come pretty near believing he hasn't any more brains *left* than to get married on nine dollars and eighty-five cents! I wouldn't put it past him! By George, I wouldn't!"

"Oh, I don't think he would," she remonstrated, feebly. "Besides, the law wouldn't permit it."

Mr. Baxter paced the floor. "Oh, I suppose they *could* manage it. They could go to some little town and give false ages and—" He broke off. "Adelia was sure he had his suit-case?"

She nodded. "Do you think we'd better go down to the Parchers'? We'd just say we came to call, of course, and if—"

"Get your hat on," he said. "I don't think there's anything in it at all, but we'd just as well drop down there. It can't *hurt* anything."

"Of course, I don't think—" she began.

"Neither do I," he interrupted, irascibly. "But with a boy of his age crazy enough to think he's in love, how do *we* know what'll happen? We're only his parents! Get your hat on."

But when the uneasy couple found themselves upon the pavement before the house of the Parchers, they paused under the shade-trees in the darkness, and presently decided that it was not necessary to go in. Suddenly their uneasiness had fallen from them. From the porch came the laughter of several young voices, and then one silvery voice, which pretended to be that of a tiny child.

"Oh, s'ame! S'ame on 'oo, big Bruvva Josie-Joe! Mus' be polite to Johnnie Jump-Up, or tant play wiv May and Lola!"

"That's Miss Pratt," whispered Mrs. Baxter. "She's talking to Johnnie Watson and Joe Bullitt and May Parcher. Let's go home; it's all right. Of course I knew it would be."

"Why, certainly," said Mr. Baxter, as they turned.

"Even if Willie were as crazy as that, the little girl would have more sense. I wouldn't have thought anything of it, if you hadn't told me about the suit-case. That looked sort of queer."

She agreed that it did, but immediately added that she had thought nothing of it. What had seemed more significant to her was William's interest in the early marriage of Genesis's father and in the Iowa beard story, she said. Then she said that it *was* curious about the suit-case.

And when they came to their own house again, there was William sitting alone and silent upon the steps of the porch.

"I thought you'd gone out, Willie," said his mother, as they paused beside him.

"Ma'am?"

"Adelia said you went out, carrying your suit-case."

"Oh yes," he said, languidly. "If you leave clothes at Schwartz's in the evening they have 'em pressed in the morning. You said I looked damp at dinner, so I took 'em over and left 'em there."

"I see." Mrs. Baxter followed her husband to the door, but she stopped on the threshold and called back:

"Don't sit there too long, Willie."

"Ma'am?"

"The dew is falling and it rained so hard to-day—I'm afraid it might be damp."

"Ma'am?"

"Come on," Mr. Baxter said to his wife. "He's down on the Parchers' porch, not out in front here. Of course he can't hear you. It's three blocks and a half."

But William's father was mistaken. Little he knew! William was not upon the porch of the Parchers, with May Parcher and Joe Bullitt and Johnnie Watson to interfere. He was far from there, in a land where time was not. Upon a planet floating in pink mist, and uninhabited— unless old Mr. Genesis and some Hindoo princes and the diligent Iowan may have established themselves in its remoter regions—William was alone with Miss Pratt, in the conservatory. And, after a time, they went together, and looked into the door of a room where an indefinite number of little boys—all over three years of age—were playing in the firelight upon a white-bear rug. For, in the roseate gossamer that boys' dreams are made of, William had indeed entered the married state.

His condition was growing worse, every day.

18. The Big Fat Lummox

IN THE MORNING sunshine, Mrs. Baxter stood at the top of the steps of the front porch, addressing her son, who listened impatiently and edged himself a little nearer the gate every time he shifted his weight from one foot to the other.

"Willie," she said, "you must really pay some attention to the laws of health, or you'll never live to be an old man."

"I don't want to live to be an old man," said William, earnestly. "I'd rather do what I please now and die a little sooner."

"You talk very foolishly," his mother returned. "Either come back and put on some heavier *things* or take your overcoat."

"My overcoat!" William groaned. "They'd think I was a lunatic, carrying an overcoat in August!"

"Not to a picnic," she said.

"Mother, it isn't a picnic, I've told you a hunderd times! You think it's one of those ole-fashion things *you* used to go to—sit on the damp ground and eat sardines with ants all over 'em! This isn't anything like that; we just go out on the trolley to this farm-house and have noon dinner, and dance all afternoon, and have supper, and then come home on the trolley. I guess we'd hardly of got up anything as out o' date as a picnic in honor of Miss *Pratt!*"

Mrs. Baxter seemed unimpressed.

"It doesn't matter whether you call it a picnic or not, Willie. It will be cool on the open trolley-car coming home, especially with only those white trousers on—"

"Ye gods!" he cried. "I've got other things on besides my trousers! I wish you wouldn't always act as if I was a perfect child! Good heavens! isn't a person my age supposed to know how much clothes to wear?"

"Well, if he is," she returned, "it's a mere supposition

and not founded on fact. Don't get so excited, Willie, please; but you'll either have to give up the picnic or come in and ch—"

"Change my 'things'!" he wailed. "I can't change my 'things'! I've got just twenty minutes to get to May Parcher's—the crowd meets there, and they're goin' to take the trolley in front of the Parchers' at exactly a quarter after 'leven. *Please* don't keep me any longer, mother—I *got* to go!"

She stepped into the hall and returned immediately. "Here's your overcoat, Willie."

His expression was of despair. "They'll think I'm a lunatic and they'll say so before everybody—and I don't blame 'em! Overcoat on a hot day like this! Except me, I don't suppose there was ever anybody lived in the world and got to be going on eighteen years old and had to carry his silly old overcoat around with him in August—because his mother made him!"

"Willie," said Mrs. Baxter, "you don't know how many thousands and thousands of mothers for thousands and thousands of years have kept their sons from taking thousands and thousands of colds—just this way!"

He moaned. "Well, and I got to be called a lunatic just because you're nervous, I s'pose. All right!"

She hung it upon his arm, kissed him; and he departed in a desperate manner.

However, having worn his tragic face for three blocks, he halted before a corner drug-store, and permitted his expression to improve as he gazed upon the window display of My Little Sweetheart All-Tobacco Cuban Cigarettes, the Package of Twenty for Ten Cents. William was not a smoker—that is to say, he had made the usual boyhood experiments, finding them discouraging; and though at times he considered it humorously man-about-town to say to a smoking friend, "Well, *I'll* tackle one o' your ole coffin-nails," he had never made a purchase of tobacco in his life. But it struck him now that it would be rather debonair to disport himself with a package of Little Sweethearts upon the excursion.

And the name! It thrilled him inexpressibly, bringing a tenderness into his eyes and a glow into his bosom. He felt that when he should smoke a Little Sweetheart it would be a tribute to the ineffable visitor for whom this party was being given—it would bring her closer to him. His young brow grew almost stern with determination, for he made up his mind, on the spot, that he would smoke oftener in the future—he would become a confirmed smoker, and all his life he would smoke My Little Sweetheart All-Tobacco Cuban Cigarettes.

He entered and managed to make his purchase in a matter-of-fact way, as if he were doing something quite unemotional; then he said to the clerk:

"Oh, by the by—ah—"

The clerk stared. "Well, what else?"

"I mean," said William, hurriedly, "there's something I wanted to 'tend to, now I happen to be here. I was on my way to take this overcoat to—to get something altered at the tailor's for next winter. 'Course I wouldn't want it till winter, but I thought I might as well get it *done*." He paused, laughing carelessly, for greater plausibility. "I thought he'd prob'ly want lots of time on the job—he's a slow worker, I've noticed—and so I decided I might just as well go ahead and let him get at it. Well, so I was on my way there, but I just noticed I only got about six minutes more to get to a mighty important engagement I got this morning, and I'd like to leave it here and come by and get it on my way home, this evening."

"Sure," said the clerk. "Hang it on that hook inside the p'scription-counter. There's one there already, b'longs to your friend, that young Bullitt fella. He was in here awhile ago and said he wanted to leave his because he didn't have time to take it to be pressed in time for next winter. Then he went on and joined that crowd in Mr. Parcher's yard, around the corner, that's goin' on a trolley-party. I says, 'I betcher mother maje carry it,' and he says, 'Oh no. Oh no,' he says. 'Honest, I was goin' to get it pressed!' You can hang yours on the same nail."

The clerk spoke no more, and went to serve another customer, while William stared after him a little uneasily. It seemed that here was a man of suspicious nature, though, of course, Joe Bullitt's shallow talk about getting an overcoat pressed before winter would not have imposed upon anybody. However, William felt strongly that the private life of the customers of a store should not be pried into and speculated about by employees, and he was conscious of a distaste for this clerk.

Nevertheless, it was with a lighter heart that he left his overcoat behind him and stepped out of the side door of the drug-store. That brought him within sight of the gaily dressed young people, about thirty in number, gathered upon the small lawn beside Mr. Parcher's house.

Miss Pratt stood among them, in heliotrope and white, Flopit nestling in her arms. She was encircled by girls who were enthusiastically caressing the bored and blinking Flopit; and when William beheld this charming group, his breath became eccentric, his knee-caps became cold and convulsive, his neck became hot, and he broke into a light perspiration.

She saw him! The small blonde head and the delirious little fluffy hat above it shimmered a nod to him. Then his mouth fell unconsciously open, and his eyes grew glassy with the intensity of meaning he put into the silent response he sent across the picket fence and through the interstices of the intervening group. Pressing with his elbow upon the package of cigarettes in his pocket, he murmured, in-audibly, "My Little Sweetheart, always for you!"—a repe-tition of his vow that, come what might, he would forever remain a loyal smoker of that symbolic brand. In fact, William's mental condition had never shown one moment's turn for the better since the fateful day of the distracting visitor's arrival.

Mr. Johnnie Watson and Mr. Joe Bullitt met him at the gate and offered him hearty greeting. All bickering and dis-sension among these three had passed. The lady was so wondrous impartial that, as time went on, the sufferers had come to be drawn together, rather than thrust asunder, by their common feeling. It had grown to be a bond uniting them; they were not so much rivals as ardent novices serv-ing a single altar, each worshipping there without visible gain over the other. Each had even come to possess, in the eyes of his two fellows, almost a sacredness as a sharer in the celestial glamor; they were tender one with another. They were in the last stages.

Johnnie Watson had with him to-day a visitor of his own—a vastly overgrown person of eighteen, who, at

Johnnie's beckoning, abandoned a fair companion of the moment and came forward as William entered the gate.

"I want to intradooce you to two of my most int'mut friends, George," said Johnnie, with the anxious gravity of a person about to do something important and unfamiliar. "Mr. Baxter, let me intradooce my cousin, Mr. Crooper. Mr. Crooper, this is my friend, Mr. Baxter."

The gentlemen shook hands solemnly, saying, " 'M very glad to meet you," and Johnnie turned to Joe Bullitt. "Mr. Croo— I mean, Mr. Bullitt, let me intradooce my friend, Mr. Crooper— I mean my cousin, Mr. Crooper. Mr. Crooper is a cousin of mine."

"Glad to make your acquaintance, Mr. Crooper," said Joe. "I suppose you're a cousin of Johnnie's, then?"

"Yep," said Mr. Crooper, becoming more informal. "Johnnie wrote me to come over for this shindig, so I thought I might as well come." He laughed loudly, and the others laughed with the same heartiness. "Yessir," he added, "I thought I might as well come, 'cause I'm pretty apt to be on hand if there's anything doin'!"

"Well, that's right," said William, and while they all laughed again, Mr. Crooper struck his cousin a jovial blow upon the back.

"Hi, ole sport!" he cried, "I want to meet that Miss Pratt before we start. The car'll be along pretty soon, and I got her picked for the girl I'm goin' to sit by."

The laughter of William and Joe Bullitt, designed to express cordiality, suddenly became flaccid and died. If Mr. Crooper had been a sensitive person he might have perceived the chilling disapproval in their glances, for they had just begun to be most unfavorably impressed with him. The careless loudness—almost the notoriety—with which he had uttered Miss Pratt's name, demanding loosely to be presented to her, regardless of the well-known law that a lady must first express some wish in such matters—these were indications of a coarse nature sure to be more than uncongenial to Miss Pratt. Its presence might make the whole occasion distasteful to her—might spoil her day. Both William and Joe Bullitt began to wonder why on earth Johnnie Watson didn't have any more sense than to invite such a big, fat lummox of a cousin to the party.

This severe phrase of theirs, almost simultaneous in the two minds, was not wholly a failure as a thumb-nail sketch of Mr George Crooper. And yet there was the impressiveness of size about him, especially about his legs and chin. At seventeen and eighteen growth is still going on, sometimes in a sporadic way, several parts seeming to have sprouted faster than others. Often the features have not quite settled down together in harmony, a mouth, for instance, appearing to have gained such a lead over the rest of a face, that even a mother may fear it can never be overtaken. Voices, too, often seem misplaced; one hears, outside the door, the bass rumble of a sinister giant, and a mild boy, thin as a cricket, walks in. The contrary was George Crooper's case; his voice was an unexpected piping tenor, half falsetto and frequently girlish—as surprising as the absurd voice of an elephant.

He had the general outwardness of a vast and lumpy child. His chin had so distanced his other features that his eyes, nose, and brow seemed almost baby-like in comparison, while his mountainous legs were the great part of the rest of him. He was one of those huge, bottle-shaped boys who are always in motion in spite of their cumbersomeness. His gestures were continuous, though difficult to interpret as bearing upon the subject of his equally continuous conversation; and under all circumstances he kept his conspicuous legs incessantly moving, whether he was going anywhere or remaining in comparatively one spot.

His expression was pathetically offensive, the result of his bland confidence in the audible opinions of a small town whereof his father was the richest inhabitant—and the one thing about him even more obvious than his chin, his legs, and his spectacular taste in flannels was his perfect trust that he was as welcome to every one as he was to his mother. This might some day lead him in the direction of great pain, but on the occasion of the "subscription party" for Miss Pratt it gave him an advantage.

"When do I get to meet that cutie?" he insisted, as Johnnie Watson moved backward from the cousinly arm, which threatened further flailing. "You intradooced me to about seven I can't do much *for*, but I want to get the howdy business over with this Miss Pratt, so I and she can get things started. I'm goin' to keep her busy all day!"

"Well, don't be in such a hurry," said Johnnie, uneasily. "You can meet her when we get out in the country—if I get a chance, George."

"No, sir!" George protested, jovially. "I guess you're sad birds over in this town, but look out! When I hit a town it don't take long till they all hear there's something doin'! You know how I am when I get started, Johnnie!" Here he turned upon William, tucking his fat arm affectionately through William's thin one. "Hi, sport! Ole Johnnie's so slow, *you* toddle me over and get me fixed up with this Miss Pratt, and I'll tell her you're the real stuff—after we get engaged!"

He was evidently a true cloud-compeller, this horrible George.

19. "I Dunno Why It Is"

WILLIAM extricated his arm, huskily muttering words which were lost in the general outcry, "Car's coming!" The young people poured out through the gate, and, as the car stopped, scrambled aboard. For a moment everything was hurried and confused. William struggled anxiously to push through to Miss Pratt and climb up beside her, but Mr. George Crooper made his way into the crowd in a beaming, though bull-like manner, and a fat back in a purple-and-white "blazer" flattened William's nose, while ponderous heels damaged William's toes; he was shoved back, and just managed to clamber upon the foot-board as the car started. The friendly hand of Joe Bullitt pulled him to a seat, and William found himself rubbing his nose and sitting between Joe and Johnnie Watson, directly behind the dashing Crooper and Miss Pratt. Mr. Crooper had already taken Flopit upon his lap.

"Dogs are always crazy 'bout me," they heard him say, for his high voice was but too audible over all other sounds. "Dogs and chuldren. I dunno why it is, but they always take to me. My name's George Crooper, Third, Johnnie Watson's cousin. He was tryin' to intradooce me before the car came along, but he never got the chance. I guess as this shindig's for you, and I'm the only other guest from out o' town, we'll have to intradooce ourselves—the two guests of honor, as it were."

Miss Pratt laughed her silvery laugh, murmured politely, and turned no freezing glance upon her neighbor. Indeed, it seemed that she was far from regarding him with the distaste anticipated by William and Joe Bullitt. "Flopit look so toot an' tunnin'," she was heard to remark. "Flopit look so 'ittle on dray, big, 'normous man's lap."

Mr. Crooper laughed deprecatingly. "He does look kind of small compared with the good ole man that's got charge of him, now! Well, I always was a good deal bigger than the fellas I went with. I dunno why it is, but I was always kind of quicker, too, as it were—and the strongest in any crowd I ever got with. I'm kind of muscle-bound, I guess, but I don't let that interfere with my quickness any. Take me in an automobile, now—I got a racin'-car at home— and I keep my head better than most people do, as it were. I can kind of handle myself better; I dunno why it is. My brains seem to work better than other people's, that's all it is. I don't mean that I got more sense, or anything like that; it's just the way my brains work; they kind of put me at an advantage, as it were. Well, f'rinstance, if I'd been livin' here in this town and joined in with the crowd to get up this party, well, it would of been done a good deal dif- f'rent. I won't say better, but diff'rent. That's always the way with me—if I go into anything, pretty soon I'm run- ning the whole shebang; I dunno why it is. The other people might try to run it their way for a while, but pretty soon you notice 'em beginning to step out of the way for good ole George. I dunno why it is, but that's the way it goes. Well, if I'd been running *this* party I'd of had auto- mobiles to go out in, not a trolley-car where you all got to sit together—and I'd of sent over home for my little racer and I'd of taken you out in her myself. I wish I'd of sent for it, anyway. We could of let the rest go out in the trolley, and you and I could of got off by ourselves: I'd like you to see that little car. Well, anyway, I bet you'd of seen something pretty different and a whole lot better if I'd of come over to this town in time to get up this party for you!"

"For us," Miss Pratt corrected him, sunnily. "Bofe strangers—party for us two—all bofe!" And she gave him one of her looks.

Mr. Crooper flushed with emotion; he was annexed; he became serious. "Say," he said, "that's a mighty smooth hat you got on." And he touched the fluffy rim of it with his forefinger. His fat shoulders leaned toward her yearningly.

"We'd cert'nly of had a lot better time sizzin' along in that little racer I got," he said. "I'd like to had you see how I handle that little car. Girls over home, they say they like to go out with me just to watch the way I handle her; they say it ain't so much just the ride, but more the way I handle that little car. I dunno why it is, but that's what they say. That's the way I do anything I make up my mind to tackle, though. I don't try to tackle everything—there's lots o' things I wouldn't take enough interest in 'em, as it were —but just lemme make up my mind once, and it's all off; I dunno why it is. There was a brakeman on the train got kind of fresh: he didn't know who I was. Well, I just put my hand on his shoulder and pushed him down in his seat like this"—he set his hand upon Miss Pratt's shoulder. "I didn't want to hit him, because there was women and chuldren in the car, so I just shoved my face up close to him, like this. 'I guess you don't know how much stock my father's got in this road,' I says. Did he wilt? Well, you ought of seen that brakeman when I got through tellin' him who I was!"

"Nassy ole brateman!" said Miss Pratt, with unfailing sympathy.

Mr. Crooper's fat hand, as if unconsciously, gave Miss Pratt's delicate shoulder a litle pat in reluctant withdrawal. "Well, that's the way with me," he said. "Much as I been around this world, nobody ever tried to put anything over on me and got away with it. They always come out the little end o' the horn; I dunno why it is. Say, that's a mighty smooth locket you got on the end o' that chain, there." And again stretching forth his hand, in a proprietor-like way, he began to examine the locket.

Three hot hearts, just behind, pulsated hatred toward him; for Johnnie Watson had perceived his error, and his sentiments were now linked to those of Joe Bullitt and William. The unhappiness of these three helpless spectators was the more poignant because not only were they witnesses of the impression of greatness which George Crooper was obviously producing upon Miss Pratt, but they were unable to prevent themselves from being likewise impressed.

They were not analytical; they dumbly accepted George at his own rating, not even being able to charge him with lack of modesty. Did he not always accompany his testimonials to himself with his deprecating falsetto laugh and "I dunno why it is," an official disclaimer of merit, "as it were"? Here was a formidable candidate, indeed—a traveler, a man of the world, with brains better and quicker than other people's brains; an athlete, yet knightly—he would not destroy even a brakeman in the presence of women and children—and, finally, most enviable and deadly, the owner and operator of a "little racer"! All this glitter was not far short of overpowering; and yet, though accepting it as fact, the woeful three shared the inconsistent belief that in spite of everything George was nothing but a big, fat lummox. For thus they even rather loudly whispered of him—almost as if hopeful that Miss Pratt, and mayhap George himself, might overhear.

Impotent their seething! The overwhelming Crooper pursued his conquering way. He leaned more and more toward the magnetic girl, his growing tenderness having that effect upon him, and his head inclining so far that his bedewed brow now and then touched the fluffy hat. He was constitutionally restless, but his movements never ended by placing a greater distance between himself and Miss Pratt, though they sometimes discommoded Miss Parcher, who sat at the other side of him—a side of him which appeared to be without consciousness. He played naïvely with Miss Pratt's locket and with the filmy border of her collar; he flicked his nose for some time with her little handkerchief, loudly sniffing its scent; and finally he became interested in a ring she wore, removed it, and tried unsuccessfully to place it upon one of his own fingers.

"I've worn lots o' girls' rings on my watch-fob. I'd let 'em wear mine on a chain or something. I guess they like to do that with me," he said. "I dunno why it is."

At this subtle hint the three unfortunates held their breath, and then lost it as the lovely girl acquiesced in the horrible exchange. As for William, life was of no more use to him. Out of the blue heaven of that bright morning's promise had fallen a pall, draping his soul in black and purple. He had been horror-stricken when first the pudgy finger of George Crooper had touched the fluffy edge of that sacred little hat; then, during George's subsequent pawings and leanings, William felt that he must either rise and murder or go mad. But when the exchange of rings was accomplished, his spirit broke and even resentment oozed away. For a time there was no room in him for anything except misery.

Dully, William's eyes watched the fat shoulders hitching and twitching, while the heavy arms flourished in gesture and in further pawings. Again and again were William's ears afflicted with "I dunno why it is," following upon tribute after tribute paid by Mr. Crooper to himself, and received with little cries of admiration and sweet child-words on the part of Miss Pratt. It was a long and accursed ride.

20. Sydney Carton

AT THE FARM-HOUSE where the party were to dine, Miss Pratt with joy discovered a harmonium in the parlor, and, seating herself, with all the girls, Flopit, and Mr. George Crooper gathered around her, she played an accompaniment, while George, in a thin tenor of detestable sweetness, sang "I'm Falling in Love with Some One."

His performance was rapturously greeted, especially by the accompanist. "Oh, wunnerfulest Untle Georgiecums!" she cried, for that was now the gentleman's name. "If Johnnie McCormack hear Untle Georgiecums he go shoot umself dead—bang!" She looked round to where three figures hovered morosely in the rear. "Tum on, sin' chorus, Big Bruvva Josie-Joe, Johnnie Jump-Up, an' Ickle Boy Baxter. All over adain, Untle Georgiecums! Boys an' dirls all sin' chorus. Tummence!"

And so the heartrending performance continued until it was stopped by Wallace Banks, the altruistic and perspiring youth who had charge of the subscription-list for the party, and the consequent collection of assessments. This entitled Wallace to look haggard and to act as master of ceremonies. He mounted a chair.

"Ladies and gentlemen," he bellowed, "I want to say—that is—ah—I am requested to announce that before dinner we're all supposed to take a walk around the farm and look at things, as this is supposed to be kind of a model farm or supposed to be something like that. There's a Swedish lady named Anna going to show us around. She's out in the yard waiting, so please follow her to inspect the farm."

To inspect a farm was probably the least of William's desires. He wished only to die in some quiet spot and to have Miss Pratt told about it in words that would show her what she had thrown away. But he followed with the others, in the wake of the Swedish lady named Anna, and as they stood in the cavernous hollow of the great barn he found his condition suddenly improved.

Miss Pratt turned to him unexpectedly and placed Flopit in his arms. "Keep p'eshus Flopit cozy," she whispered. "Flopit love ole friends best!"

William's heart leaped, while a joyous warmth spread all over him. And though the execrable lummox immediately propelled Miss Pratt forward—by her elbow—to hear the descriptive remarks of the Swedish lady named Anna, William's soul remained uplifted and entranced. She had not said "like"; she had said, "Flopit *love* ole friends best"! William pressed forward valiantly, and placed himself as close as possible upon the right of Miss Pratt, the lummox being upon her left. A moment later, William wished that he had remained in the rear.

This was due to the unnecessary frankness of the Swedish lady named Anna, who was briefly pointing out the efficiency of various agricultural devices. Her attention being diverted by some effusions of pride on the part of a passing hen, she thought fit to laugh and say:

"She yust laid egg."

William shuddered. This grossness in the presence of Miss Pratt was unthinkable. His mind refused to deal with so impossible a situation; he could not accept it as a fact that such words had actually been uttered in such a presence. And yet it was the truth; his incredulous ears still sizzled. "She yust laid egg!" His entire skin became flushed; his averted eyes glazed themselves with shame.

He was not the only person shocked by the ribaldry of

the Swedish lady named Anna. Joe Bullitt and Johnnie Watson, on the outskirts of the group, went to Wallace Banks, drew him aside, and, with feverish eloquence, set his responsibilities before him. It was his duty, they urged, to have an immediate interview with this free-spoken Anna and instruct her in the proprieties. Wallace had been almost as horrified as they by her loose remark, but he declined the office they proposed for him, offering, however, to appoint them as a committee with authority in the matter—whereupon they retorted with unreasonable indignation, demanding to know what he took them for.

Unconscious of the embarrassment she had caused in these several masculine minds, the Swedish lady named Anna led the party onward, continuing her agricultural lecture. William walked mechanically, his eyes averted and looking at no one. And throughout this agony he was burningly conscious of the blasphemed presence of Miss Pratt beside him.

Therefore, it was with no little surprise, when the party came out of the barn, that William beheld Miss Pratt, not walking at his side, but, on the contrary, sitting too cozily with George Crooper upon a fallen tree at the edge of a peach-orchard just beyond the barn-yard. It was Miss Parcher who had been walking beside him, for the truant couple had made their escape at the beginning of the Swedish lady's discourse.

In vain William murmured to himself, "Flopit love ole friends best." Purple and black again descended upon his soul, for he could not disguise from himself the damnatory fact that George had flitted with the lady, while he, wretched William, had been permitted to take care of the dog!

A spark of dignity still burned within him. He strode to the barn-yard fence, and, leaning over it, dropped Flopit rather brusquely at his mistress's feet. Then, without a word—even without a look—William walked haughtily away, continuing his stern progress straight through the barn-yard gate, and thence onward until he found himself in solitude upon the far side of a smoke-house, where his hauteur vanished.

Here, in the shade of a great walnut-tree which sheltered the little building, he gave way—not to tears, certainly, but to faint murmurings and little heavings under impulses as ancient as young love itself. It is to be supposed that William considered his condition a lonely one, but if all the seventeen-year-olds who have known such half-hours could have shown themselves to him then, he would have fled from the mere horror of billions. Alas! he considered his sufferings a new invention in the world, and there was now inspired in his breast a monologue so eloquuently bitter that it might deserve some such title as A Passion Beside the Smoke-house. During the little time that William spent in this sequestration he passed through phases of emotion which would have kept an older man busy for weeks and left him wrecked at the end of them.

William's final mood was one of beautiful resignation with a kick in it; that is, he nobly gave her up to George and added irresistibly that George was a big, fat lummox! Painting pictures, such as the billions of other young sufferers before him have painted, William saw himself a sad, gentle old bachelor at the family fireside, sometimes making the sacrifice of his reputation so that *she* and the children might never know the truth about George; and he gave himself the solace of a fierce scene or two with George: "Remember, it is for them, not you—you *thing!*"

After this human little reaction he passed .to a higher field of romance. He would die for George—and then she would bring the little boy she had named William to the lonely headstone— Suddenly William saw himself in his true and fitting character—Sydney Carton! He had lately read *A Tale of Two Cities,* immediately re-reading until, as he would have said, he "knew it by heart"; and even at the time he had seen resemblances between himself and the appealing figure of Carton. Now that the sympathy between them was perfected by Miss Pratt's preference for another, William decided to mount the scaffold in place of George Crooper. The scene became actual to him, and, setting one foot upon a tin milk-pail which some one had carelessly left beside the smoke-house, he lifted his eyes to the pitiless blue sky and unconsciously assumed the familiar attitude of Carton on the steps of the guillotine. He spoke aloud those great last words:

"It is a far, far better thing that I do, than I have ever done; it is a far, far better rest that I go to—"

A whiskered head on the end of a long, corrugated red neck protruded from the smoke-house door.

"What say?" it inquired, huskily.

"Nun-nothing!" stammered William.

Eyes above whiskers became fierce. "You take your feet off that milk-bucket. Say! This here's a sanitary farm. 'Ain't you got any more sense 'n to go an'——"

But William had abruptly removed his foot and departed.

He found the party noisily established in the farm-house at two long tables piled with bucolic viands already being violently depleted. Johnnie Watson had kept a chair beside himself vacant for William. Johnnie was in no frame of mind to sit beside any "chattering girl," and he had protected himself by Joe Bullitt upon his right and the empty seat upon his left. William took it, and gazed upon the nearer foods with a slight renewal of animation.

He began to eat; he continued to eat; in fact, he did well. So did his two comrades. Not that the melancholy of these three was dispersed—far from it! With ineffaceable gloom they ate chicken, both white meat and dark, drumsticks, wishbones, and liver; they ate corn-on-the-cob, many ears, and fried potatoes and green peas and stringbeans; they ate peach preserves and apricot preserves and preserved pears; they ate biscuits with grape jelly and biscuits with crab-apple jelly; they ate apple sauce and apple butter and apple pie. They ate pickles, both cucumber pickles and pickles made of watermelon rind; they ate pickled tomatoes, pickled peppers, also pickled onions. They ate lemon pie.

At that, they were no rivals to George Crooper, who was a real eater. Love had not made his appetite ethereal today, and even the attending Swedish lady named Anna felt some apprehension when it came to George and the gravy, though she was accustomed to the prodigies performed in this line by the robust hinds on the farm. George laid waste his section of the table, and from the beginning he allowed himself scarce time to say, "I dunno why it is." The pretty companion at his side at first gazed dumfounded; then, with growing enthusiasm for what promised to be a really magnificent performance, she began to utter little ejaculations of wonder and admiration. With this music in his ears,

George outdid himself. He could not resist the temptation to be more and more astonishing as a heroic comedian, for these humors sometimes come upon vain people at country dinners.

George ate when he had eaten more than he needed; he ate long after every one understood why he was so vast; he ate on and on sheerly as a flourish—as a spectacle. He ate even when he himself began to understand that there was daring in what he did, for his was a toreador spirit so long as he could keep bright eyes fastened upon him.

Finally, he ate to decide wagers made upon his gorging, though at times during this last period his joviality deserted him. Anon his damp brow would be troubled, and he knew moments of thoughtfulness.

21. My Little Sweetheart

WHEN GEORGE did stop, it was abruptly, during one of these intervals of sobriety, and he and Miss Pratt came out of the house together rather quietly, joining one of the groups of young people chatting with after-dinner languor under the trees. However, Mr. Crooper began to revive presently, in the sweet air of outdoors, and, observing some of the more dashing gentlemen lighting cigarettes, he was moved to laughter. He had not smoked since his childhood—having then been bonded through to twenty-one with a pledge of gold—and he feared that these smoking youths might feel themselves superior. Worse, Miss Pratt might be impressed; therefore he laughed in scorn, saying:

"Burnin' up ole trash around here, I expect!" He sniffed searchingly. "Somebody's set some ole rags on fire." Then, as in discovery, he cried, "Oh no, only cigarettes!"

Miss Pratt, that tactful girl, counted four smokers in the group about her, and only one abstainer, George. She at once defended the smokers, for it is to be feared that numbers always had weight with her. "Oh, but cigarettes is lubly smell!" she said. "Untle Georgiecums maybe be too 'ittle boy for smokings!"

This archness was greeted loudly by the smokers, and Mr. Crooper was put upon his mettle. He spoke too quickly to consider whether or no the facts justified his assertion. "Me? I don't smoke paper and ole carpets. I smoke cigars!"

He had created the right impression, for Miss Pratt clapped her hands. "Oh, 'plendid! Light one, Untle Georgiecums! Light one ever 'n' ever so quick! P'eshus Flopit an' me we want see dray, big, 'normous man smoke dray, big, 'normous cigar!"

William and Johnnie Watson, who had been hovering morbidly, unable to resist the lodestone, came nearer, Johnnie being just in time to hear his cousin's reply.

"I—I forgot my cigar-case."

Johnnie's expression became one of biting skepticism. "What you talkin' about, George? Didn't you promise Uncle George you'd never smoke till you're of age, and Uncle George said he'd give you a thousand dollars on your twenty-first birthday? What'd you say about your 'cigar-case'?"

George felt that he was in a tight place, and the lovely eyes of Miss Pratt turned upon him questioningly. He could not flush, for he was already so pink after his exploits with unnecessary nutriment that more pinkness was impossible. He saw that the only safety for him lay in boisterous prevarication. "A thousand dollars!" he laughed loudly. "I thought that was real money when I was ten years old! It didn't stand in *my* way very long, I guess! Good ole George wanted his smoke, and he went after it! You know how I am, Johnnie, when I go after anything. I been smokin' cigars I dunno how long!" Glancing about him, his eye became reassured; it was obvious that even Johnnie had accepted this airy statement as the truth, and to clinch plausibility he added: "When I smoke, I smoke! I smoke cigars straight along—light one right on the stub of the other. I only wish I had some with me, because I miss 'em after a meal. I'd give a good deal for something to smoke right now! I don't mean cigarettes; I don't want any paper —I want something that's all tobacco!"

William's pale, sad face showed a hint of color. With a pang he remembered the package of My Little Sweetheart All-Tobacco Cuban Cigarettes (the Package of Twenty for Ten Cents) which still reposed, untouched, in the breast pocket of his coat. His eyes smarted a little as he recalled the thoughts and hopes that had accompanied the purchase; but he thought, "What would Sydney Carton do?"

William brought forth the package of My Little Sweetheart All-Tobacco Cuban Cigarettes and placed it in the large hand of George Crooper. And this was a noble act, for William believed that George really wished to smoke. "Here," he said, "take these; they're all tobacco. I'm goin' to quit smokin', anyway." And, thinking of the name, he added, gently, with a significance lost upon all his hearers, "I'm sure you ought to have 'em instead of me."

Then he went away and sat alone upon the fence.

"Light one, light one!" cried Miss Pratt. "Ev'ybody mus' be happy, an' dray, big, 'normous man tan't be happy 'less he have his all-tobatto smote. Light it, light it!"

George drew as deep a breath as his diaphragm, strangely oppressed since dinner, would permit, and then bravely lit a Little Sweetheart. There must have been some valiant blood in him, for, as he exhaled the smoke, he covered a slight choking by exclaiming, loudly: *"That's good! That's the ole stuff! That's what I was lookin' for!"*

Miss Pratt was entranced. "Oh, 'plendid!" she cried, watching him with fascinated eyes. "Now take dray, big, 'normous puffs! Take dray, big *'normous* puffs!"

George took great, big, enormous puffs.

She declared that she loved to watch men smoke, and William's heart, as he sat on the distant fence, was wrung and wrung again by the vision of her playful ecstasies. But when he saw her holding what was left of the first Little Sweetheart for George to light a second at its expiring spark, he could not bear it. He dropped from the fence and moped away to be out of sight once more. This was his darkest hour.

Studiously avoiding the vicinity of the smoke-house, he sought the little orchard where he had beheld her sitting with George; and there he sat himself in sorrowful reverie upon the selfsame fallen tree. How long he remained there is uncertain, but he was roused by the sound of music which came from the lawn before the farm-house. Bitterly he smiled, remembering that Wallace Banks had engaged Italians with harp, violin, and flute, promising great things for dancing on a fresh-clipped lawn—a turf floor being no impediment to seventeen's dancing. Music! To see her whirling and smiling sunnily in the fat grasp of that dancing bear! He would stay in this lonely orchard; *she* would not miss him.

But though he hated the throbbing music and the sound of the laughing voices that came to him, he could not keep away—and when he reached the lawn where the dancers were, he found Miss Pratt moving rhythmically in the thin grasp of Wallace Banks. Johnnie Watson approached, and spoke in a low tone, tinged with spiteful triumph.

"Well, anyway, ole fat George didn't get the first dance with her! She's the guest of honor, and Wallace had a right to it because he did all the work. He came up to 'em and ole fat George couldn't say a thing. Wallace just took her right away from him. George didn't say anything at all, but I s'pose after this dance he'll be rushin' around again and nobody else'll have a chance to get near her the rest of the afternoon. My mother told me I ought to invite him over here, but I had no business to do it; he don't know the first principles of how to act in a town he don't live in!"

"Where'd he go?" William asked, listlessly, for Mr. Crooper was nowhere in sight.

"I don't know—he just walked off without sayin' anything. But he'll be back, time this dance is over, never you fear, and he'll grab her again and— What's the matter with Joe?"

Joseph Bullitt had made his appearance at a corner of the house, some distance from where they stood. His face was alert under the impulse of strong excitement, and he beckoned fiercely. "Come here!" And, when they had obeyed, "He's around back of the house by a kind of shed," said Joe. "I think something's wrong. Come on, I'll show him to you."

But behind the house, whither they followed him in vague, strange hope, he checked them. *"Look there!"* he said.

His pointing finger was not needed. Sounds of paroxysm drew their attention sufficiently—sounds most poignant, soul-rending, and lugubrious. William and Johnnie perceived the large person of Mr. Crooper; he was seated upon the ground, his back propped obliquely against the smoke-house, though this attitude was not maintained constantly.

Facing him, at a little distance, a rugged figure in homely garments stood leaning upon a hoe and regarding George with a cold interest. The apex of this figure was a volcanic straw hat, triangular in profile and coned with an open crater emitting reddish wisps, while below the hat were several features, but more whiskers, at the top of a long, corrugated red neck of sterling worth. A husky voice issued from the whiskers, addressing George.

"I seen you!" it said. "I seen you eatin'! This here farm is supposed to be a sanitary farm, and you'd ought of knew better. Go it, doggone you! Go it!"

George complied. And three spectators, remaining aloof, but watching zealously, began to feel lost faith in Providence returning into them; their faces brightened slowly, and without relapse. It was a visible thing how the world became fairer and better in their eyes during that little while they stood there. And William saw that his Little Sweethearts had been an inspired purchase, after all; they had delivered the final tap upon a tottering edifice. George's deeds at dinner had unsettled, but Little Sweethearts had overthrown—and now there was awful work among the ruins, to an ironical accompaniment of music from the front yard, where people danced in heaven's sunshine!

This accompaniment came to a stop, and Johnnie Watson jumped. He seized each of his companions by a sleeve and spoke eagerly, his eyes glowing with a warm and brotherly light. "Here!" he cried. "We better get around there—this looks like it was goin' to last all afternoon. Joe, you get the next dance with her, and just about time the music slows up you dance her around so you can stop right near where Bill will be standin', so Bill can get her quick for the dance after that. Then, Bill, you do the same for me, and I'll do the same for Joe again, and then, Joe, you do it for Bill again, and then Bill for me—and so on. If we go in right now and work together we can crowd the rest out, and there won't anybody else get to dance with her the whole day! Come on quick!"

United in purpose, the three ran lightly to the dancing-lawn, and Mr. Bullitt was successful, after a little debate, in obtaining the next dance with the lovely guest of the day. "I did promise big Untle Georgiecums," she said, looking about her.

"Well, I don't think he'll come," said Joe. "That is, I'm pretty sure he won't."

A shade fell upon the exquisite face. "No'ty. Bruvva Josie-Joe! The Men *always* tum when Lola promises dances. Mustn't be rude!"

"Well—" Joe began, when he was interrupted by the Swedish lady named Anna, who spoke to them from the steps of the house. Of the merrymakers they were the nearest.

"Dot pick fella," said Anna, "dot one dot eats—we make him in a petroom. He holler! He tank he neet some halp."

"Does he want a doctor?" Joe asked.

"Doctor? No! He want make him in a amyoulance for hospital!"

"I'll go look at him," Johnnie Waston volunteered, running up. "He's my cousin, and I guess I got to take the responsibility."

Miss Pratt paid the invalid the tribute of one faintly commiserating glance toward the house. "Well," she said, "if people would rather eat too much than dance!" She meant "dance with *me!*" though she thought it prettier not to say so. "Come on, Bruvva Josie-Joe!" she cried, joyously.

And a little later Johnnie Watson approached her where she stood with a restored and refulgent William, about to begin the succeeding dance. Johnnie dropped into her hand a ring, receiving one in return. "I thought I better *get* it," he said, offering no further explanation. "I'll take care of his until we get home. He's all right," said Johnnie, and then perceiving a sudden advent of apprehension upon the sensitive brow of William, he went on reassuringly: "He's doin' as well as anybody could expect; that is—after the crazy way he *did!* He's always been considered the dumbest one in all our relations—never did know how to act. I don't mean he's exactly not got his senses, or ought to be watched, anything like that—and of course he belongs to an awful good family—but he's just kind of the black sheep when it comes to intelligence, or anything like that. I got him as comfortable as a person could be, and they're givin' him hot water and mustard and stuff, but what he needs now is just to be kind of quiet. It'll do him a lot o' good,"

Johnnie concluded, with a spark in his voice, "to lay there the rest of the afternoon and get quieted down, kind of."

"You don't think there's any—" William began, and, after a pause, continued—"any hope—of his getting strong enough to come out and dance afterwhile?"

Johnnie shook his head. "None in the world!" he said, conclusively. "The best we can do for him is to let him entirely alone till after supper, and then ask nobody to sit on the back seat of the trolley-car goin' home, so we can make him comfortable back there, and let him kind of stretch out by himself."

Then gaily tinkled harp, gaily sang flute and violin! Over the greensward William lightly bore his lady, while radiant was the cleared sky above the happy dancers. William's fingers touched those delicate fingers; the exquisite face smiled rosily up to him; undreamable sweetness beat rhythmically upon his glowing ears; his feet moved in a rhapsody of companionship with hers. They danced and danced and danced!

Then Joe danced with her, while William and Johnnie stood with hands upon each other's shoulders and watched, mayhap with longing, but without spite; then Johnnie danced with her while Joe and William watched—and then William danced with her again.

So passed the long, ineffable afternoon away—ah, Seventeen!

". . . 'Jav a good time at the trolley-party?" the clerk in the corner drug-store inquired that evening.

"Fine!" said William, taking his overcoat from the hook where he had left it.

"How j' like them Little Sweethearts I sold you?"

"Fine!" said William.

22. Foreshadowings

NOW THE LAST rose had blown; the dandelion globes were long since on the wind; gladioli and golden-glow and salvia were here; the season moved toward asters and the golden-rod. This haloed summer still idled on its way, yet all the

while sped quickly; like some languid lady in an elevator.
There came a Sunday—very hot.

Mr. and Mrs. Baxter, having walked a scorched half-
mile from church, drooped thankfully into wicker chairs
upon their front porch, though Jane, who had accompanied
them, immediately darted away, swinging her hat by its
ribbon and skipping as lithesomely as if she had just come
forth upon a cool morning.

"I don't know how she does it!" her father moaned,
glancing after her and drying his forehead temporarily
upon a handkerchief. "That would merely kill me dead,
after walking in this heat."

Then, for a time, the two were content to sit in silence,
nodding to occasional acquaintances who passed in the
desultory after-church procession. Mr. Baxter fanned himself with sporadic little bursts of energy which made his
straw hat creak, and Mrs. Baxter sighed with the heat, and
gently rocked her chair.

But as a group of five young people passed along the
other side of the street Mr. Baxter abruptly stopped fan-
ning himself, and, following the direction of his gaze, Mrs.
Baxter ceased to rock. In half-completed attitudes they
leaned slightly forward, sharing one of those pauses of
parents who unexpectedly behold their offspring.

"My soul!" said William's father. "Hasn't that girl gone
home *yet?*"

"He looks pale to me," Mrs. Baxter murmured, absently.
"I don't think he seems at all well, lately."

During seventeen years Mr. Baxter had gradually
learned not to protest anxieties of this kind, unless he desired to argue with no prospect of ever getting a decision.
"Hasn't she got any *home?*" he demanded, testily. "Isn't
she ever going to quit visiting the Parchers and let people
have a little peace?"

Mrs. Baxter disregarded this outburst as he had disregarded her remark about William's pallor. "You mean
Miss Pratt?" she inquired, dreamily, her eyes following the
progress of her son. "No, he really doesn't look well at all."

"Is she going to visit the Parchers all summer?" Mr.
Baxter insisted.

"She already has, about," said Mrs. Baxter.

"Look at that boy!" the father grumbled. "Mooning

along with those other moon-calves—can't even let her go to church alone! I wonder how many weeks of time, counting it out in hours, he's wasted that way this summer?"

"Oh, I don't know! You see, he never goes there in the evening."

"What of that? He's there all day, isn't he? What do they find to talk about? That's the mystery to me! Day after day; hours and hours— My soul! What do they *say?*"

Mrs. Baxter laughed indulgently. "People are always wondering that about the other ages. Poor Willie! I think that a great deal of the time their conversation would be probably about as inconsequent as it is now. You see Willie and Joe Bullitt are walking one on each side of Miss Pratt, and Johnnie Watson has to walk behind with May Parcher. Joe and Johnnie are there about as much as Willie is, and, of course, it's often his turn to be nice to May Parcher. He hasn't many chances to be tête-à-tête with Miss Pratt."

"Well, she ought to go home. I want that boy to get back into his senses. He's in an awful state."

"I think she is going soon," said Mrs. Baxter. "The Parchers are to have a dance for her Friday night, and I understand there's to be a floor laid in the yard and great things. It's a farewell party."

"That's one mercy, anyhow!"

"And if you wonder what they say," she resumed, "why, probably they're all talking about the party. And when Willie *is* alone with her—well, what does anybody say?" Mrs. Baxter interrupted herself to laugh. "Jane, for instance—she's always fascinated by that darky, Genesis, when he's at work here in the yard, and they have long, long talks; I've seen them from the window. What on earth do you suppose they talk about? That's where Jane is now. She knew I told Genesis I'd give him something if he'd come and freeze the ice-cream for us to-day, and when we got here she heard the freezer and hopped right around there. If you went out to the back porch you'd find them talking steadily—but what on earth about I couldn't guess to save my life!"

And yet nothing could have been simpler: as a matter of fact, Jane and Genesis (attended by Clematis) were talking about society. That is to say, their discourse was not sociologic; rather it was of the frivolous and elegant. Watteau prevailed with them over John Stuart Mill—in a word, they spoke of the *beau monde*.

Genesis turned the handle of the freezer with his left hand, allowing his right the freedom of gesture which was an intermittent necessity when he talked. In the matter of dress, Genesis had always been among the most informal of his race, but to-day there was a change almost unnerving to the Caucasian eye. He wore a balloonish suit of purple, strangely scalloped at pocket and cuff, and more strangely decorated with lines of small parasite buttons, in color blue, obviously buttons of leisure. His bulbous new shoes flashed back yellow fire at the embarrassed sun, and his collar (for he had gone so far) sent forth other sparkles, playing upon a polished surface over an inner graining of soot. Beneath it hung a simple, white, soiled evening tie, draped in a manner unintended by its manufacturer, and heavily overburdened by a green glass medallion of the Emperor Tiberius, set in brass.

"Yesm," said Genesis. "Now I'm in 'at Swim—flyin' roun' ev'y night wif all lem blue-vein people—I say, 'Mus' go buy me some blue-vein clo'es! Ef I'm go'n' a *start*, might's well start *high!*' So firs', I buy me thishere gol' necktie pin wi' thishere lad's face carved out o' green di'mon', sittin' in the middle all 'at gol'. 'Nen I buy me pair Royal King shoes. I got a frien' o' mine, thishere Blooie Bowers; he say Royal King shoes same kine o' shoes *he* wear, an' I walk straight in 'at sto' where they keep 'em at. 'Don' was'e my time showin' me no ole-time shoes,' I say. 'Run out some them big, yella, lump-toed Royal Kings befo' my eyes, an' firs' pair fit me I pay price, an' wear 'em right off on me!' 'Nen I got me thishere suit o' clo'es—*oh, oh!* Sign on 'em in window: 'Ef you wish to be bes'-dress' man in town take me home fer six dulluhs ninety-sevum cents.' ' 'At's kine o' suit Genesis need,' I say. 'Ef Genesis go'n' a start dressin' high, might's well start top!' "

Jane nodded gravely, comprehending the reasonableness of this view. "What made you decide to start, Genesis?" she asked, earnestly. "I mean, how did it happen you began to get this way?"

"Well, suh, 'tall come 'bout right like kine o' slidin' into it 'stid o' hoppin' an' jumpin'. I'z spen' the even' at 'at lady's house, Fanny, what cook nex' do', las' year. Well, suh, 'at lady Fanny, she quit privut cookin', she kaytliss—"

"She's what?" Jane asked. "What's that mean, Genesis —kaytliss?"

"She kaytuhs," he explained. "Ef it's a man you call him kaytuh; ef it's a lady, she's a kaytliss. She does kaytun fer all lem blue-vein fam'lies in town. She makes ref'es-mums, bring waituhs—'at's kaytun. You' maw give big dinnuh, she have Fanny kaytuh, an' don't take no trouble 'tall herself. Fanny take all 'at trouble."

"I see," said Jane. "But I don't see how her bein' a kaytliss started you to dressin' so high, Genesis."

"Thishere way. Fanny say, 'Look here, Genesis, I got big job t'morra night an' I'm man short, 'count o' havin' to have a 'nouncer.' "

"A what?"

"Fanny talk jes' that way. Goin' be big dinnuh-potty, an' thishere blue-vein fam'ly tell Fanny they want whole lot extry sploogin'; tell her put fine-lookin' cullud man stan' by drawin'-room do'—ask ev'body name an' holler out whatever name they say, jes' as they walk in. Thishere fam'ly say they goin' show what's what, 'nis town, an' they boun' Fanny go git 'em a 'nouncer. 'Well, what's mattuh *you* doin' 'at 'nouncin'?' Fanny say. 'Who—me?' I tell her. 'Yes, you kin, too!' she say, an' she say she len' me 'at waituh suit yoosta b'long ole Henry Gimlet what die' when he owin' Fanny sixteen dolluhs—an' Fanny tuck an' keep 'at waituh suit. She use 'at suit on extry waituhs when she got some on her hands what 'ain't got no waituh suit. 'You wear 'at suit,' Fanny say, 'an' you be good 'nouncer, 'cause you' a fine, big man, an' got a big, gran' voice; 'nen you learn befo' long be a waituh, Genesis, an' git dolluh an' half ev'y even' you waitin', 'sides all 'at money you make cuttin' grass daytime.' Well, suh, I'z stan' up doin' 'at 'nouncin' ve'y nex' night. White lady an' ge'lmun walk todes my do', I step up to 'em—I step up to 'em thisaway."

Here Genesis found it pleasant to present the scene with some elaboration. He dropped the handle of the freezer, rose, assumed a stately, but ingratiating, expression, and "stepped up" to the imagined couple, using a pacing and rhythmic gait—a conservative prance, which plainly indicated the simultaneous operation of an orchestra. Then bending graciously, as though the persons addressed were of dwarfish stature, " 'Scuse me," he said, "but kin I please be so p'lite as to 'quiah you' name?" For a moment he listened attentively, then nodded, and, returning with the same aristocratic undulations to an imaginary doorway near the freezer, "Misto an' Missuz Orlosko Rinktum!" he proclaimed, sonorously.

"Who?" cried Jane, fascinated. "Genesis, 'nounce that again, right away!"

Genesis heartily complied.

"Misto an' Missuz Orlosko Rinktum!" he bawled.

"Was that really their names?" she asked, eagerly.

"Well, I kine o' fergit," Genesis admitted, resuming his work with the freezer. "Seem like I rickalect *somebody* got name good deal like what I say, 'cause some mighty bluevein names at 'at dinnuh-potty, yessuh! But I on'y git to be 'nouncer one time, 'cause Fanny tellin' me nex' fam'ly have dinnuh-potty make heap o' fun. Say I done my 'nouncin' *good,* but say what's use holler'n names jes' fer some the neighbors or they own aunts an' uncles to walk in, when ev'ybody awready knows 'em? So Fanny pummote me to waituh, an' I roun' right in amongs' big doin's mos' ev'y night. Pass ice-cream, lemonade, lemon-ice, cake, samwitches. 'Lemme han' you li'l' mo' chicken salad, ma'am'— ' 'Low me be so kine as to git you f'esh cup coffee, suh'— 'S way ole Genesis talkin' ev'y even' 'ese days!"

Jane looked at him thoughtfully. "Do you like it better than cuttin' grass, Genesis?" she asked.

He paused to consider. "Yes'm—when ban' play all lem *tunes!* My goo'ness, do soun' gran'!"

"You can't do it to-night, though, Genesis," said Jane. "You haf to be quiet on Sunday nights, don't you?"

"Yes'm. 'Ain' got no mo' kaytun till nex' Friday even'."

"Oh, I bet that's the party for Miss Pratt at Mr. Parcher's!" Jane cried. "Didn't I guess right?"

"Yes'm. I reckon I'm a-go'n' a see one you' fam'ly 'at night; see him dancin'—wait on him at ref'eshmuns."

Jane's expression became even more serious than usual. "Willie? I don't know whether he's goin', Genesis."

"Lan' name!" Genesis exclaimed. "He die ef he don' git *in*vite to 'at ball!"

"Oh, he's invited," said Jane. "Only I think maybe he won't go."

"My goo'ness! Why ain' he goin'?"

Jane looked at her friend studiously before replying. "Well, it's a secret," she said, finally, "but it's a very inter'sting one, an' I'll tell you if you never tell."

"Yes'm; I ain' tellin' nobody."

Jane glanced round, then stepped a little closer and told the secret with the solemnity it deserved. "Well, when Miss Pratt first came to visit Miss May Parcher, Willie used to keep papa's evening clo'es in his window-seat, an' mamma wondered what *had* become of 'em. Then, after dinner, he'd slip up there an' put 'em on him, an' go out through the kitchen an' call on Miss Pratt. Then mamma found 'em, an' she thought he oughtn't to do that, so she didn't tell him or anything, an' she didn't even tell papa, but she had the tailor make 'em ever an' ever so much bigger, 'cause they were gettin' too tight for papa. An' well, so after that, even if Willie could get 'em out o' mamma's clo'es-closet where she keeps 'em now, he'd look so funny in 'em he couldn't wear 'em. Well, an' then he couldn't go to pay calls on Miss Pratt in the evening since then, because mamma says after he started to go there in that suit he couldn't go without it, or maybe Miss Pratt or the other ones that's in love of her would think it was pretty queer, an' maybe kind of expeck it was papa's all the time. Mamma says she thinks Willie must have worried a good deal over reasons to say why he'd always go in the daytime after that, an' never came in the evening, an' now they're goin' to have this party, an' she says he's been gettin' paler and paler every day since he heard about it. Mamma says he's pale *some* because Miss Pratt's goin' away, but she thinks it's a good deal more because, well, if he would wear those evening clo'es just to go *callin'*, how would it be to go to that *party* an' not have any! That's what mamma thinks—an', Genesis, you promised you'd never tell as long as you live!"

"Yes'm. *I* ain' tellin'," Genesis chuckled. "I'm a-go'n a git me one nem waituh suits befo' long, myse'f, so's I kin quit wearin' at' ole Henry Gimlet suit what b'long to Fanny, an' have me a privut suit o' my own. They's a secon'-han' sto' ovuh on the avynoo, where they got

swaller-tail suits all way f'um sevum dolluhs to nineteem
dolluhs an' ninety-eight cents. I'm a—"

Jane started, interrupting him. " *'Sh!'* " she whispered,
laying a finger warningly upon her lips.

William had entered the yard at the back gate, and approaching over the lawn, had arrived at the steps of the
porch before Jane perceived him. She gave him an apprehensive look, but he passed into the house absent-mind-
edly, not even flinching at sight of Clematis—and Mrs.
Baxter was right, William did look pale.

"I guess he didn't hear us," said Jane, when he had disappeared into the interior. "He acks awful funny!" she
added, thoughtfully. "First when he was in love of Miss
Pratt, he'd be mad about som'p'm almost every minute he
was home. Couldn't anybody say *anything* to him but he'd
just behave as if it was frightful, an' then if you'd see him
out walkin' with Miss Pratt, well, he'd look like—like—"
Jane paused; her eye fell upon Clematis and by a happy
inspiration she was able to complete her simile with remarkable accuracy. "He'd look like the way Clematis looks
at people! That's just *exactly* the way he'd look, Genesis,
when he was walkin' with Miss Pratt; and' then when he
was home he got so quiet he couldn't answer questions an'
wouldn't hear what anybody said to him at table or anywhere, an' papa'd nearly almost bust. Mamma 'n' papa'd
talk an' talk about it, an' "—she lowered her voice—"an' I
knew what they were talkin' about. Well, an' then he'd
hardly ever get mad any more; he'd just sit in his room,
an' sometimes he'd sit in there without any light, or he'd sit
out in the yard all by himself all evening, maybe; an'
th'other evening after I was in bed I heard 'em, an' papa
said—well, this is what papa told mamma." And again
lowering her voice, she proffered the quotation from her
father in a tone somewhat awe-struck: "Papa said, by Gosh!
if he ever 'a' thought a son of his could make such a Word
idiot of himself he almost wished we'd both been girls!"

Having completed this report in a violent whisper, Jane
nodded repeatedly, for emphasis, and Genesis shook his
head to show that he was as deeply impressed as she
wished him to be. "I guess," she added, after a pause—"I
guess Willie didn't hear anything you an' I talked about
him, or clo'es, or anything.'

She was mistaken in part. William had caught no reference to himself, but he had overheard something and he was now alone in his room, thinking about it almost feverishly. "A secon'-han' sto' ovuh on the avynoo, where they got swaller-tail suits all way f'um sevem dolluhs to nineteem dolluhs an' ninety-eight cents."

. . . Civilization is responsible for certain longings in the breast of man—artificial longings, but sometimes as poignant as hunger and thirst. Of these the strongest are those of the maid for the bridal veil, of the lad for long trousers, and of the youth for a tailed coat of state. To the gratification of this, only a few of the early joys in life are comparable. Indulged youths, too rich, can know, to the unctuous full, neither the longing nor the gratification; but one such as William, in "moderate circumstances," is privileged to pant for his first evening clothes as the hart panteth after the water-brook—and sometimes, to pant in vain. Also, this was a crisis in William's life: in addition to his yearning for such apparel, he was racked by a passionate urgency.

As Jane had so precociously understood, unless he should somehow manage to obtain the proper draperies he could not go to the farewell dance for Miss Pratt. Other unequipped boys could go in their ordinary "best clothes," but William could not; for, alack! he had dressed too well too soon!

He was in desperate case.

The sorrow of the approaching great departure was but the heavier because it had been so long deferred. To William it had seemed that this flower-strewn summer could actually end no more than he could actually die, but Time had begun its awful lecture, and even Seventeen was listening.

Miss Pratt, that magic girl, was going home.

23. Fathers Forget

To THE competent twenties, hundreds of miles suggesting no impossibilities, such departures may be rending, but not tragic. Implacable, the difference to Seventeen! Miss Pratt was going home, and Seventeen could not follow; it could only mourn upon the lonely shore, tracing little angelic footprints left in the sand.

To Seventeen such a departure is final; it is a vanishing.

And now it seemed possible that Willie might be deprived even of the last romantic consolations: of the "last waltz together," of the last, last "listening to music in the moonlight together"; of all those sacred lasts of the "last evening together."

He had pleaded strongly for a "dress-suit" as a fitting recognition of his seventeenth birthday anniversary, but he had been denied by his father with a jocularity more crushing than rigor. Since then—in particular since the arrival of Miss Pratt—Mr. Baxter's temper had been growing steadily more and more even. That is, as affected by William's social activities, it was uniformly bad. Nevertheless, after heavy brooding. William decided to make one final appeal before he resorted to measures which the necessities of despair had caused him to contemplate.

He wished to give himself every chance for a good effect; therefore, he did not act hastily, but went over what he intended to say, rehearsing it with a few appropriate gestures, and even taking some pleasure in the pathetic dignity of this performance, as revealed by occasional glances at the mirror of his dressing-table. In spite of these little alleviations, his trouble was great and all too real, for, unhappily, the previous rehearsal of an emotional scene does not prove the emotion insincere.

Descending, he found his father and mother still sitting upon the front porch. Then, standing before them, solemn-eyed, he uttered a preluding cough, and began:

"Father," he said in a loud voice, "I have come to—"

"Dear me!" Mrs. Baxter exclaimed, not perceiving that she was interrupting an intended oration. "Willie, you *do* look pale! Sit down, poor child; you oughtn't to walk so much in this heat."

"Father," William repeated. "Fath—"

"I suppose you got her safely home from church," Mr. Baxter said. "She might have been carried off by footpads if you three boys hadn't been along to take care of her!"

But William persisted heroically. "Father—" he said. "Father, I have come to—"

"What on earth's the matter with you?" Mr. Baxter ceased to fan himself; Mrs. Baxter stopped rocking, and both stared, for it had dawned upon them that something unusual was beginning to take place.

William backed to the start and tried it again. "Father, I have come to—" He paused and gulped, evidently expecting to be interrupted, but both of his parents remained silent, regarding him with puzzled surprise. "Father," he began once more, "I have come—I have come to—to place before you something I think it's your duty as my father to undertake, and I have thought over this step before laying it before you."

"My soul!" said Mr. Baxter, under his breath. "My soul!'

"At my age," William continued, swallowing, and fixing his earnest eyes upon the roof of the porch, to avoid the disconcerting stare of his father—"at my age there's some things that ought to be done and some things that ought not to be done. If you asked me what I thought *ought* to be done, there is only one answer: When anybody as old as I am has to go out among other young men his own age that already got one, like anyway half of them *have*, who I go with, and their fathers have already taken such a step, because they felt it was the only right thing to do, because at my age and the young men I go with's age, it *is* the only right thing to do, because that is something nobody could deny, at my age—" Here William drew a long breath, and, deciding to abandon that sentence as irrevocably tangled, began another: "I have thought over this step, because there comes a time to every young man when they must lay a step before their father before something happens that they would be sorry for. I have thought this undertaking over, and I am certain it would be your honest duty—"

"My soul!" gasped Mr. Baxter. "I thought I knew you pretty well, but you talk like a stranger to *me!* What is all this? What you *want?*"

"A dress-suit!" said William.

He had intended to say a great deal more before coming to the point, but, although through nervousness he had lost some threads of his rehearsed plea, it seemed to him that he was getting along well and putting his case with some

distinction and power. He was surprised and hurt, therefore, to hear his father utter a wordless shout in a tone of
wondering derision.

"I have more to say—" William began.

But Mr. Baxter cut him off. "A dress-suit!" he cried.
"Well, I'm glad you were talking about *something,* because
I honestly thought it must be too much sun."

At this, the troubled William brought his eyes down
from the porch roof and forgot his rehearsal. He lifted his
hand appealingly. "Father," he said, "I *got* to have one!"

" 'Got to'!" Mr. Baxter laughed a laugh that chilled the
supplicant through and through. "At your age I thought I
was lucky if I had *any* suit that was fit to be seen in. You're
too young, Willie. I don't want you to get your mind on
such stuff, and if I have my way, you won't have a dress-
suit for four years more, anyhow."

"Father, I *got* to have one. I got to have one right away!"
The urgency in William's voice was almost tearful. "I
don't ask you to have it made, or to go to expensive tailors,
but there's plenty of good ready-made ones that only cost
about forty dollars; they're advertised in the paper. Father,
wouldn't you spend just forty dollars? I'll pay it back when
I'm in business. I'll work—"

Mr. Baxter waved all this aside. "It's not the money. It's
the principle that I'm standing for, and I don't intend—"

"Father, *won't* you do it?"

"No, I will not!"

William saw that sentence had been passed and all
appeals for a new trial denied. He choked, and rushed into
the house without more ado.

"Poor boy!" his mother said.

"Poor boy nothing!" fumed Mr. Baxter. "He's about lost
his mind over that Miss Pratt. Think of his coming out here
and starting a regular debating society declamation before
his mother and father! Why, I never heard anything like
it in my life! I don't like to hurt his feelings, and I'd give
him anything I could afford that would do him any good,
but all he wants it for now is to splurge around in at this
party before that little yellow-haired girl! I guess he can
wear the kind of clothes most of the other boys wear—the
kind *I* wore at parties—and never thought of wearing any-

thing else. What's the world getting to be like? Seventeen years old and throws a fit because he can't have a dress-suit!"

Mrs. Baxter looked thoughtful. "But—but suppose he felt he couldn't go to the dance unless he wore one, poor boy—"

"All the better," said Mr. Baxter, firmly. "Do him good to keep away and get his mind on something else."

"Of course," she suggested, with some timidity, "forty dollars isn't a great deal of money, and a ready-made suit, just to begin with—"

Naturally, Mr. Baxter perceived whither she was drifting. "Forty dollars isn't a thousand," he interrupted, "but what you want to throw it away for? One reason a boy of seventeen oughtn't to have evening clothes is the way he behaves with *any* clothes. Forty dollars! Why, only this summer he sat down on Jane's open paint-box, twice in one week!"

"Well—Miss Pratt *is* going away, and the dance will be her last night. I'm afraid it would really hurt him to miss it. I remember once, before we were engaged—that evening before papa took me abroad, and you—"

"It's no use, mamma," he said. "We were both in the twenties—why, *I* was six years older than Willie, even then. There's no comparison at all. I'll let him order a dress-suit on his twenty-first birthday and not a minute before. I don't believe in it, and I intend to see that he gets all this stuff out of his system. He's got to learn some hard sense!"

Mrs. Baxter shook her head doubtfully, but she said no more. Perhaps she regretted a little that she had caused Mr. Baxter's evening clothes to be so expansively enlarged—for she looked rather regretful. She also looked rather incomprehensible, not to say cryptic, during the long silence which followed, and Mr. Baxter resumed his rocking, unaware of the fixity of gaze which his wife maintained upon him—a thing the most loyal will do sometimes.

The incomprehensible look disappeared before long; but the regretful one was renewed in the mother's eyes whenever she caught glimpses of her son, that day, and at the table, where William's manner was gentle—even toward his heartless father.

Underneath that gentleness, the harried self of William was no longer debating a desperate resolve, but had fixed upon it, and on the following afternoon Jane chanced to be a witness of some resultant actions. She came to her mother with an account of them.

"Mamma, what you s'pose Willie wants of those two ole market-baskets that were down cellar?"

"Why, Jane?"

"Well, he carried 'em in his room, an' then he saw me lookin'; an' he said, 'G'way from here!' an' shut the door. He looks so funny! What's he want of those ole baskets, mamma?"

"I don't know. Perhaps he doesn't even know, himself, Jane."

But William did know, definitely. He had set the baskets upon chairs, and now, with pale determination, he was proceeding to fill them. When his task was completed the two baskets contained:

One "heavy-weight winter suit of clothes."

One "light-weight summer suit of clothes."

One cap.

One straw hat.

Two pairs of white flannel trousers.

Two Madras shirts.

Two flannel shirts.

Two silk shirts.

Seven soft collars.

Three silk neckties.

One crocheted tie.

Eight pairs of socks.

One pair of patent-leather shoes.

One pair of tennis-shoes.

One overcoat.

Some underwear.

One two-foot shelf of books, consisting of several sterling works upon mathematics, in a damaged condition; five of Shakespeare's plays, expurgated for schools and colleges, and also damaged; a work upon political economy, and another upon the science of physics; *Webster's Collegiate Dictionary; How to Enter a Drawing-Room and Five Hundred Other Hints; Witty sayings from Here and*

There; Lorna Doone; Quentin Durward; The Adventures of Sherlock Holmes, a very old copy of *Moths,* and a small Bible.

William spread handkerchiefs upon the two over-bulging cargoes, that their nature might not be disclosed to the curious, and, after listening a moment at his door, took the baskets, one upon each arm, then went quickly down the stairs and out of the house, out of the yard, and into the alley—by which route he had modestly chosen to travel.

. . . After an absence of about two hours he returned empty-handed and anxious. "Mother, I want to speak to you," he said, addressing Mrs. Baxter in a voice which clearly proved the strain of these racking days. "I want to speak to you about something important."

"Yes, Willie?"

"Please send Jane away. I can't talk about important things with a child in the room."

Jane naturally wished to stay, since he was going to say something important. "Mamma, do I *haf* to go?"

"Just a few minutes, dear."

Jane walked submissively out of the door, leaving it open behind her. Then, having gone about six feet farther, she halted and, preserving a breathless silence, consoled herself for her banishment by listening to what was said, hearing it all as satisfactorily as if she had remained in the room. Quiet, thoughtful children, like Jane, avail themselves of these little pleasures oftener than is suspected.

"Mother," said William, with great intensity, "I want to ask you please to lend me three dollars and sixty cents."

"What for, Willie?"

"Mother, I just ask you to lend me the three dollars and sixty cents."

"But what *for?*"

"Mother, I don't feel I can discuss it any; I simply ask you: Will you lend me three dollars and sixty cents?"

Mrs. Baxter laughed gently. "I don't think I could, Willie, but certainly I should want to know what for."

"Mother, I am going on eighteen years of age, and when I ask for a small sum of money like three dollars and sixty cents I think I might be trusted to know how to use it for my own good without having to answer questions like a ch—"

"Why, Willie," she exclaimed, "you ought to have plenty of money of your own!"

"Of course I ought," he agreed, warmly. "If you'd ask father to give me a regular allow—"

"No, no; I mean you ought to have plenty left out of that old junk and furniture I let you sell last month. You had over nine dollars!"

"That was five weeks ago," William explained, wearily.

"But you certainly must have some of it left. Why, it was *more* than nine dollars, I believe! I think it was nearer ten. Surely you haven't—"

"Ye gods!" cried the goaded William. "A person going on eighteen years old ought to be able to spend nine dollars in five weeks without everybody's acting like it was a crime! Mother, I ask you the simple question: Will you please lend me three dollars and sixty cents?"

"I don't think I ought to, dear. I'm sure your father wouldn't wish me to, unless you'll tell me what you want it for. In fact, I won't consider it at all unless you do tell me."

"You won't do it?" he quavered.

She shook her head gently. "You see, dear, I'm afraid the reason you don't tell me is because you know that I wouldn't give it to you if I knew what you wanted it for."

This perfect diagnosis of the case so disheartened him that after a few monosyllabic efforts to continue the conversation with dignity he gave it up, and left in such a preoccupation with despondency that he passed the surprised Jane in the hall without suspecting what she had been doing.

That evening, after dinner, he addressed to his father an impassioned appeal for three dollars and sixty cents, laying such stress of pathos on his principal argument that if he couldn't have a dress-suit, at least he ought to be given three dollars and sixty *cents* (the emphasis is William's) that Mr. Baxter was moved in the direction of consent— but not far enough. "I'd like to let you have it, Willie," he said, excusing himself for refusal, "but your mother felt *she* oughtn't to do it unless you'd say what you wanted it for, and I'm sure she wouldn't like me to do it. I can't let you have it unless you get her to say she wants me to."

Thus advised, the unfortunate made another appeal to his mother the next day, and having brought about no relaxation of the situation, again petitioned his father, on the following evening. So it went; the torn and driven William turning from parent to parent; and surely, since the world began, the special sum of three dollars and sixty cents has never been so often mentioned in any one house and in the same space of time as it was in the house of the Baxters during Monday, Tuesday, Wednesday, and Thursday of that oppressive week.

But on Friday William disappeared after breakfast and did not return to lunch.

24. Clothes Make the Man

MRS. BAXTER was troubled. During the afternoon she glanced often from the open window of the room where she had gone to sew, but the peaceful neighborhood continued to be peaceful, and no sound of the harassed footsteps of William echoed from the pavement. However, she saw Genesis arrive (in his week-day costume) to do some weeding, and Jane immediately skip forth for mingled purposes of observation and conversation.

"What *do* they say?" thought Mrs. Baxter, observing that both Jane and Genesis were unusually animated. But for once that perplexity was to be dispersed. After an exciting half-hour Jane came flying to her mother, breathless.

"Mamma," she cried, "I know where Willie is! Genesis told me, 'cause he saw him, an' he talked to him while he was doin' it."

"Doing what? Where?"

"Mamma, listen! What you think Willie's doin'? I bet you can't g—"

"Jane!" Mrs. Baxter spoke sharply. "Tell me what Genesis said, at once."

"Yes'm. Willie's sittin' in a lumber-yard that Genesis comes by on his way from over on the avynoo where all the colored people live—an' he's countin' knot-holes in shingles."

"He is *what?*"

"Yes'm. Genesis knows all about it, because he was thinkin' of doin' it himself, only he says it would be too slow. This is the way it is, mamma. Listen, mamma, because this is just exackly the way it is. Well, this lumber-yard man got into some sort of a fuss because he bought millions an' millions of shingles, mamma, that had too many knots in, an' the man don't want to pay for 'em, or else the store where he bought 'em won't take 'em back, an' they got to prove how many shingles are bad shingles, or somep'm, an' anyway, mamma, that's what Willie's doin'. Every time he comes to a bad shingle, mamma, he puts it somewheres else, or somep'm like that, mamma, an' every time he's put a thousand bad shingles in this other place they give him six cents. He gets the six cents to keep, mamma—an' that's what he's been doin' all day!"

"Good gracious!"

"Oh, but that's nothing, mamma—just you wait till you hear the rest. *That* part of it isn't anything a *tall,* mamma! You wouldn't hardly notice that part of it if you knew the other part of it, mamma. Why, that isn't *anything!*" Jane made demonstrations of scorn for the insignificant information already imparted.

"Jane!'

"Yes'm?"

"I want to know everything Genesis told you," said her mother, "and I want you to tell it as quickly as you can."

"Well, I *am* tellin' it, mamma!" Jane protested. "I'm just *beginning* to tell it. I can't tell it unless there's a beginning, can I? How could there be *anything* unless you had to begin it, mamma?"

"Try your best to go on, Jane!"

"Yes'm. Well, Genesis says— Mamma!" Jane interrupted herself with a little outcry. "Oh! I bet *that's* what he had those two market-baskets for! Yes, sir! That's just what he did! An' then he needed the rest o' the money an' you an' papa wouldn't give him any, an' so he began countin' shingles to-day 'cause to-night's the night of the party an' he just *hass* to have it!"

Mrs. Baxter, who had risen to her feet, recalled the
episode of the baskets and sank into a chair. "How did
Genesis know Willie wanted forty dollars, and if Willie's
pawned something how did Genesis know *that?* Did Willie
tell Gen—"

"Oh no, mamma, Willie didn't want forty dollars—only
fourteen!"

"But he couldn't get even the cheapest ready-made
dress-suit for fourteen dollars."

"Mamma, you're gettin' it all mixed up!" Jane cried.
"Listen, mamma! Genesis knows all about a second-hand
store over on the avynoo; an' it keeps 'most everything, an'
Genesis says it's the nicest store! It keeps waiter suits all
the way up to nineteen dollars and ninety-nine cents. Well,
an' Genesis wants to get one of those suits, so he goes in
there all the time, an' talks to the man an' bargains an'
bargains with him, 'cause Genesis says this man is the bar-
gainest man in the wide worl', mamma! That's what Genesis says. Well, an' so this man's name is One-eye Beljus,
mamma. That's his name, an' Genesis says so. Well, an' so
this man that Genesis told me about, that keeps the store—
I mean One-eye Beljus, mamma—well, One-eye Beljus
had Willie's name written down in a book, an' he knew
Genesis worked for fam'lies that have boys like Willie in
'em, an' this morning One-eye Beljus showed Genesis
Willie's name written down in this book, an' One-eye Beljus asked Genesis if he knew anybody by that name an' all
about him. Well, an' so at first Genesis pretended he was
tryin' to remember, because he wanted to find out what
Willie went there for. Genesis didn't tell any stories,
mamma; he just pretended he couldn't remember, an' so,
well, One-eye Beljus kept talkin' an' pretty soon Genesis
found out all about it. One-eye Beljus said Willie came in
there an' tried on the coat of one of those waiter suits—"

"Oh no!" gasped Mrs. Baxter.

"Yes'm an' One-eye Beljus said it was the only one that
would fit Willie, an' One-eye Beljus told Willie that suit
was worth fourteen dollars, an' Willie said he didn't have
any money, but he'd like to trade something else for it.
Well, an' so One-eye Beljus said this was an awful fine suit
an' the only one he had that had b'longed to a white
gentleman. Well, an' so they bargained, an' bargained, an'

bargained, an' *bargained!* An' then, well, an' so at last
Willie said he'd go an' get everything that b'longed to him,
an' One-eye Beljus could pick out enough to make fourteen
dollars' worth, an' then Willie could have the suit. Well, an'
so Willie came home an' put everything he had that
b'longed to him into those two baskets, mamma—that's
just what he did, 'cause Genesis says he told One-eye
Beljus it was everything that b'longed to him, an' that
would take two baskets, mamma. Well, then, an' so he
told One-eye Beljus to pick out fourteen dollars' worth,
an' One-eye Beljus ast Willie if he didn't have a watch.
Well, Willie took out his watch, an' One-eye Beljus said it
was an awful bad watch, but he would put it in for a
dollar; an' he said, 'I'll put your necktie pin in for forty
cents more,' so Willie took it out of his necktie; an' then
One-eye Beljus said it would take all the things in the
baskets to make I forget how much, mamma, an' the watch
would be a dollar more, an' the pin forty cents, an' that
would leave just three dollars an' sixty cents more for
Willie to pay before he could get the suit."

Mrs. Baxter's face had become suffused with high color,
but she wished to know all that Genesis had said, and,
mastering her feelings with an effort, she told Jane to proceed—a command obeyed after Jane had taken several
long breaths.

"Well, an' so the worst part of it is, Genesis says, it's
because that suit is haunted."

"What!"

"Yes'm," said Jane, solemnly; "Genesis says it's
haunted. Genesis says everybody over on the avynoo
knows all about that suit, an' he says that's why One-eye
Beljus never could sell it before. Genesis says One-eye
Beljus tried to sell it to a colored man for three dollars, but
the man said he wouldn't put it on for three hundred dollars, an' Genesis says *he* wouldn't, either, because it belonged to a Dago waiter that—that—" Jane's voice sank
to a whisper of unctuous horror. She was having a wonderful time! "Mamma, this Dago waiter, he lived over on the
avynoo, an' he took a case-knife he'd sharpened—*an' he
cut a lady's head off with it!*"

Mrs. Baxter screamed faintly.

"An' he got hung, mamma! If you don't believe it, you

can ask One-eye Beljus—I guess *he* knows! An' you can ask—"

"Hush!"

"An' he sold this suit to One-eye Beljus when he was in jail, mamma. He sold it to him before he got hung, mamma."

"Hush, Jane!"

But Jane couldn't hush now. "An' he had that suit on when he cut the lady's head off, mamma, an' that's why it's haunted. They cleaned it all up excep' a few little spots of bl—"

"*Jane!*" shouted her mother. "You must not talk about such things, and Genesis mustn't tell you stories of that sort!"

"Well, how could he help it, if he told me about Willie?" Jane urged, reasonably.

"Never mind! Did that crazy ch— Did Willie *leave* the baskets in that dreadful place?"

"Yes'm—an' his watch an' pin," Jane informed her, impressively. "An' One-eye Beljus wanted to know if Genesis knew Willie, because One-eye Beljus wanted to know if Genesis thought Willie could get the three dollars an' sixty cents, an' One-eye Beljus wanted to know if Genesis thought he could get anything more out of him besides that. He told Genesis he hadn't told Willie he *could* have the suit, after all; he just told him he *thought* he could, but he wouldn't say for certain till he brought him the three dollars an' sixty cents. So Willie left all his things there, an' his watch an'—"

"That will do!" Mrs. Baxter's voice was sharper than it had ever been in Jane's recollection. "I don't need to hear any more—and I don't *want* to hear any more!"

Jane was justly aggrieved. "But, mamma, it isn't *my* fault!"

Mrs. Baxter's lips parted to speak, but she checked herself. "Fault?" she said, gravely. "I wonder whose fault it really is!"

And with that she went hurriedly into William's room and made a brief inspection of his clothes-closet and dressing-table. Then, as Jane watched her in awed silence, she strode to the window, and called, loudly:

"Genesis!"

"Yes'm?" came the voice from below.

"Go to that lumber-yard where Mr. William is at work and bring him here to me at once. If he declines to come, tell him—" Her voice broke oddly; she choked, but Jane could not decide with what emotion. "Tell him—tell him I ordered you to use force if necessary! Hurry!"

"*Yes'm!*"

Jane ran to the window in time to see Genesis departing seriously through the back gate.

"Mamma—"

"Don't talk to me now, Jane," Mrs. Baxter said, crisply. "I want you to go down in the yard, and when Willie comes tell him I'm waiting for him here in his own room. And don't come with him, Jane. Run!"

"Yes, mamma." Jane was pleased with this appointment; she anxiously desired to be the first to see how Willie "looked."

. . . He looked flurried and flustered and breathless, and there were blisters upon the reddened palms of his hands. "What on earth's the matter, mother?" he asked, as he stood panting before her. "Genesis said something was wrong, and he said you told him to hit me if I wouldn't come."

"Oh *no!*" she cried. "I only meant I thought perhaps you wouldn't obey any ordinary message—"

"Well, well, it doesn't matter, but please hurry and say what you want to, because I got to get back and—"

"No," Mrs. Baxter said, quietly, "you're not going back to count any more shingles, Willie. How much have you earned?"

He swallowed, but spoke bravely. "Thirty-six cents. But I've been getting lots faster the last two hours and there's a good deal of time before six o'clock. Mother—"

"No," she said. "You're going over to that horrible place where you've left your clothes and your watch and all those other things in the two baskets, and you're going to bring them home at once."

"Mother!" he cried, aghast. "Who told you?"

"It doesn't matter. You don't want your father to find out, do you? Then get those things back here as quickly as you can. They'll have to be fumigated after being in that den."

"They've never been out of the baskets," he protested, hotly, "except just to be looked at. They're *my* things, mother, and I had a right to do what I needed to with 'em, didn't I?" His utterance became difficult. "You and father just *can't* understand—and you won't do anything to help me—"

"Willie, you can go to the party," she said, gently. "You didn't need those frightful clothes at all."

"I do!" he cried. "I *got* to have 'em! I *can't* go in my day clo'es! There's a reason you wouldn't understand why I can't. I just *can't!*"

"Yes," she said, "you can go to the party."

"I can't, either! Not unless you give me three dollars and twenty-four cents, or unless I can get back to the lumber-yard and earn the rest before—"

"No!" And the warm color that had rushed over Mrs. Baxter during Jane's sensational recital returned with a vengeance. Her eyes flashed. "If you'd rather I sent a policeman for those baskets, I'll send one. I should prefer to do it—much! And to have that rascal arrested. If you don't want me to send a policeman you can go for them yourself, but you must start within ten minutes, because if you don't I'll telephone headquarters. Ten minutes, Willie, and I mean it!"

He cried out, protesting. She would make him a thing of scorn forever and soil his honor, if she sent a policeman. Mr. Beljus was a fair and honest tradesman, he explained, passionately, and had not made the approaches in this matter. Also, the garments in question, though not entirely new, nor of the highest mode, were of good material and in splendid condition. Unmistakably they were evening clothes, and such a bargain at fourteen dollars that William would guarantee to sell them for twenty after he had worn them this one evening. Mr. Beljus himself had said that he would not even think of letting them go at fourteen to anybody else, and as for the two poor baskets of worn and useless articles offered in exchange, and a bent scarfpin and a worn-out old silver watch that had belonged to great-uncle Ben —why, the ten dollars and forty cents allowed upon them was beyond all ordinary liberality; it was almost charity. There was only one place in town where evening clothes were rented, and the suspicious persons in charge had insisted that William obtain from his father a guarantee to insure the return of the garments in perfect condition. So that was hopeless. And wasn't it better, also, to wear clothes which had known only one previous occupant (as was the case with Mr. Beljus's offering) than to hire what chance hundreds had hired? Finally, there was only one thing to be considered and this was the fact that William *had* to have those clothes!

"Six minutes," said Mrs. Baxter, glancing implacably at her watch. "When it's ten I'll telephone."

And the end of it was, of course, victory for the woman —victory both moral and physical. Three-quarters of an hour later she was unburdening the contents of the two baskets and putting the things back in place, illuminating these actions with an expression of strong distaste—in spite of broken assurances that Mr. Beljus had not more than touched any of the articles offered to him for valuation.

. . . At dinner, which was unusually early that evening, Mrs. Baxter did not often glance toward her son; she kept her eyes from that white face and spent most of her time in urging upon Mr. Baxter that he should be prompt in dressing for a card-club meeting which he and she were to attend that evening. These admonitions of hers were continued so pressingly that Mr. Baxter, after protesting that there was no use in being a whole hour too early, groaningly went to dress without even reading his paper.

William had retired to his own room, where he lay upon his bed in the darkness. He heard the evening noises of the house faintly through the closed door: voices and the clatter of metal and china from the far-away kitchen, Jane's laugh in the hall, the opening and closing of the doors. Then his father seemed to be in distress about something. William heard him complaining to Mrs. Baxter, and though the words were indistinct, the tone was vigorously plaintive. Mrs. Baxter laughed and appeared to make light of his troubles, whatever they were—and presently their footsteps were audible from the stairway; the front door closed emphatically, and they were gone.

Everything was quiet now. The open window showed as a greenish oblong set in black, and William knew that in a little while there would come through the stillness of that window the distant sound of violins. That was a moment he dreaded with a dread that ached. And as he lay on his dreary bed he thought of brightly lighted rooms where other boys were dressing eagerly, faces and hair shining, hearts beating high—boys who would possess this last evening and the "last waltz together," the last smile and the last sigh.

It did not once enter his mind that he could go to the dance in his "best suit," or that possibly the other young people at the party would be too busy with their own affairs to notice particularly what he wore. It was the unquestionable and granite fact, to his mind, that the whole derisive World would know the truth about his earlier appearances in his father's clothes. And that was a form of ruin not to be faced. In the protective darkness and seclusion of William's bedroom, it is possible that smarting eyes relieved themselves by blinking rather energetically; it is even possible that there was a minute damp spot upon the pillow. Seventeen cannot always manage the little boy yet alive under all the coverings.

Now arrived that moment he had most painfully anticipated, and dance-music drifted on the night—but there came a tapping upon his door and a soft voice spoke.

"Will-ee?"

With a sharp exclamation William swung his legs over the edge of the bed and sat up. Of all things he desired not, he desired no conversation with, or on the part of Jane. But he had forgotten to lock his door—the handle turned, and a dim little figure marched in.

"Willie, Adelia's goin' to put me to bed."

"You g'way from here," he said, huskily. "I haven't got time to talk to you. I'm busy."

"Well, you can wait a minute, can't you?" she asked, reasonably. "I haf to tell you a joke on mamma."

"I don't want to hear any jokes!"

"Well, I *haf* to tell you this one 'cause she told me to! Oh!" Jane clapped her hand over her mouth and jumped up and down, offering a fantastic silhouette against the light of the open door. "Oh, oh, *oh!*"

"What's matter?"

"She said I mustn't, *mustn't* tell that she told me to tell! My goodness! I forgot that! Mamma took me off alone right after dinner, an' she told me to tell you this joke on her a little after she an' papa had left the house, but she said, 'Above all *things,*' she said *'don't* let Willie know *I* said to tell him.' That's just what she said, an' here that's the very first thing I had to go an' do!"

"Well, what of it?"

Jane quieted down. The pangs of her remorse were lost in her love of sensationalism, and her voice sank to the thrilling whisper which it was one of her greatest pleasures to use. "Did you hear what a fuss papa was makin' when he was dressin' for the card-party?"

"*I* don't care if—"

"He had to go in his reg'lar clo'es!" whispered Jane, triumphantly. "An' this is the joke on mamma: you know that tailor that let papa's dress-suit 'way, 'way out; well, mamma thinks that tailor must think she's crazy, or somep'm, 'cause she took papa's dress-suit to him last Monday to get it pressed for this card-party, an' she guesses he must of understood her to tell him to do lots beside just pressin' it. Anyway, he went an' altered it, an' he took it 'way, 'way *in* again; an' this afternoon when it came back it was even tighter'n what it was in the first place, an' papa couldn't *begin* to get into it! Well, an' so it's all pressed an' ev'ything, an' she stopped on the way out, an' whispered to me that she'd got so upset over the joke on her that she couldn't remember where she put it when she took it out o' papa's room after he gave up tryin' to get inside of it. An' that," cried Jane—"that's the funniest thing of all! Why, it's layin' right on her bed this very minute!"

In one bound William leaped through the open door. Two seconds sufficed for his passage through the hall to his mother's bedroom—and there, neatly spread upon the lace coverlet and brighter than coronation robes, fairer than Joseph's holy coat, It lay!

25. Youth and Mr. Parcher

As a HURRIED worldling, in almost perfectly fitting evening clothes, passed out of his father's gateway and hurried toward the place whence faintly came the sound of dance-music, a child's voice called sweetly from an unidentified window of the darkened house behind him:

"Well, *anyway*, you try and have a good time, Willie!"

William made no reply; he paused not in his stride. Jane's farewell injunction, though obviously not ill-intended, seemed in poor taste, and a reply might have encouraged her to believe that, in some measure at least, he condescended to discuss his inner life with her. He departed rapidly, but with hauteur. The moon was up, but shade-trees were thick along the sidewalk, and the hauteur was invisible to any human eye; nevertheless, William considered it necessary.

Jane's friendly but ill-chosen *"anyway"* had touched doubts already annoying him. He was certain to be late to the party—so late, indeed, that it might prove difficult to obtain a proper number of dances with the sacred girl in whose honor the celebration was being held. Too many were steeped in a sense of her sacredness, well he wot! and he was unable to find room in his apprehensive mind for any doubt that these others would be accursedly diligent.

But as he hastened onward his spirits rose, and he did reply to Jane, after all, though he had placed a hundred yards between them.

"Yes, and you can bet your bottom dollar I will, too!" he muttered, between his determined teeth.

The very utterance of the words increased the firmness of his decision, and at the same time cheered him. His apprehensions fell away, and a glamorous excitement took their place, as he turned a corner and the music burst more loudly upon his tingling ear. For there, not half-way to the next street, the fairy scene lay spread before him.

Spellbound groups of uninvited persons, most of them colored, rested their forearms upon the upper rail of the Parchers' picket fence, offering to William's view a silhouette like that of a crowd at a fire. Beyond the fence, bright forms went skimming, shimmering, wavering over a white platform, while high overhead the young moon sprayed a thinner light down through the maple leaves, to where processions of rosy globes hung floating in the blue night. The mild breeze trembled to the silver patterings of a harp, to the sweet, barbaric chirping of plucked strings of violin and 'cello—and swooned among the maple leaves to the rhythmic crooning of a flute. And, all the while, from the platform came the sounds of little cries in girlish voices, and the cadenced shuffling of young feet, where the witching dance-music had its way, as ever and forever, with big and little slippers.

The heart of William had behaved tumultuously the summer long, whenever his eyes beheld those pickets of the Parchers' fence, but now it outdid all its previous riotings. He was forced to open his mouth and gasp for breath, so deep was his draught of that young wine, romance. Yonder—somewhere in the breath-taking radiance—danced his Queen with all her Court about her. Queen and Court, thought William, and nothing less exorbitant could have expressed his feeling. For seventeen needs only some paper lanterns, a fiddle, and a pretty girl—and Versailles is all there!

The moment was so rich that William crossed the street with a slower step. His mood changed: an exaltation had come upon him, though he was never for an instant unaware of the tragedy beneath all this worldly show and glamor. It was the last night of the divine visit; to-morrow the town would lie desolate, a hollow shell in the dust, without her. Miss Pratt would be gone—gone utterly—gone away on the *train!* But to-night was just beginning, and tonight he would dance with her; he would dance and dance with her—he would dance and dance like mad! He and she, poetic and fated pair, would dance on and on! They would be intoxicated by the lights—the lights, the flowers, and the music. Nay, the flowers might droop, the lights might go out, the music cease and dawn come—she and he would dance recklessly on—on—on!

A sense of picturesqueness—his own picturesqueness—made him walk rather theatrically as he passed through the groups of humble onlookers outside the picket fence. Many of these turned to stare at the belated guest, and William was unconscious of neither their low estate nor his own quality as a patrician man-about-town in almost perfectly fitting evening dress. A faint, cold smile was allowed to appear upon his lips, and a fragment from a story he had read came momentarily to his mind. . . . "Through the gaping crowds the young Augustan noble was borne down from the Palatine, scornful in his jeweled litter. . . ."

An admiring murmur reached William's ear. *"Oh,* oh, honey! Look attem long-tail suit! 'At's a rich boy, honey!"

"Yessum, so! Bet he got his pockets pack' full o' twenty-dolluh gol' pieces right iss minute!"

"You right, honey!"

William allowed the coldness of his faint smile to increase—to become scornful. These poor sidewalk creatures little knew what seethed inside the alabaster of the young Augustan noble! What was it to *them* that this was Miss Pratt's last night and that he intended to dance and dance with her, on and on?

Almost sternly he left these squalid lives behind him and passed to the festal gateway.

Upon one of the posts of that gateway there rested the elbow of a contemplative man, middle-aged or a little worse. Of all persons having pleasure or business within the bright inclosure, he was, that evening, the least important; being merely the background parent who paid the bills. However, even this unconsidered elder shared a thought in common with the Augustan now approaching: Mr. Parcher had just been thinking that there was true romance in the scene before him.

But what Mr. Parcher contemplated as romance arose from the fact that these young people were dancing on a spot where their great-grandfathers had scalped Indians. Music was made for them by descendants, it might well be, of Romulus, of Messalina, of Benvenuto Cellini, and, around behind the house, waiting to serve the dancers with light food and drink, lounged and gossiped grandchildren of the Congo, only a generation or so removed from dances for which a chance stranger furnished both the occasion and the refreshments. Such, in brief, was Mr. Parcher's peculiar view of what constituted the romantic element.

And upon another subject preoccupying both Mr. Parcher and William, their two views, though again founded upon one thought, had no real congeniality. The preoccupying subject was the imminence of Miss Pratt's departure—neither Mr. Parcher nor William forgot it for an instant. No matter what else played upon the surface of their attention, each kept saying to himself, underneath: "This is the last night—the last night! Miss Pratt is going away—going away to-morrow!"

Mr. Parcher's expression was peaceful. It was more peaceful than it had been for a long time. In fact, he wore the look of a man who had been through the mill but now contemplated a restful and health-restoring vacation. For there are people in this world who have no respect for the memory of Ponce de León, and Mr. Parcher had come to be of their number. The elimination of William from his evenings had lightened the burden; nevertheless, Mr. Parcher would have stated freely and openly to any responsible party that a yearning for the renewal of his youth had not been intensified by his daughter's having as a visitor, all summer long, a howling belle of eighteen who talked baby-talk even at breakfast and spread her suitors all over the small house—and its one veranda—from eight in the morning until hours of the night long after their mothers (in Mr. Parcher's opinion) should have sent their fathers to march them home. Upon Mr. Parcher's optimism the effect of so much unavoidable observation of young love had been fatal; he declared repeatedly that his faith in the human race was about gone. Furthermore, his physical constitution had proved pathetically vulnerable to nightly quartets, quintets, and even octets, on the porch below his bedchamber window, so that he was wont to tell his wife that never, never could he expect to be again the man he had been in the spring before Miss Pratt came to visit May. And, referring to conversations which he almost continuously overheard, perforce, Mr. Parcher said that if this was the way *he* talked at that age, he would far prefer to drown in an ordinary fountain, and be dead and done with it, than to bathe in Ponce de León's.

Altogether, the summer had been a severe one; he doubted that he could have survived much more of it. And now that it was virtually over, at last, he was so resigned to the departure of his daughter's lovely little friend that he felt no regret for the splurge with which her visit was closing. Nay, to speed the parting guest—such was his lavish mood—twice and thrice over would he have paid for the lights, the flowers, the music, the sandwiches, the coffee, the chicken salad, the cake, the lemonade-punch, and the ice-cream.

Thus did the one thought divide itself between William and Mr. Parcher, keeping itself deep and pure under all their other thoughts. "Miss Pratt is going away!" thought William and Mr. Parcher. "Miss *Pratt* is going away—to-morrow!"

The unuttered words advanced tragically toward the gate in the head of William at the same time that they moved contentedly away in the head of Mr. Parcher; for Mr. Parcher caught sight of his wife just then, and went to join her as she sank wearily upon the front steps.

"Taking a rest for a minute?" he inquired. "By George! we're both entitled to a good *long* rest, after to-night! If we could afford it, we'd go away to a quiet little sanitarium in the hills, somewhere, and—" He ceased to speak and there was the renewal of an old bitterness in his expression as his staring eyes followed the movements of a stately young form entering the gateway. "Look at it!" said Mr. Parcher in a whisper. "Just look at it!"

"Look at what?" asked his wife.

"That Baxter boy!" said Mr. Parcher, as William passed on toward the dancers. "What's he think he's imitating—Henry Irving? Look at his walk!"

"He walks that way a good deal, lately, I've noticed," said Mrs. Parcher in a tired voice. "So do Joe Bullitt and—"

"He didn't even come to say good evening to you," Mr. Parcher interrupted. "Talk about *manners,* nowadays! These young—"

"He didn't see us."

"Well, we're used to that," said Mr. Parcher. "None of 'em see us. They've worn holes in all the cane-seated chairs, they've scuffed up the whole house, and I haven't been able to sit down anywhere down-stairs for three months without sitting on some dam boy; but they don't even know we're alive! Well, thank the Lord, it's over—after to-night!" His voice became reflective. "That Baxter boy was the worst, until he took to coming in the daytime when I was down-town. I *couldn't* have stood it if he'd kept on coming in the evening. If I'd had to listen to any more of his talking or singing, either the embalmer or the lunatic-asylum would have had me, sure! I see he's got hold of his daddy's dress-suit again for to-night."

"Is it Mr. Baxter's dress-suit?" Mrs. Parcher inquired. "How do you know?"

Mr. Parcher smiled. "How I happen to know is a secret," he said. "I forgot about that. His little sister, Jane, told me that Mrs. Baxter had hidden it, or something, so that Willie couldn't wear it, but I guess Jane wouldn't mind my telling *you* that she told me—especially as they're letting him use it again to-night. I suppose he feels grander 'n the King o' Siam!"

"No," Mrs. Parcher returned, thoughtfully. "I don't think he does, just now." Her gaze was fixed upon the dancing-platform, which most of the dancers were abandoning as the music fell away to an interval of silence. In the center of the platform there remained one group, consisting of Miss Pratt and five orators, and of the orators the most impassioned and gesticulative was William.

"They all seem to want to dance with her all the time," said Mrs. Parcher. "I heard her telling one of the boys, half an hour ago, that all she could give him was either the twenty-eighth regular dance or the sixteenth 'extra.' "

"The what?" Mr. Parcher demanded, whirling to face her. "Do they think this party's going to keep running till day after to-morrow?" And then, as his eyes returned to the group on the platform, "That boy seems to have quite a touch of emotional insanity," he remarked, referring to William. "What *is* the matter with him?"

"Oh, nothing," his wife returned. "Only trying to arrange a dance with her. He seems to be in difficulties."

26. Miss Boke

NOTHING COULD have been more evident than William's difficulties. They continued to exist, with equal obviousness, when the group broke up in some confusion, after a few minutes of animated discussion; Mr. Wallace Banks, that busy and executive youth, bearing Miss Pratt triumphantly off to the lemonade-punch-bowl, while William pursued Johnnie Watson and Joe Bullitt. He sought to detain them near the edge of the platform, though they appeared far from anxious to linger in his company; and he was able to arrest their attention only by clutching an arm

of each. In fact, the good feeling which had latterly prevailed among these three appeared to be in danger of dis-
integrating. The occasion was too vital; and the watchword
for "Miss Pratt's last night" was Devil-Take-the-Hindmost!

"Now you look here, Johnnie," William said, vehemently, "and you listen, too, Joe! You both got seven
dances apiece with her, anyway, all on account of my not
getting here early enough, and you got to—"

"It wasn't because of any such reason," young Mr. Watson protested. "I asked her for mine two days ago."

"Well, *that* wasn't fair, was it?" William cried. "Just
because I never thought of sneaking in ahead like that, you
go and—"

"Well, you ought to thought of it," Johnnie retorted,
jerking his arm free of William's grasp. "I can't stand here
gabbin' all night!" And he hurried away.

"Joe," William began, fastening more securely upon Mr.
Bullitt—"Joe, I've done a good many favors for you, and
—"

"I've got to see a man," Mr. Bullitt interrupted. "Lemme go, Silly Bill. There's somebody I got to see right away
before the next dance begins. I *got* to! Honest I have!"

William seized him passionately by the lapels of his coat.
"Listen, Joe. For goodness' sake can't you listen a *minute?*
You *got* to give me—"

"Honest, Bill," his friend expostulated, backing away as
forcefully as possible, "I got to find a fellow that's here
to-night and ask him about something important before—"

"Ye gods! Can't you wait a *minute?*" William cried,
keeping his grip upon Joe's lapels. "You *got* to give me
anyway *two* out of all your dances with her! You heard her
tell me, yourself, that she'd be willing if you or Johnnie
or—"

"Well, I only got five or six with her, and a couple ex-
tras. Johnnie's got seven. Whyn't you go after Johnnie?
I bet he'd help you out, all right, if you kept after him.
What you want to pester *me* for, Bill?"

The brutal selfishness of this speech, as well as its cold-
blooded insincerity, produced in William the impulse to
smite. Fortunately, his only hope lay in persuasion, and
after a momentary struggle with his own features he was
able to conceal what he desired to do to Joe's.

He swallowed, and, increasing the affectionate desperation of his clutch upon Mr. Bullitt's lapels, "Joe," he began,
huskily—"Joe, if *I*'d got six reg'lar and two extras with
Miss Pratt her last night here, and you got here late, and
it wasn't your fault—I couldn't help being late, could I?
It wasn't my fault I was late, I guess, was it? Well, if I
was in *your* place I wouldn't act the way you and Johnnie
do—not in a thousand years I wouldn't! I'd say, 'You want
a couple o' my dances with Miss Pratt, ole man? Why, *certainly*—' "

"Yes, you would!" was the cynical comment of Mr. Bullitt, whose averted face and reluctant shoulders indicated a
strong desire to conclude the interview. "To-night, especially!" he added.

"Look here, Joe," said William desperately, "don't you
realize that this is the very last night Miss Pratt's going to
be in this town?"

"You bet I do!" These words, though vehement, were
inaudible; being formed in the mind of Mr. Bullitt, but,
for diplomatic reasons, not projected upon the air by his
vocal organs.

William continued: "Joe, you and I have been friends
ever since you and I were boys." He spoke with emotion,
but Joe had no appearance of being favorably impressed.
"And when I look back," said William, "I expect I've done
more favors for you than I ever have for any oth—"

But Mr. Bullitt briskly interrupted this appealing remi-
niscence. "Listen here, Silly Bill," he said, becoming all at
once friendly and encouraging—"Bill, there's other girls
here you can get dances with. There's one or two of 'em
sittin' around in the yard. You can have a bully time, even
if you did come late." And, with the air of discharging
happily all the obligations of which William had reminded
him, he added, "I'll tell you *that* much, Bill!"

"Joe, you got to give me anyway *one* da—"

"Look!" said Mr. Bullitt, eagerly. "Look sittin' yonder,
over under that tree all by herself! That's a visiting girl
named Miss Boke; she's visiting some old uncle or something she's got livin' here, and I bet you could—"

"Joe, you *got* to—"

"I bet that Miss Boke's a good dancer, Bill," Joe continued, warmly. "May Parcher says so. She was tryin' **to**

get me to dance with her myself, but I couldn't, or I would
of. Honest, Bill, I would of! Bill, if I was you I'd sail right
in there before anybody else got a start, and I'd—"

"Ole man," said William, gently, "you remember the
time Miss Pratt and I had an engagement to go walkin',
and you wouldn't of seen her for a week on account of
your aunt dyin' in Kansas City, if I hadn't let you go along
with us? Ole man, if you—"

But the music sounded for the next dance, and Joe felt
that it was indeed time to end this uncomfortable conversation. "I got to go, Bill," he said. "I *got* to!"

"Wait just one minute," William implored. "I want to
say just this: if—"

"Here!" exclaimed Mr. Bullitt. "I got to *go*"!

"I know it. That's why—"

Heedless of remonstrance, Joe wrenched himself free,
for it would have taken a powerful and ruthless man to
detain him longer. "What you take me for?" he demanded,
indignantly. "I got this with Miss *Pratt!*"

And evading a hand which still sought to clutch him, he
departed hotly.

. . . Mr. Parcher's voice expressed wonder, a little later,
as he recommended his wife to turn her gaze in the direction of "that Baxter boy" again. "Just look at him!" said
Mr. Parcher. "His face has got more genuine idiocy in it
than I've seen around here yet, and God knows I've been
seeing some miracles in that line this summer!"

"He's looking at Lola Pratt," said Mrs. Parcher.

"Don't you suppose I can see that?" Mr. Parcher returned, with some irritation. "That's what's the trouble
with him. Why don't he *quit* looking at her?"

"I think probably he feels badly because she's dancing
with one of the other boys," said his wife, mildly.

"Then why can't he dance with somebody else himself?"
Mr. Parcher inquired, testily. "Instead of standing around
like a calf looking out of the butcher's wagon! By George!
he looks as if he was just going to *moo!*"

"Of course he ought to be dancing with somebody,"
Mrs. Parcher remarked, thoughtfully. "There are one or
two more girls than boys here, and he's the only boy not
dancing. I believe I'll—" And, not stopping to complete
the sentence, she rose and walked across the interval of

grass to William. "Good evening, William," she said, pleasantly. "Don't you want to dance?"

"Ma'am?" said William, blankly, and the eyes he turned upon her were glassy with anxiety. He was still determined to dance on and on with Miss Pratt, but he realized that there were great obstacles to be overcome before he could begin the process. He was feverishly awaiting the next interregnum between dances—then he would show Joe Bullitt and Johnnie Watson and Wallace Banks, and some others who had set themselves in his way, that he was "abs'lutely not goin' to stand it!"

He couldn't stand it, he told himself, even if he wanted to—not to-night! He had "been through enough" in order to get to the party, he thought, thus defining sufferings connected with his costume, and now that he was here he *would* dance and dance, on and on, with Miss Pratt. Anything else was unthinkable.

He *had* to!

"Don't you want to dance?" Mrs. Parcher repeated. "Have you looked around for a girl without a partner?"

He continued to stare at her, plainly having no comprehension of her meaning.

"Girl?" he echoed, in a tone of feeble inquiry.

She smiled and nodded, taking his arm. "You come with me," she said. *"I'll* fix you up!"

William suffered her to conduct him across the yard. Intensely preoccupied with what he meant to do as soon as the music paused, he was somewhat hazy, but when he perceived that he was being led in the direction of a girl, sitting solitary under one of the maple-trees, the sudden shock of fear aroused his faculties.

"What—where—" he stammered, halting and seeking to detach himself from his hostess.

"What is it?" she asked.

"I got—I got to—" William began, uneasily. "I got to—"

His purpose was to excuse himself on the ground that he had to find a man and tell him something important before the next dance, for in the confusion of the moment his powers refused him greater originality. But the vital part of his intended excuse remained unspoken, being disregarded and cut short, as millions of other masculine diplomacies have been, throughout the centuries, by the decisive action of ladies.

Miss Boke had been sitting under the maple-tree for a long time—so long, indeed, that she was acquiring a profound distaste for forestry and even for maple syrup. In fact, her state of mind was as desperate, in its way, as William's; and when a hostess leads a youth (in almost perfectly fitting conventional black) toward a girl who has been sitting alone through dance after dance, that girl knows what that youth is going to have to do.

It must be confessed for Miss Boke that her eyes had been upon William from the moment Mrs. Parcher addressed him. Nevertheless, as the pair came toward her she looked casually away in an indifferent manner. And yet this may have been but a seeming unconsciousness, for upon the very instant of William's halting, and before he had managed to stammer "I got to—" for the fourth time, Miss Boke sprang to her feet and met Mrs. Parcher more than half-way.

"Oh, Mrs. Parcher!" she called, coming forward.

"I got—" the panic-stricken William again hastily began. "I got to—"

"Oh, Mrs. Parcher," cried Miss Boke, "I've been *so* worried! There's a candle in that Japanese lantern just over your head, and I think it's going out."

"I'll run and get a fresh one in a minute," said Mrs. Parcher, smiling benevolently and retaining William's arm with a little difficulty. "We were just coming to find you. I've brought—"

"I got to—I got to find a m—" William made a last, stricken effort.

"Miss Boke, this is Mr. Baxter," said Mrs. Parcher, and she added, with what seemed to William hideous garrulity, "He and you both came late, dear, and he hasn't any dances engaged, either. So run and dance, and have a nice time together."

Thereupon this disastrous woman returned to her husband. Her look was conscientious; she thought she had done something pleasant!

The full horror of his position was revealed to William in the relieved, confident, proprietor's smile of Miss Boke.

For William lived by a code from which no previous experience had taught him any means of escape. Mrs. Parcher
had made the statement—so needless and so ruinous—that
he had no engagements; and in his dismay he had been
unable to deny this fatal truth; he had been obliged to let
it stand. Henceforth, he was committed absolutely to Miss
Boke until either someone else asked her to dance, or
(while yet in her close company) William could obtain
an engagement with another girl. The latter alternative presented certain grave difficulties, also contracting William
to dance with the other girl before once more obtaining his
freedom, but undeniably he regarded it from the first as
the more hopeful.

He had to give form to the fatal invitation. "M'av this
dance 'thyou?" he muttered, doggedly.

"Vurry pleased to!" Miss Boke responded, whereupon
they walked in silence to the platform, stepped upon its
surface, and embraced.

They made a false start.

They made another.

They stood swaying to catch the time; then made another. After that they tried again, and were saved from a
fall only by spasmodic and noticeable contortions.

Miss Boke laughed tolerantly, as if forgiving William
for his awkwardness, and his hot heart grew hotter with
that injustice. She was a large, ample girl, weighing more
than William (this must be definitely claimed in his be-
half), and she had been spending the summer at a lakeside
hotel where she had constantly danced "man's part." To
paint William's predicament at a stroke, his partner was
a determined rather than a graceful dancer—and their efforts to attune themselves to each other and to the music
were in a fair way to attract general attention.

A coarse chuckle, a half-suppressed snort, assailed William's scarlet ear, and from the corner of his eye he caught
a glimpse of Joe Bullitt gliding by, suffused; while over
Joe's detested shoulder could be seen the adorable and
piquant face of the One girl—also suffused.

"Doggone it!" William panted.

"Oh, you mustn't be discouraged with yourself," said
Miss Boke, genially. "I've met lots of Men that had trou-

ble to get started and turned out to be right good dancers, after all. It seems to me we're kind of workin' against each other. I'll tell you—you kind of let me do the guiding and I'll get you going fine. Now! *One,* two, *one,* two! There!"

William ceased to struggle for dominance, and their efforts to "get started" were at once successful. With a muscular power that was surprising, Miss Boke bore him out into the circling current, swung him round and round, walked him backward half across the platform, then swung him round and round and round again. For a girl, she "guided" remarkably well; nevertheless, a series of collisions, varying in intensity, marked the path of the pair upon the rather crowded platform. In such emergencies Miss Boke proved herself deft in swinging William to act as a buffer, and he several times found himself heavily stricken from the rear; anon his face would be pressed suffocatingly into Miss Boke's hair, without the slightest wish on his part for such intimacy. He had a helpless feeling, fully warranted by the circumstances. Also, he soon became aware that Miss Boke's powerful "guiding" was observed by the public; for, after one collision, more severe than others, a low voice hissed in his ear:

"She won't hurt you much, Silly Bill. She's only in fun!"

This voice belonged to the dancer with whom he had just been in painful contact, Johnnie Watson. However, Johnnie had whirled far upon another orbit before William found a retort, and then it was a feeble one.

"I wish *you'd* try a few dances with her!" he whispered, inaudibly, but with unprecedented bitterness, as the masterly arm of his partner just saved him from going over the edge of the platform. "I bet she'd kill you!"

More than once he tried to assert himself and resume his natural place as guide, but each time he did so he immediately got out of step with his partner, their knees collided embarrassingly, they staggered and walked upon each other's insteps—and William was forced to abandon the unequal contest.

"I just love dancing," said Miss Boke, serenely. "Don't you, Mr. Baxter?"

"What?" he gulped. "Yeh."

"It's a beautiful floor for dancing, isn't it?"

"Yeh."

"I just love dancing," Miss Boke thought proper to declare again. "Don't you love it, Mr. Baxter?"

This time he considered his enthusiasm to be sufficiently indicated by a nod. He needed all his breath.

"It's lovely," she murmured. "I hope they don't play 'Home, Sweet Home' very early at parties in this town. I could keep on like this all night!"

To the gasping William it seemed that she already had kept on like this all night, and he expressed himself in one great, frank, agonized moan of relief when the music stopped. "I sh' think those musicians'd be dead!" he said, as he wiped his brow. And then discovering that May Parcher stood at his elbow, he spoke hastily to her. "M'av the next 'thyou?"

But Miss Parcher had begun to applaud the musicians for an encore. She shook her head. "Next's the third extra," she said. "And, anyhow, this one's going to be encored now. You can have the twenty-second—if there *is* any!"

William threw a wild glance about him, looking for other girls, but the tireless orchestra began to play the encore, and Miss Boke, who had been applauding, instantly cast herself upon his bosom. "Come on!" she cried. "Don't let's miss a second of it. It's just glorious!"

When the encore was finished she seized William's arm, and, mentioning that she'd left her fan upon the chair under the maple-tree, added, "Come on! Let's go get it *quick!*"

Under the maple-tree she fanned herself and talked of her love for dancing until the music sounded again. "Come on!" she cried, then. "Don't let's miss a second of it! It's just glorious!"

And grasping his arm, she propelled him toward the platform with a merry little rush.

So passed five dances. Long, long dances.

Likewise five encores. Long encores.

27. Marooned

AT EVERY POSSIBLE opportunity William hailed other girls with a hasty "M'av the next 'thyou?" but he was indeed unfortunate to have arrived so late.

The best he got was a promise of "the nineteenth—if there *is* any!"

After each dance Miss Boke conducted him back to the maple-tree, aloof from the general throng, and William found the intermissions almost equal to his martyrdoms upon the platform. But, as there was a barely perceptible balance in their favor, he collected some fragments of his broken spirit, when Miss Boke would have borne him to the platform for the sixth time, and begged to "sit this one out," alleging that he had "kind of turned his ankle, or something," he believed.

The cordial girl at once placed him upon the chair and gallantly procured another for herself. In her solicitude she sat close to him, looking fondly at his face, while William, though now and then rubbing his ankle for plausibility's sake, gazed at the platform with an expression which Gustave Doré would gratefully have found suggestive. William was conscious of a voice continually in action near him, but not of what it said. Miss Boke was telling him of the dancing "up at the lake" where she had spent the summer, and how much she had loved it, but William missed all that. Upon the many-colored platform the ineffable One drifted to and fro, back and forth; her little blonde head, in a golden net, glinting here and there like a bit of tinsel blowing across a flower-garden.

And when that dance and its encore were over she went to lean against a tree, while Wallace Banks fanned her, but she was so busy with Wallace that she did not notice William, though she passed near enough to waft a breath of violet scent to his wan nose. A fragment of her silver speech tinkled in his ear.

"Oh, Wallie Banks! Bid pid s'ant have Bruvva Josie-Joe's dance 'less Joe say so. Lola *mus'* be fair. Wallie mustn't—"

"That's that Miss Pratt," observed Miss Boke, following William's gaze with some interest. "You met her yet?"

"Yeh," said William.

"She's been visiting here all summer," Miss Boke informed him. "I was at a little tea this afternoon, and some of the girls said this Miss Pratt said she'd never *dream* of getting engaged to any man that didn't have seven hundred and fifty thousand dollars. I don't know if it's true or not, but I expect so. Anyway, they said they heard her say so."

William lifted his right hand from his ankle and passed it, time after time, across his damp forehead. He did not believe that Miss Pratt could have expressed herself in so mercenary a manner, but if she *had*—well, one fact in British history had so impressed him that he remembered it even after Examination: William Pitt, the younger, had been Prime Minister of England at twenty-one.

If an Englishman could do a thing like that, surely a bright, energetic young American needn't feel worried about seven hundred and fifty thousand dollars! And although William, at seventeen, had seldom possessed more than seven hundred and fifty cents, four long years must pass, and much could be done, before he would reach the age at which William Pitt attained the premiership—coincidentally a good, ripe, marriageable age. Still, seven hundred and fifty thousand dollars is a stiffish order, even allowing four long years to fill it; and undoubtedly Miss Boke's bit of gossip added somewhat to the already sufficient anxieties of William's evening.

"Up at the lake," Miss Boke chattered on, "we got to use the hotel dining-room for the hops. It's a floor a good deal like this floor is to-night—just about oily enough and as nice a floor as ever I danced on. We have awf'ly good times up at the lake. 'Course there aren't so many Men up there, like there are here to-night, and I *must* say I *am* glad to get a chance to dance with a Man again! I told you you'd dance all right, once we got started, and look at the way it's turned out: our steps just suit exactly! If I must say it, I could scarcely think of anybody I *ever* met I'd rather dance with. When anybody's step suits in with mine, that way, why, I *love* to dance straight through an evening with one person, the way we're doing."

Dimly, yet with strong repulsion, William perceived

that their interminable companionship had begun to affect Miss Boke with a liking for him. And as she chattered chummily on, revealing this increasing cordiality all the while—though her more obvious topics were dancing, dancing-floors, and "the lake"—the reciprocal sentiment roused in his breast was that of Sindbad the Sailor for the Old Man of the Sea.

He was unable to foresee a future apart from her; and when she informed him that she preferred his style of dancing to all other styles shown by the Men at this party, her thus singling him out for praise only emphasized, in his mind, that point upon which he was the most embittered.

"Yes!" he reflected. "It had to be *me!*" With all the crowd to choose from, Mrs. Parcher had to go and pick on *him!* All, all the others went about, free as air, flitting from girl to girl—girls that danced like girls! All, all except William, danced with Miss *Pratt!* What Miss Pratt had offered *him* was a choice between the thirty-second dance and the twenty-first extra. *That* was what he had to look forward to: the thirty-second reg'lar or the twenty-first extra!

Meanwhile, merely through eternity, he was sealed unto Miss Boke.

The tie that bound them oppressed him as if it had been an ill-omened matrimony, and he sat beside her like an unwilling old husband. All the while, Miss Boke had no appreciation whatever of her companion's real condition, and, when little, spasmodic, sinister changes appeared in his face (as they certainly did from time to time) she attributed them to pains in his ankle. However, William decided to discard his ankle, after they had "sat out" two dances on account of it. He decided that he preferred dancing, and said he guessed he must be better.

So they danced again—and again.

When the fourteenth dance came, about half an hour before midnight, they were still dancing together.

It was upon the conclusion of this fourteenth dance that Mr. Parcher mentioned to his wife a change in his feelings toward William. "I've been watching him," said Mr. Parcher, "and I never saw true misery show plainer. He's having a really horrible time. By George! I hate him, but

I've begun to feel kind of sorry for him! Can't you trot up somebody else, so he can get away from that fat girl?"

Mrs. Parcher shook her head in a discouraged way. "I've tried, and I've tried, and I've tried!" she said.

"Well, try again."

"I can't now." She waved her hand toward the rear of the house. Round the corner marched a short procession of Negroes, bearing trays; and the dancers were dispersing themselves to chairs upon the lawn "for refreshments."

"Well, do something," Mr. Parcher urged. "We don't want to find him in the cistern in the morning!"

Mrs. Parcher looked thoughtful, then brightened. "*I* know!" she said. "I'll make May and Lola and their partners come sit in this little circle of chairs here, and then I'll go and bring Willie and Miss Boke to sit with them. I'll give Willie the seat at Lola's left. You keep the chairs."

Straightway she sped upon her kindly errand. It proved successful, so successful, indeed, that without the slightest effort—without even a hint on her part—she brought not only William and his constant friend to sit in the circle with Miss Pratt, Miss Parcher and their escorts, but Mr. Bullitt, Mr. Watson, Mr. Banks, and three other young gentlemen as well. Nevertheless, Mrs. Parcher managed to carry out her plan, and, after a little display of firmness, saw William satisfactorily established in the chair at Miss Pratt's left.

At last, at last, he sat beside the fairy-like creature, and filled his lungs with infinitesimal particles of violet scent. More: he was no sooner seated than the little blonde head bent close to his; the golden net brushed his cheek. She whispered:

"No'ty ickle boy Batster! Lola's last night, an' ickle boy Batster fluttin'! Flut all night wif dray bid dirl!"

William made no reply.

There are occasions, infrequent, of course, when even a bachelor is not flattered by being accused of flirting. William's feelings toward Miss Boke had by this time come to such a pass that he regarded the charge of flirting with her as little less than an implication of grave mental deficiency. And well he remembered how Miss Pratt, beholding his subjugated gymnastics in the dance, had grown pink with laughter! But still the rose-leaf lips whispered:

"Lola saw! Lola saw bad boy Batster under dray bid tree fluttin' wif dray bid dirl. Fluttin' all night wif dray bid 'normous dirl!"

Her cruelty was all unwitting; she intended to rally him sweetly. But seventeen is deathly serious at such junctures, and William was in a sensitive condition. He made no reply in words. Instead, he drew himself up (from the waist, that is, because he was sitting) with a kind of proud dignity. And that was all.

"Oo tross?" whispered Lola.

He spake not.

" 'Twasn't my fault about dancing," she said. "Bad boy! What made you come so late?"

He maintained his silence and the accompanying icy dignity, whereupon she made a charming little pout.

"Oo be so tross," she said, "Lola talk to nice Man uvver side of her!"

With that she turned her back upon him and prattled merrily to the gentleman of sixteen upon her right.

Still and cold sat William. Let her talk to the Man at the other side of her as she would, and never so gaily, William knew that she was conscious every instant of the reproachful presence upon her left. And somehow these moments of quiet and melancholy dignity became the most satisfactory he had known that evening. For as he sat, so silent, so austere, and not yet eating, though a plate of chicken salad had been placed upon his lap, he began to feel that there was somewhere about him a mysterious superiority which set him apart from other people—and above them. This quality, indefinable and lofty, had carried him through troubles, that very night, which would have wrecked the lives of such simple fellows as Joe Bullitt and Johnnie Watson. And although Miss Pratt continued to make merry with the Man upon her right, it seemed to William that this was but outward show. He had a strange, subtle impression that the mysterious superiority which set him apart from others was becoming perceptible to her— that she was feeling it, too.

Alas! Such are the moments Fate seizes upon to play the clown!

Over the chatter and laughter of the guests rose a too

familiar voice. "Lemme he'p you to nice tongue samwich, lady. No'm? Nice green lettuce samwich, lady?"

Genesis!

"Nice tongue samwich, suh? Nice lettuce samwich, lady?" he could be heard vociferating—perhaps a little too much as if he had sandwiches for sale. "Lemme jes' lay this nice green lettuce samwich on you' plate fer you, lady."

His wide-spread hand bore the tray of sandwiches high overhead, for his style in waiting was florid, though polished. He walked with a faint, shuffling suggestion of a prance, a lissome pomposity adopted in obedience to the art-sense within him which bade him harmonize himself with occasions of state and fashion. His manner was the super-supreme expression of graciousness, but the graciousness was innocent, being but an affectation and nothing inward—for inwardly Genesis was humble. He was only pretending to be the kind of waiter he would like to be.

And because he was a new waiter he strongly wished to show familiarity with his duties—familiarity, in fact, with everything and everybody. This yearning, born of self-doubt, and intensified by a slight touch of gin, was beyond question the inspiration of his painful behavior when he came near the circle of chairs where sat Mr. and Mrs. Parcher, Miss Parcher, Miss Pratt, Miss Boke, Mr. Watson, Mr. Bullitt, others—and William.

"Nice tongue samwich, lady!" he announced, semi-cake-walking beneath his high-borne tray. "Nice green lettuce sam—" He came suddenly to a dramatic dead-stop as he beheld William sitting before him, wearing that strange new dignity, and Mr. Baxter's evening clothes. "Name o' goo'ness!" Genesis exclaimed, so loudly that every one looked up. "How in the livin' worl' *you* evuh come to git here? You' daddy sut'ny mus' 'a' weakened 'way down 'fo' he let you wear his low-cut ves' an' pants an' long-tail coat! I bet any man fifty cents you gone an' stole 'em out aftuh he done went to bed!"

And he burst into a wild, free African laugh.

At seventeen such things are not embarrassing; they are catastrophical. But, mercifully, catastrophes often produce a numbness in the victims. More as in a trance than actually William heard the outbreak of his young companions; and, during the quarter of an hour subsequent to Genesis's performance, the oft-renewed explosions of their mirth made but a kind of horrid buzzing in his ears. Like sounds borne from far away were the gaspings of Mr. and Mrs. Parcher, striving with all their strength to obtain mastery of themselves once more.

. . . A flourish of music challenged the dancers. Couples appeared upon the platform.

The dreadful supper was over.

The ineffable One, supremely pink, rose from her seat at William's side and moved toward the platform with the glowing Joe Bullitt. Then William, roused to action by this sight, sprang to his feet and took a step toward them. But it was only one weak step.

A warm and ample hand placed itself firmly inside the crook of his elbow. "Let's get started for this one before the floor gets all crowded up," said Miss Boke.

Miss Boke danced and danced with him; she danced him on—and on—and on—

At half past one the orchestra played "Home, Sweet Home." As the last bars sounded, a group of earnest young men who had surrounded the lovely guest of honor, talking vehemently, broke into loud shouts, embraced one another and capered variously over the lawn. Mr. Parcher beheld from a distance these manifestations, and then, with an astonishment even more profound, took note of the tragic William, who was running toward him, radiant— Miss Boke hovering futilely in the far background.

"What's all the hullabaloo?" Mr. Parcher inquired.

"Miss Pratt!" gasped William. "Miss Pratt!"

"Well, what about her?"

And upon receiving William's reply, Mr. Parcher might well have discerned behind it the invisible hand of an ironic but recompensing Providence making things even— taking from the one to give to the other.

"She's going to stay!" shouted the happy William. "She's promised to stay another week!"

And then, mingling with the sounds of rejoicing, there ascended to heaven the stricken cry of an elderly man plunging blindly into the house in search of his wife.

28. Rannie Kirsted

OBSERVING the monotonously proper behavior of the sun, man had an absurd idea and invented Time. Becoming still more absurd, man said, "So much shall be a day; such and such shall be a week. All weeks shall be the same length." Yet every baby knows better! How long for Johnnie Watson, for Joe Bullitt, for Wallace Banks—how long for William Sylvanus Baxter was the last week of Miss Pratt? No one can answer. How long was that week for Mr. Parcher? Again the mind is staggered.

Many people, of course, considered it to be a week of average size. Among these was Jane.

Throughout seven days which brought some tense moments to the Baxter household, Jane remained calm; and she was still calm upon the eighth morning as she stood in the front yard of her own place of residence, gazing steadily across the street. The object of her brave attention was an ample brick house, newly painted white after repairs and enlargements so inspiring to Jane's faculty for suggesting better ways of doing things, that the workmen had learned to address her, with a slight bitterness, as "Madam President."

Throughout the process of repair, and until the very last of the painting, Jane had considered this house to be as much her property as anybody's; for children regard as ownerless all vacant houses and all houses in course of construction or radical alteration. Nothing short of furniture—intimate furniture in considerable quantity—hints that the public is not expected. However, such a hint, or warning, was conveyed to Jane this morning, for two "express wagons" were standing at the curb with their backs impolitely toward the brick house; and powerful-voiced men went surging to and fro under fat arm-chairs, mahogany tables, disarticulated bedsteads, and baskets of china and glassware; while a harassed lady appeared in the outer doorway, from time to time, with gestures of lamentation and entreaty. Upon the sidewalk, between the wagons and the gate, was a broad wet spot, vaguely circular, with a partial circumference of broken glass and extinct goldfish.

Jane was forced to conclude that the brick house did belong to somebody, after all. Wherefore, she remained in her own yard, a steadfast spectator, taking nourishment into her system at regular intervals. This was beautifully automatic: in each hand she held a slice of bread, freely plastered over with butter, apple sauce, and powdered sugar; and when she had taken somewhat from the right hand, that hand slowly descended with its burden, while, simultaneously, the left began to rise, reaching the level of her mouth precisely at the moment when a little wave passed down her neck, indicating that the route was clear. Then, having made delivery, the left hand sank, while the right began to rise again. And, so well had custom trained Jane's members, never once did she glance toward either of these faithful hands or the food that it supported; her gaze was all the while free to remain upon the house across the way and the great doings before it.

After a while, something made her wide eyes grow wider almost to their utmost. Nay, the event was of that importance her mechanical hands ceased to move and stopped stock-still, the right half-way up, the left half-way down, as if because of sudden motor trouble within Jane. Her mouth was equally affected, remaining open at a visible crisis in the performance of its duty. These were the tokens of her agitation upon beholding the removal of a dolls' house from one of the wagons. This dolls' house was at least five feet high, of proportionate breadth and depth; the customary absence of a façade disclosing an interior of four luxurious floors, with stairways, fireplaces, and wall-paper. Here was a mansion wherein doll-duchesses, no less, must dwell.

Straightway, a little girl ran out of the open doorway of the brick house and, with a self-importance concentrated to the point of shrewishness, began to give orders concerning the disposal of her personal property, which included (as she made clear) not only the dolls' mansion, but also three dolls' trunks and a packing-case of fair size. She was a thin little girl, perhaps half a year younger than Jane; and she was as soiled, particularly in respect to hands, brow, chin, and the knees of white stockings, as could be expected of any busybodyish person of nine or ten whose mother is house-moving. But she was gifted—if we choose to put the matter in the hopeful, sweeter way—she was gifted with an unusually loud and shrill voice; and she made herself heard over the strong-voiced men to such emphatic effect that one of the latter, with the dolls' mansion upon his back, paused in the gateway to acquaint her with his opinion that of all the bossy little girls he had ever seen, heard, or heard of, she was the bossiest.

"*The* worst!" he added.

The little girl across the street was of course instantly aware of Jane, though she pretended not to be; and from the first her self-importance was in large part assumed for the benefit of the observer. After a momentary silence, due to her failure to think of any proper response to the workman who so pointedly criticized her, she resumed the peremptory direction of her affairs. She ran in and out of the house, her brow dark with frowns, her shoulders elevated; and by every means at her disposal she urged her audience to behold the frightful responsibilities of one who must keep a thousand things in her head at once, and yet be ready for decisive action at any instant.

There may have been one weakness in this strong performance: the artistic sincerity of it was a little discredited by the increasing frequency with which the artist took note of her effect. During each of her most impressive moments, she flashed, from the far corner of her eye, two questions at Jane: "How about *that* one? Are you still watching Me?"

Then, apparently in the very midst of her cares, she suddenly and without warning ceased to boss, walked out into the street, halted, and stared frankly at Jane.

Jane had begun her automatic feeding again. She continued it, meanwhile seriously returning the stare of the new neighbor. For several minutes this mutual calm and inoffensive gaze was protracted; then Jane, after swallowing the last morsel of her supplies, turned her head away and looked at a tree. The little girl, into whose eyes some wistfulness had crept, also turned her head and looked at a tree. After a while, she advanced to the curb on Jane's side of the street, and, swinging her right foot, allowed it to kick the curbstone repeatedly.

Jane came out to the sidewalk and began to kick one of the fence-pickets.

"You see that ole fatty?" asked the little girl, pointing to one of the workmen, thus sufficiently identified.

"Yes."

"That's the one broke the goldfish," said the little girl. There was a pause during which she continued to scuff the curbstone with her shoe, Jane likewise scuffing the fence-picket. "I'm goin' to have papa get him arrested," added the stranger.

"My papa got two men arrested once," Jane said, calmly. "Two or three."

The little girl's eyes, wandering upward, took note of Jane's papa's house, and of a fierce young gentleman framed in an open window up-stairs. He was seated, wore ink upon his forehead, and tapped his teeth with a red penholder.

"Who is that?" she asked.

"It's Willie."

"Is it your papa?"

"*No-o-o-o!*" Jane exclaimed. "It's *Willie!*"

"Oh," said the little girl, apparently satisfied.

Each now scuffed less energetically with her shoe; feet slowed down; so did conversation, and, for a time, Jane and the stranger wrapped themselves in stillness, though there may have been some silent communing between them. Then the new neighbor placed her feet far apart and leaned backward upon nothing, curving her front outward and her remarkably flexible spine inward until a profile view of her was grandly semicircular.

Jane watched her attentively, but without comment. However, no one could have doubted that the processes of acquaintance were progressing favorably.

"Let's go in our yard," said Jane.

The little girl straightened herself with a slight gasp, and accepted the invitation. Side by side, the two passed through the open gate, walked gravely forth upon the lawn, and halted, as by common consent. Jane thereupon placed her feet wide apart and leaned backward upon nothing, attempting the feat in contortion just performed by the stranger.

"Look," she said. "Look at *me!*"

But she lacked the other's genius, lost her balance, and fell. Born persistent, she immediately got to her feet and made fresh efforts.

"No! Look at *me!*" the little girl cried, becoming semicircular again. "This is the way. I call it 'puttin' your stummick out o' joint.' You haven't got yours out far enough."

"Yes, I have," said Jane, gasping.

"Well, to do it right, you must *walk* that way. As soon as you get your stummick out o' joint, you must begin an' walk. Look! Like this." And the little girl, having achieved a state of such convexity that her braided hair almost touched the ground behind her, walked successfully in that singular attitude.

"I'm walkin'," Jane protested, her face not quite upside down. "Look! *I'm* walkin' that way, too. My stummick——"

There came an outraged shout from above, and a fierce countenance, stained with ink, protruded from the window.

"Jane!"

"What?"

"Stop that! Stop putting your stomach out in front of you like that! It's disgraceful!"

Both young ladies, looking rather oppressed, resumed the perpendicular. "Why doesn't he like it?" the stranger asked in a tone of pure wonder.

"I don't know," said Jane. "He doesn't like much of anything. He's seventeen years old."

After that, the two stared moodily at the ground for a little while, chastened by the severe presence above; then Jane brightened.

"*I* know!" she exclaimed, cozily. "'Let's play callers. Right here by this bush'll be my house. You come to call on me, an' we'll talk about our chuldren. You be Mrs. Smith an' I'm Mrs. Jones." And in the character of a hospitable matron she advanced graciously toward the new neighbor. "Why, my dear Mrs. *Smith,* come right *in!* I *thought* you'd call this morning. I want to tell you about my lovely little daughter. She's only ten years old, an' says the brightest *things!* You really must——"

But here Jane interrupted herself abruptly, and, hopping behind the residential bush, peeped over it, not at Mrs. Smith, but at a boy of ten or eleven who was passing along the sidewalk. Her expression was gravely interested, somewhat complacent; and Mrs. Smith was not so lacking in perception that she failed to understand how completely —for the time being, at least—calling was suspended.

The boy whistled briskly, "My country, 'tis of thee," and though his knowledge of the air failed him when he finished the second line, he was not disheartened, but began at the beginning again, continuing repeatedly after this fashion to offset monotony by patriotism. He whistled loudly; he walked with ostentatious intent to be at some heavy affair in the distance; his ears were red. He looked neither to the right nor to the left.

That is, he looked neither to the right nor to the left until he had passed the Baxters' fence. But when he had gone as far as the upper corner of the fence beyond, he turned his head and looked back, without any expression— except that of a whistler—at Jane. And thus, still whistling "My country, 'tis of thee," and with blank pink face over his shoulder, he proceeded until he was out of sight.

"Who was that boy?" the new neighbor then inquired.

"It's Freddie," said Jane, placidly. "He's in our Sunday-school. He's in love of me."

"JANE!"

Again the outraged and ink-stained countenance glared down from the window.

"What do you want?" Jane asked.

"What you *mean* talking about such things?" William demanded. "In all my life I never heard anything as disgusting! Shame on you!"

The little girl from across the street looked upward thoughtfully. "He's mad," she remarked, and, regardless of Jane's previous information, "It *is* your papa, isn't it?" she insisted.

"No!" said Jane, testily. "I told you five times it's my brother Willie."

"Oh," said the little girl, and, grasping, the fact that William's position was, in dignity and authority, negligible, compared with that which she had persisted in imagining, she felt it safe to tint her upward gaze with disfavor. "He acts kind of crazy," she murmured.

"He's in love of Miss Pratt," said Jane. "She's goin'

away to-day. She said she'd go before, but to-day she *is!*
Mr. Parcher, where she visits, he's almost dead, she's
stayed so long. She's awful, I think."

William, to whom all was audible, shouted, hoarsely,
"I'll see to *you!*" and disappeared from the window.

"Will he come down here?" the little girl asked, taking
a step toward the gate.

"No. He's just gone to call mamma. All she'll do'll be
to tell us to go play somewheres else. Then we can go talk
to Genesis."

"Who?"

"Genesis. He's puttin' a load of coal in the cellar window with a shovel. He's nice."

"What's he put the coal in the window for?"

"He's a colored man," said Jane.

"Shall we go talk to him now?"

"No," Jane said, thoughtfully. "Let's be playin' callers
when mamma comes to tell us to go 'way. What was your
name?"

"Rannie."

"No, it wasn't."

"It is too, Rannie," the little girl insisted. "My whole
name's Mary Randolph Kirsted, but my short name's
Rannie."

Jane laughed. "What a funny name!" she said. "I didn't
mean your real name; I meant your callers' name. One of
us was Mrs. Jones, and one was—"

"I want to be Mrs. Jones," said Rannie.

"Oh, my *dear* Mrs. Jones," Jane began at once, "I want
to tell you about my lovely chuldren. I have two, one only
seven years old, and the other—"

"Jane!" called Mrs. Baxter from William's window.

"Yes'm?"

"You must go somewhere else to play. Willie's trying
to work at his studies up here, and he says you've disturbed
him very much."

"Yes'm."

The obedient Jane and her friend turned to go, and as
they went, Miss Mary Randolph Kirsted allowed her uplifted eyes to linger with increased disfavor upon William,
who appeared beside Mrs. Baxter at the window.

"I tell you what let's do," Rannie suggested in a lowered voice. "He got so fresh with us, an' made your mother
come, an' all, let's—let's—"

She hesitated.

"Let's what?" Jane urged her, in an eager whisper.

"Let's think up somep'n he won't like—an' *do* it!"

They disappeared round a corner of the house, their
heads close together.

29. "Don't Forget"

UP-STAIRS, Mrs. Baxter moved to the door of her son's
room, pretending to be unconscious of the gaze he maintained upon her. Mustering courage to hum a little tune
and affecting inconsequence, she had nearly crossed the
threshold when he said, sternly:

"And this is all you intend to say to that child?"

"Why, yes, Willie."

"And yet I told you what she said!" he cried. "I told
you I *heard* her stand there and tell that dirty-faced little
girl how that idiot boy that's always walkin' past here four
or five times a day, whistling and looking back, was in
'love of' her! Ye gods! What kind of person will she grow
up into if you don't punish her for havin' ideas like that
at her age?"

Mrs. Baxter regarded him mildly, not replying, and he
went on, with loud indignation:

"I never heard of such a thing! That Worm walkin' past
here four or five times a day just to look at *Jane!* And her
standing there, calmly tellin' that sooty-faced little girl,
'He's in love of me'! Why, it's enough to sicken a man!
Honestly, if I had my way, I'd see that both she and that
little Freddie Banks got a first-class whipping!"

"Don't you think, Willie," said Mrs. Baxter—"don't you
think that, considering the rather noncommittal method
of Freddie's courtship, you are suggesting extreme measures?"

"Well, *she* certainly ought to be punished!" he insisted,
and then, with a reversal to agony, he shuddered. "That's
the least of it!" he cried. "It's the insulting things you

always allow her to say of one of the noblest girls in the United States—*that's* what counts! On the very last day— yes, almost the last hour—that Miss Pratt's in this town, you let your only daughter stand there and speak disre- spectfully of her—and then all you do is tell her to 'go and play somewhere else'! I don't understand your way of bringing up a child," he declared, passionately. "I do *not!*"

"There, there, Willie," Mrs. Baxter said. "You're all wrought up—"

"I am NOT wrought up!" shouted William. "Why should I be charged with—"

"Now, now!" she said. "You'll feel better to-morrow."

"What do you mean by that?" he demanded, breathing deeply.

For reply she only shook her head in an odd little way, and in her parting look at him there was something at once compassionate, amused, and reassuring.

"You'll be all right, Willie," she said, softly, and closed the door.

Alone, William lifted clenched hands in a series of tu- multuous gestures at the ceiling; then he moaned and sank into a chair at his writing-table. Presently a comparative calm was restored to him, and with reverent fingers he took from a drawer a one-pound box of candy, covered with white tissue-paper, girdled with blue ribbon. He set the box gently beside him upon the table; then from beneath a large, green blotter drew forth some scribbled sheets. These he placed before him, and, taking infinite pains with his handwriting, slowly copied:

DEAR LOLA—I presume when you are reading these lines it will be this afternoon and you will be on the train moving rapidly away from this old place here farther and farther from it all. As I sit here at my old desk and look back upon it all while I am writing this farewell letter I hope when you are reading it you also will look back upon it all and think of one you called (Alias) Little Boy Baxter. As I sit here this morn- ing that you are going away at last I look back and I cannot remember any summer in my whole life which has been like this summer, because a great change has come over me this summer. If you would like to know what this means it was something like I said when John Watson got there yesterday afternoon and interupted what I said. May you enjoy this candy and think of the giver. I will put something in with this letter. It is something maybe you would like to have and in exchange I would give all I possess for one of you if you would send it to me when you get home. Please do this for now my heart is braking.

Yours sincerely,
WILLIAM S. BAXTER (ALIAS) LITTLE BOY BAXTER.

William opened the box of candy and placed the letter upon the top layer of chocolates. Upon the letter he placed a small photograph (wrapped in tissue-paper) of himself. Then, with a pair of scissors, he trimmed an oblong of white cardboard to fit into the box. Upon this piece of cardboard he laboriously wrote, copying from a tortured, inky sheet before him:

IN DREAM

BY WILLIAM S. BAXTER

The sunset light
Fades into night
But never will I forget
The smile that haunts me yet
Through the future four long years
I hope you will remember with tears
Whate'er my rank or station
Whilst receiving my education
Though far away you seem
I will see thee in dream.

He placed his poem between the photograph and the letter, closed the box, and tied the tissue-paper about it again with the blue ribbon. Throughout these rites (they were rites both in spirit and in manner) he was subject to little catchings of the breath, half gulp, half sigh. But the dolorous tokens passed, and he sat with elbows upon the table, his chin upon his hands, reverie in his eyes. Tragedy had given way to gentler pathos—beyond question, something had measurably soothed him. Possibly, even in this hour preceding the hour of parting, he knew a little of that proud amazement which any poet is entitled to feel over each new lyric miracle just wrought.

Perhaps he was helped, too, by wondering what Miss

Pratt would think of him when she read "In Dream," on the train that afternoon. For reasons purely intuitive, and decidedly without foundation in fact, he was satisfied that no rival farewell poem would be offered her, and so it may be that he thought "In Dream" might show her at last, in one blaze of light, what her eyes had sometimes fleetingly intimated she did perceive in part—the difference between William and such every-day, rather well-meaning, fairly good-hearted people as Joe Bullitt, Wallace Banks, Johnnie Watson, and others. Yes, when she came to read "In Dream," and to "look back upon it all," she would surely know—at last!

And then, when the future four long years (while receiving his education) had passed, he would go to her. He would go to her, and she would take him by the hand, and lead him to her father, and say, "Father, this is William."

But William would turn to her, and, with the old, dancing light in his eyes, "No, Lola," he would say, "not William, but Ickle Boy Baxter! Always and always, just that for you; oh, my dear!"

And then, as in story and film and farce and the pleasanter kinds of drama, her father would say, with kindly raillery, "Well, when you two young people get *through,* you'll find me in the library, where I have a pretty good *business* proposition to lay before *you,* young man!"

And when the white-waistcoated, white-sideburned old man had, chuckling, left the room, William would slowly lift his arms; but Lola would move back from him a step—only a step—and after laying a finger archly upon her lips to check him, "Wait, sir!" she would say. "I have a question to ask you, sir!"

"What question, Lola?"

"*This* question, sir!" she would reply. "In all that sum·mer, sir, so long ago, why did you never tell me what you *were,* until I had gone away and it was too late to show you what I felt? Ah, Ickle Boy Baxter, I never understood until I looked back upon it all, after I had read 'In Dream,' on the train that day! *Then* I *knew!*"

"And now, Lola?" William would say. "Do you understand me, *now?*"

Shyly she would advance the one short step she had put between them, while he, with lifted, yearning arms, this time destined to no disappointment—

At so vital a moment did Mrs. Baxter knock at his door and consoling reverie cease to minister unto William. Out of the rosy sky he dropped, falling miles in an instant, landing with a bump. He started, placed the sacred box out of sight, and spoke gruffly.

"What do you want?"

"I'm not coming in, Willie," said his mother. "I just wanted to know—I thought maybe you were looking out of the window and noticed where those children went."

"What children?"

"Jane and that little girl from across the street—Kirsted, her name must be."

"No. I did not."

"I just wondered," Mrs. Baxter said, timidly. "Genesis thinks he heard the little Kirsted girl telling Jane she had plenty of money for carfare. He thinks they went somewhere on a street-car. I thought maybe you noticed wheth—"

"I told you I did not."

"All right," she said, placatively. "I didn't mean to bother you, dear."

Following this there was a silence; but no sound of receding footsteps indicated Mrs. Baxter's departure from the other side of the closed door.

"Well, what you *want?*" William shouted.

"Nothing—nothing at all," said the compassionate voice. "I just thought I'd have lunch a little later than usual; ot till half past one. That is if—well, I thought probably you meant to go to the station to see Miss Pratt off on the one-o'clock train."

Even so friendly an interest as this must have appeared to the quivering William an intrusion in his affairs, for he demanded, sharply:

"How'd you find out she's going at one o'clock?"

"Why—why, Jane mentioned it," Mrs. Baxter replied, with obvious timidity. "Jane said—"

She was interrupted by the loud, desperate sound of William's fist smiting his writing-table, so sensitive was his condition. "This is just unbearable!" he cried. "Nobody's business is safe from that child!"

"Why, Willie, I don't see how it matters if—"

He uttered a cry. "No! Nothing matters! Nothing matters at all! Do you s'pose I want that child, with her insults, discussing when Miss Pratt is or is not going away? Don't you know there are *some* things that have no business to be talked about by every Tom, Dick, and Harry?"

"Yes, dear," she said. "I understand, of course. Jane only told me she met Mr. Parcher on the street, and he mentioned that Miss Pratt was going at one o'clock to-day. That's all I—"

"You say you understand," he wailed, shaking his head drearily at the closed door, "and yet, even on such a day as this, you keep *talking!* Can't you see sometimes there's times when a person can't stand to—"

"Yes, Willie," Mrs. Baxter interposed, hurriedly. "Of course! I'm going now. I have to go hunt up those children, anyway. You try to be back for lunch at half past one—and don't worry, dear; you really *will* be all right!

She departed, a sigh from the abyss following her as she went down the hall. Her comforting words meant nothing pleasant to her son, who felt that her optimism was out of place and tactless. He had no intention to be "all right, ' and he desired nobody to interfere with his misery.

He went to his mirror, and, gazing long—long and piercingly—at the William there limned, enacted, almost unconsciously, a little scene of parting. The look of suffering upon the mirrored face slowly altered; in its place came one still sorrowful, but tempered with sweet indulgence.

He stretched out his hand, as if he set it upon a head at about the height of his shoulder.

"Yes, it may mean—it may mean forever!" he said in a low, tremulous voice. "Little girl, we *must* be brave!"

And the while his eyes gazed into the mirror, they became expressive of a momentary pleased surprise, as if, even in the arts of sorrow, he found himself doing better than he knew. But his sorrow was none the less genuine because of that.

Then he noticed the ink upon his forehead, and went away to wash. When he returned he did an unusual thing

—he brushed his coat thoroughly, removing it for this special purpose. After that, he earnestly combed and brushed his hair, and retied his tie. Next, he took from a drawer two clean handkerchiefs. He placed one in his breast pocket, part of the colored border of the handkerchief being left on exhibition; and with the other he carefully wiped his shoes. Finally, he sawed it back and forth across them, and, with a sigh, languidly dropped it upon the floor, where it remained.

Returning to the mirror, he again brushed his hair—he went so far, this time, as to brush his eyebrows, which seemed not much altered by the operation. Suddenly, he was deeply affected by something seen in the glass.

"By George!" he exclaimed aloud.

Seizing a small hand-mirror, he placed it in juxtaposition to his right eye, and closely studied his left profile as exhibited in the larger mirror. Then he examined his right profile, subjecting it to a like scrutiny—emotional, yet attentive and prolonged.

"By George!" he exclaimed, again. "By George!"

He had made a discovery. There was a downy shadow upon his upper lip. What he had just found out was that this down could be seen projecting beyond the line of his lip, like a tiny nimbus. It could be seen in *profile*.

"By *George!*" William exclaimed.

He was still occupied with the two mirrors when his mother again tapped softly upon his door, rousing him as from a dream (brief but engaging) to the heavy realities of that day.

"What you want now?"

"I won't come in," said Mrs. Baxter. "I just came to see."

"See what?"

"I wondered—I thought perhaps you needed something. I knew your watch was out of order—"

"F'r 'eaven's sake what if it is?"

She offered a murmur of placative laughter as her apology, and said: "Well, I just thought I'd tell you—because if you did intend going to the station, I thought you probably wouldn't want to miss it and get there too late. I've got your hat here—all nicely brushed for you. It's nearly twenty minutes of one, Willie."

"*What?*"

"Yes, it is. It's—"

She had no further speech with him.

Breathless, William flung open his door, seized the hat, racketed down the stairs, and out through the front door, which he left open behind him. Eight seconds later he returned at a gallop, hurtled up the stairs and into his room, emerging instantly with something concealed under his coat. Replying incoherently to his mother's inquiries, he fell down the stairs as far as the landing, used the impetus thus given as a help to greater speed for the rest of the descent—and passed out of hearing.

Mrs. Baxter sighed, and went to a window in her own room, and looked out.

William was already more than half-way to the next corner, where there was a car-line that ran to the station; but the distance was not too great for Mrs. Baxter to comprehend the nature of the symmetrical white parcel now carried in his right hand. Her face became pensive as she gazed after the flying slender figure—there came to her mind the recollection of a seventeen-year-old boy who had brought a box of candy (a small one, like William's) to the station, once, long ago, when she had been visiting in another town. For just a moment she thought of that boy she had known, so many years ago, and a smile cam⁑ vaguely upon her lips. She wondered what kind of a woman he had married, and how many children he had—and whether he was a widower——

The fleeting recollection passed; she turned from the window and shook her head, puzzled.

"Now where on earth could Jane and that little Kirsted girl have gone?" she murmured.

... At the station, William, descending from the streetcar, found that he had six minutes to spare. Reassured of so much by the great clock in the station tower, he entered the building, and, with calm and dignified steps, crossed the large waiting-room. Those calm and dignified steps were taken by feet which little betrayed the tremulousness of the knees above them. Moreover, though William's face was red, his expression—cold, and concentrated upon high matters—scorned the stranger, and warned the lower classes that the mission of this bit of gentry was not to them.

With but one sweeping and repellent glance over the canaille present, he made sure that the person he sought was not in the waiting-room. Therefore he turned to the doors which gave admission to the tracks, but before he went out he paused for an instant of displeasure. Hard by the doors stood a telephone-booth, and from inside this booth a little girl of nine or ten was peering eagerly out at William, her eyes just above the lower level of the glass window in the door.

Even a prospect thus curtailed revealed her as a smudged and dusty little girl; and, evidently, her mother must have been preoccupied with some important affair that day; but to William she suggested nothing familiar. As his glance happened to encounter hers, the peering eyes grew instantly brighter with excitement—she exposed her whole countenance at the window, and impulsively made a face at him.

William had not the slightest recollection of ever having seen her before.

He gave her one stern look and went on; though he felt that something ought to be done. The affair was not a personal one—patently, this was a child who played about the station and amused herself by making faces at everybody who passed the telephone-booth—still, the authorities ought not to allow it. People did not come to the station to be insulted.

Three seconds later the dusty-faced little girl and her *moue* were sped utterly from William's mind. For, as the doors swung together behind him, he saw Miss Pratt. There were no gates nor iron barriers to obscure the view; there was no train-shed to darken the air. She was at some distance, perhaps two hundred feet, along the tracks, where the sleeping-cars of the long train would stop. But there she stood, mistakable for no other on this wide earth!

There she stood—a glowing little figure in the hazy September sunlight, her hair an amber mist under the adorable little hat; a small bunch of violets at her waist; a larger bunch of fragrant but less expensive sweet peas in her right hand; half a dozen pink roses in her left; her little dog Flopit in the crook of one arm; and a one-pound box of candy in the crook of the other—ineffable, radiant, starry, there she stood!

Near her also stood her young hostess, and Wallace

Banks, Johnnie Watson, and Joe Bullitt—three young gentlemen in a condition of solemn tensity. Miss Parcher saw William as he emerged from the station building, and she waved her parasol in greeting, attracting the attention of the others to him, so that they all turned and stared.

Seventeen sometimes finds it embarrassing (even in a state of deep emotion) to walk two hundred feet, or there-about, toward a group of people who steadfastly watch the long approach. And when the watching group contains the lady of all the world before whom one wishes to appear most debonair, and contains not only her, but several rivals, who, though *fairly* good-hearted, might hardly be trusted to neglect such an opportunity to murmur something jocular about one—No, it cannot be said that William appeared to be wholly without self-consciousness.

In fancy he had prophesied for this moment something utterly different. He had seen himself parting from her, the two alone as within a cloud. He had seen himself gently placing his box of candy in her hands, some of his fingers just touching some of hers and remaining thus lightly in contact to the very last. He had seen himself bending toward the sweet blonde head to murmur the few last words of simple eloquence, while her eyes lifted in mysterious appeal to his—and he had put no other figures, not even Miss Parcher's, into this picture.

Parting is the most dramatic moment in young love; and if there is one time when the lover wishes to present a lofty but graceful appearance it is at the last. To leave with the loved one, for recollection, a final picture of manly dignity in sorrow—that, above all things, is the lover's desire. And yet, even at the beginning of William's two-hundred-foot advance (later so much discussed) he felt the heat surging over his ears, and, as he took off his hat, thinking to wave it jauntily in reply to Miss Parcher, he made but an uncertain gesture of it, so that he wished he had not tried it. Moreover, he had covered less than a third of the distance, when he became aware that all of the group were staring at him with unaccountable eagerness, and had begun to laugh.

William felt certain that his attire was in no way disordered, nor in itself a cause for laughter—all of these people had often seen him dressed as he was to-day, and had preserved their gravity. But, in spite of himself, he took off his hat again, and looked to see if anything about it might explain this mirth, which, at his action, increased. Nay, the laughter began to be shared by strangers; and some set down their hand-luggage for greater pleasure in what they saw.

William's inward state became chaotic.

He tried to smile carelessly, to prove his composure, but he found that he had lost almost all control over his features. He had no knowledge of his actual expression except that it hurt him. In desperation he fell back upon hauteur; he managed to frown, and walked proudly. At that they laughed the more, Wallace Banks rudely pointing again and again at William; and not till the oncoming sufferer reached a spot within twenty feet of these delighted people did he grasp the significance of Wallace's repeated gesture of pointing. Even then he understood only when the gesture was supplemented by half-articulate shouts:

"Behind you! Look *behind* you!"

The stung youth turned.

There, directly behind him, he beheld an exclusive little procession consisting of two damsels in single file, the first soiled with house-moving, the second with apple sauce.

For greater caution they had removed their shoes; and each damsel, as she paraded, dangled from each far-extended hand a shoe. And both damsels, whether beneath apple sauce or dust smudge, were suffused with the rapture of a great mockery.

They were walking with their stummicks out o' joint.

At sight of William's face they squealed. They turned and ran. They got themselves out of sight.

Simultaneously, the air filled with solid thunder and the pompous train shook the ground. Ah, woe's the word! This was the thing that meant to bear away the golden girl and honeysuckle of the world—meant to, and would, not abating one iron second!

Now a porter had her hand-bag.

Dear Heaven! to be a porter—yes, a colored one! What of that, *now?* Just to be a simple porter, and journey with her to the far, strange pearl among cities whence she had come!

The gentle porter bowed her toward the steps of his car;

but first she gave Flopit into the hands of May Parcher, for a moment, and whispered a word to Wallace Banks; then to Joe Bullitt; then to Johnnie Watson—then she ran to William.

She took his hand.

"Don't forget!" she whispered. "Don't forget Lola!" He stood stock-still. His face was blank, his hand limp. He said nothing.

She enfolded May Parcher, kissed her devotedly; then, with Flopit once more under her arm, she ran and jumped upon the steps just as the train began to move. She stood there, on the lowest step, slowly gliding away from them, and in her eyes there was a sparkle of tears, left, it may be, from her laughter at poor William's pageant with Jane and Rannie Kirsted—or, it may be, not.

She could not wave to her friends, in answer to their gestures of farewell, for her arms were too full of Flopit and roses and candy and sweet peas; but she kept nodding to them in a way that showed them how much she thanked them for being sorry she was going—and made it clear that she was sorry, too, and loved them all.

"Good-by!" she meant.

Faster she glided; the engine passed from sight round a curve beyond a culvert, but for a moment longer they could see the little figure upon the steps—and, to the very last glimpse they had of her, the small, golden head was still nodding "Good-by!" Then those steps whereon she stood passed in their turn beneath the culvert, and they saw her no more.

Lola Pratt was gone!

Wet-eyed, her young hostess of the long summer turned away, and stumbled against William. "Why, Willie Baxter!" she cried, blinking at him.

The last car of the train had rounded the curve and disappeared, but William was still waving farewell—not with his handkerchief, but with a symmetrical, one-pound parcel, wrapped in white tissue-paper, girdled with blue ribbon.

"Never mind!" said May Parcher. "Let's all walk uptown together, and talk about her on the way, and we'll go by the express-office, and you can send your candy to her by express, Willie."

30. The Bride-to-Be

IN THE SMALLISH house which all summer long, from
morning until late at night, had resounded with the voices
of young people, echoing their songs, murmurous with
their theories of love, or vibrating with their glee, sometimes shaking all over during their more boisterous moods
—in that house, now comparatively so vacant, the proprietor stood and breathed deep breaths.

"Hah!" he said, inhaling and exhaling the air profoundly.
His wife was upon the porch outside, sewing. The
silence was deep. He seemed to listen to it—to listen with
gusto; his face slowly broadening, a pinkish tint over-
spreading it. His flaccid cheeks appeared to fill, to grow
firm again, a smile finally widening them.

"Hah!" he breathed, sonorously. He gave himself several
resounding slaps upon the chest, then went out to the
porch and sat in a rocking-chair near his wife. He spread
himself out expansively. "My Glory!" he said. "I believe
I'll take off my coat! I haven't had my coat off, outside of
my own room, all summer. I believe I'll take a vacation!
By George, I believe I'll stay home this afternoon!"

"That's nice," said Mrs. Parcher.

"Hah!" he said. "My Glory! I believe I'll take off my
shoes!"

And, meeting no objection, he proceeded to carry out
this plan.

"Hah-*ah!*" he said, and placed his stockinged feet upon
the railing, where a number of vines, running upon strings,
made a screen between the porch and the street. He lit a
large cigar. "Well, well!" he said. "That tastes good! If
this keeps on, I'll be in as good shape as I was last spring
before you know it!" Leaning far back in the rocking-chair,
his hands behind his head, he smoked with fervor; but
suddenly he jumped in a way which showed that his nerves
were far from normal. His feet came to the floor with a
thump, he jerked the cigar out of his mouth, and turned a
face of consternation upon his wife.

"What's the matter?"

"Suppose," said Mr. Parcher, huskily—"suppose she missed her train."

Mrs. Parcher shook her head.

"Think not?" he said brightening. "I ordered the livery-stable to have a carriage here in lots of time."

"They did," said Mrs. Parcher, severely. "About five dollars' worth."

"Well, I don't mind that," he returned, putting his feet up again. "After all, she was a mighty fine little girl in her way. The only trouble with me was that crowd of boys; —having to listen to them certainly liked to killed me, and I believe if she'd stayed just one more day I'd been a goner! Of all the damn boys I ever—" He paused, listening.

"Mr. Parcher!" a youthful voice repeated.

He rose, and, separating two of the vines which screened the end of the porch from the street, looked out. Two small maidens had paused upon the sidewalk, and were peering over the picket fence.

"Mr. Parcher," said Jane, as soon as his head appeared between the vines—"Mr. Parcher, Miss Pratt's gone. She's gone away on the cars."

"You think so?" he asked, gravely.

"We saw her," said Jane. "Rannie an' I were there. Willie was goin' to chase us, I guess, but we went in the baggage-room behind trunks, an' we saw her go. She got on the cars, an' it went with her in it. Honest, she's gone away, Mr. Parcher."

Before speaking, Mr. Parcher took a long look at this telepathic child. In his fond eyes she was a marvel and a darling.

"Well— *thank* you, Jane!" he said.

Jane, however, had turned her head and was staring at the corner, which was out of his sight.

"Oo-oo-ooh!" she murmured.

"What's the trouble, Jane?"

"Willie!" she said. "It's Willie an' that Joe Bullitt, an' Johnnie Watson, an' Mr. Wallace Banks. They're with Miss May Parcher. They're comin' right here!"

Mr. Parcher gave forth a low moan, and turned pathetically to his wife, but she cheered him with a laugh.

"They've only walked up from the station with May," she said. "They won't come in. You'll see!"

Relieved, Mr. Parcher turned again to speak to Jane—but she was not there. He caught but a glimpse of her, running up the street as fast as she could, hand in hand with her companion.

"Run, Rannie, run!" panted Jane. "I got to get home an' tell mamma about it before Willie. I bet I ketch Hail Columbia, anyway, when he does get there!"

And in this she was not mistaken: she caught Hail Columbia. It lasted all afternoon.

It was still continuing after dinner, that evening, when an oft-repeated yodel, followed by a shrill-wailed, "Jane-ee! Oh, Jane-*nee*-ee!" brought her to an open window downstairs. In the early dusk she looked out upon the washed face of Rannie Kirsted, who stood on the lawn below.

"Come on out, Janie. Mamma says I can stay outdoors an' play till half past eight."

Jane shook her head. "I can't. I can't go outside the house till to-morrow. It's because we walked after Willie with our stummicks out o' joint."

"Pshaw!" Rannie cried, lightly. "My mother didn't do anything to me for that."

"Well, nobody told her on you," said Jane, reasonably.

"Can't you come out at all?" Rannie urged. "Go ask your mother. Tell her—"

"How can I," Janie inquired, with a little heat, "when she isn't here to ask? She's gone out to play cards—she and papa."

Rannie swung her foot. "Well," she said, "I guess I haf to find *some*p'n to do! G' night!"

With head bowed in thought she moved away, disappearing into the gray dusk, while Jane, on her part, left the window and went to the open front door. Conscientiously, she did not cross the threshold, but restrained herself to looking out. On the steps of the porch sat William, alone, his back toward the house.

"Willie?" said Jane, softly; and as he made no response, she lifted her voice a little. "Will-ee!"

"Whatchwant!" he grunted, not moving.

"Willie, I told mamma I was sorry I made you feel so bad."

"All right!" he returned, curtly.

"Well, when I haf to go to bed, Willie," she said,

"mamma told me because I made you feel bad I haf to go up-stairs by myself, to-night."

She paused, seeming to hope that he would say something, but he spake not.

"Willie, I don't haf to go for a while yet, but when I do—maybe in about a half an hour—I wish you'd come stand at the foot of the stairs till I get up there. The light's lit up-stairs, but down around here it's kind of dark."

He did not answer.

"Will you, Willie?"

"Oh, all *right!*" he said.

This contented her, and she seated herself so quietly upon the floor, just inside the door, that he ceased to be aware of her, thinking she had gone away. He sat staring vacantly into the darkness, which had come on with that abruptness which begins to be noticeable in September. His elbows were on his knees, and his body was sunk far forward in an attitude of desolation.

The small noises of the town—that town so empty to-night—fell upon his ears mockingly. It seemed to him incredible that so hollow a town could go about its nightly affairs just as usual. A man and a woman, going by, laughed loudly at something the man had said: the sound of their laughter was horrid to William. And from a great distance—from far out in the country—there came the faint, long-drawn whistle of an engine.

That was the sorrowfulest sound of all to William. His lonely mind's eye sought the vasty spaces to the east; crossed prairie, and river, and hill, to where a long train whizzed onward through the dark—farther and farther and farther away. William uttered a sigh, so hoarse, so deep from the tombs, so prolonged, that Jane, who had been relaxing herself at full length upon the floor, sat up straight with a jerk.

But she was wise enough not to speak.

Now the full moon came masquerading among the branches of the shade-trees; it came in the likeness of an enormous football, gloriously orange. Gorgeously it rose higher, cleared the trees, and resumed its wonted impersonation of a silver disk. Here was another mockery: What was the use of a moon *now?*

Its use appeared straightway.

In direct coincidence with that rising moon, there came from a little distance down the street the sound of a young male voice, singing. It was not a musical voice, yet sufficiently loud; and it knew only a portion of the words and air it sought to render, but, upon completing the portion it did know, it instantly began again, and sang that portion over and over with brightest patience. So the voice approached the residence of the Baxter family, singing what the shades of night gave courage to sing—instead of whistle, as in the abashing sunlight.

Thus:

My countree, 'tis of thee,
Sweet land of liber-tee,
My countree, 'tis of thee,
Sweet land of liber-tee,
My countree, 'tis of thee,
Sweet land of liber-tee,
My countree, 'tis of thee,
Sweet land of liber-tee,
My countree, 'tis—

Jane spoke unconsciously. "It's Freddie," she said.

William leaped to his feet; this was something he could *not* bear! He made a bloodthirsty dash toward the gate, which the singer was just in the act of passing.

"You get out o' here!" William roared.

The song stopped. Freddie Banks fled like a rag on the wind.

. . . Now here is a strange matter.

The antique prophets prophesied successfully; they practised with some ease that art since lost but partly rediscovered by M. Maeterlinck, who proves to us that the future already exists, simultaneously with the present. Well, if his proofs be true, then at this very moment when William thought menacingly of Freddie Banks, the bright air of a happy June evening—an evening ordinarily reckoned ten years, nine months and twenty-one days in advance of this present sorrowful evening—the bright air of that happy June evening, so far in the future, was actually already trembling to a wedding-march played upon a church organ, and this selfsame Freddie, with a white flower in his buttonhole, and in every detail accoutered as a wedding usher, was an usher for this very William who now (as we ordinarily count time) threatened his person.

But for more miracles:

As William turned again to resume his meditations upon the steps, his incredulous eyes fell upon a performance amazingly beyond fantasy, and without parallel as a means to make scorn of him. Not ten feet from the porch—and in the white moonlight that made brilliant the path to the gate—Miss Mary Randolph Kirsted was walking. She was walking wih insulting pomposity in her most pronounced semicircular manner.

"You get out o' here!" she said, in a voice as deep and hoarse as she could make it. *"You get out o' here!"*

Her intention was as plain as the moon. She was presenting in her own person a sketch of William, by this means expressing her opinion of him and avenging Jane.

"You get out o' here!" she croaked.

The shocking audacity took William's breath. He gasped; he sought for words.

"Why, you—you—" he cried. "You—you sooty-faced little girl!"

In this fashion he directly addressed Miss Mary Randolph Kirsted for the first time in his life.

And that was the strangest thing of this strange evening. Strangest because, as with life itself, here was nothing remarkable upon the surface of it. But if M. Maeterlinck has the right of the matter, and if the bright air of that June evening, almost eleven years in the so-called future, was indeed already trembling to "Lohengrin," then William stood with Johnnie Watson against a great bank of flowers at the door of a church aisle; that aisle was roped with white-satin ribbons; and William and Johnnie were waiting for something important to happen. And then, to the strains of "Here Comes the Bride," it did—a stately, solemn, roseate, gentle young thing with bright eyes seeking through a veil for William's eyes.

Yes, if great M. Maeterlinck is right, it seems that William ought to have caught at least some eerie echo of that wedding-march, however faint—some bars or strains adrift before their time upon the moonlight of this September night in his eighteenth year.

For there, beyond the possibility of any fate to intervene, or of any later vague, fragmentary memory of even Miss Pratt to impair, there in that moonlight was his future before him.

He started forward furiously. "You—you—you little—" But he paused, not wasting his breath upon the empty air. His bride-to-be was gone.